A corner of the man's wide mouth lifted slightly, slowly.

Not even Zirak could decipher the expression-shift.

"How about a chance to spring my friends?" the huge human said.

Zirak nodded slowly, pretending to ponder. For once his subject's unlooked-for quickness of wit—so belying his brutal appearance—was helpful rather than the reverse. Zirak had been struggling with how best to broach this very subject.

"It might be," he said, "just possibly, that you could prove instrumental in rescuing them."

Grant nodded. "I'm in."

Zirak blinked again. "Like that?"

"Like that."

Other titles in this series:

James Axler
Outlanders®

REFUGE

A GOLD EAGLE BOOK FROM
WORLDWIDE®

TORONTO • NEW YORK • LONDON
AMSTERDAM • PARIS • SYDNEY • HAMBURG
STOCKHOLM • ATHENS • TOKYO • MILAN
MADRID • WARSAW • BUDAPEST • AUCKLAND

*For Shelley Thomson for invaluable
knowledge and friendship*

First edition February 2006

ISBN 0-373-63849-3

REFUGE

Special thanks to Victor Milán for his contribution to
this work.

Lord, Thou hast made this world below the shadow of a dream, An', taught by time, I tak' it so—exceptin' always Steam.
                    —Rudyard Kipling,
                       McAndrew's Hymn

In My Father's house are many mansions.
                    —*John* 14:2

The Road to Outlands—
From Secret Government Files to the Future

Almost two hundred years after the global holocaust, Kane, a former Magistrate of Cobaltville, often thought the world had been lucky to survive at all after a nuclear device detonated in the Russian embassy in Washington, D.C. The aftermath— forever known as skydark—reshaped continents and turned civilization into ashes.

Nearly depopulated, America became the Deathlands— poisoned by radiation, home to chaos and mutated life forms. Feudal rule reappeared in the form of baronies, while remote outposts clung to a brutish existence.

What eventually helped shape this wasteland were the redoubts, the secret preholocaust military installations with stores of weapons, and the home of gateways, the locational matter-transfer facilities. Some of the redoubts hid clues that had once fed wild theories of government cover-ups and alien visitations.

Rearmed from redoubt stockpiles, the barons consoli- dated their power and reclaimed technology for the villes. Their power, supported by some invisible authority, extended beyond their fortified walls to what was now called the Outlands. It was here that the rootstock of humanity survived, living with hellzones and chemical storms, hounded by Magistrates.

In the villes, rigid laws were enforced—to atone for the sins of the past and prepare the way for a better future. That was the barons' public credo and their right-to-rule.

Kane, along with friend and fellow Magistrate Grant, had upheld that claim until a fateful Outlands expedition. A displaced piece of technology…a question to a keeper of the archives…a vague clue about alien masters—and their world shifted radically. Suddenly, Brigid Baptiste, the archivist, faced summary execution, and Grant a quick termination. For

Kane there was forgiveness if he pledged his unquestioning allegiance to Baron Cobalt and his unknown masters and abandoned his friends.

But that allegiance would make him support a mysterious and alien power and deny loyalty and friends. Then what else was there?

Kane had been brought up solely to serve the ville. Brigid's only link with her family was her mother's red-gold hair, green eyes and supple form. Grant's clues to his lineage were his ebony skin and powerful physique. But Domi, she of the white hair, was an Outlander pressed into sexual servitude in Cobaltville. She at least knew her roots and was a reminder to the exiles that the outcasts belonged in the human family.

Parents, friends, community—the very rootedness of humanity was denied. With no continuity, there was no forward momentum to the future. And that was the crux—when Kane began to wonder if there *was* a future.

For Kane, it wouldn't do. So the only way was out—way, way out.

After their escape, they found shelter at the forgotten Cerberus redoubt headed by Lakesh, a scientist, Cobaltville's head archivist, and secret opponent of the barons.

With their past turned into a lie, their future threatened, only one thing was left to give meaning to the outcasts. The hunger for freedom, the will to resist the hostile influences. And perhaps, by opposing, end them.

Chapter 1

"My dear friends," said Dr. Mohandas Lakesh Singh, his tone somber, "I have brought you together to hear tidings not of the gravest import—nevertheless, we must always prepare for the worst."

"Tell us something new," Grant grumbled.

"Yeah," Kane added. "I could be catching up on my sleep."

They sat together for the briefing session in the Cerberus redoubt's dining hall. Brigid Baptiste and Domi were present, Domi gnawing on a piece of dried fruit. Sally Wright was likewise on hand, looking mild and owlish behind her big round glasses.

"Sadly," Lakesh continued, "though they have been absent for sometime, we cannot dismiss the threat they pose. I refer to the overlords, who have occupied the bodies of the nine barons."

"With all due respect," Brigid said crisply, "the barons' apotheosis is hardly a recent development, either." She was a tall, strikingly beautiful woman with a flow of hair like molten gold.

Lakesh drew in a deep breath. Brigid, former archivist in Cobaltville, was his most frequent defender and ally among the core Cerberus operatives: the ones who had escaped together from Cobaltville, and who handled the bulk of the dirty, dangerous missions in the campaign to free humanity from inhuman domination. If Brigid was dubious, he might face a tough task. Nonetheless, he reset his ingratiating smile and persevered.

"It is simply that, while we have received ample evidence of the terrible power of the overlords, it is also most painfully clear that we have as yet had but a glimpse of the totality of that power. Indeed, I daresay it likely they themselves do not yet appreciate the full extent of their powers. Therefore the potential threat they constitute to us—to this redoubt—can only be considered extreme. And only likely to mount.

"I have come to feel a strong need for a substantially remote place of refuge.

"Where?" Grant asked. His voice was like a volcano trying to decide whether to get serious about erupting. Given the impressive size of his chest that was not surprising. He was a black man who made Kane seem small, and Kane was neither short nor weakly built. He had close-cropped hair, dusted gray at the temples, and an impressive handlebar mustache. "Madagascar?"

"Interesting that you should suggest that, Grant, my friend," Lakesh said.

Kane raised an eyebrow. He was a dangerous-looking man, dark of hair and beard, light of eye, lean and sinewy as a wolf. If anything, his appearance understated his men-

ace. "Oh? Is that where you want us to grab you a new va-
cation hideaway?"

"No. Or at least, not directly."

Finishing off her fruit, Domi licked her fingers and fa-
vored Lakesh with a scowl almost worthy of Grant, who
was past master of the menacing scowl. She was a small,
slender albino woman with hair shorn to a snowy fuzz and
startling bloodred eyes. Despite her slimness she seldom
ran any risk of being mistaken for a boy.

"Don't walk all around the blaster," she said. "Get to
the trigger."

Lakesh nodded. "Cogently if idiomatically said, dearest Domi. The ideal location for an alternate base of operations is not on Earth at all."

"You are *not* moving us to Manitius," Kane said. It was
emphatically not a question. Neither he nor his companions
had fond memories of the lunar base—from which many
of Cerberus's current personnel had arrived as refugees.

"Oh, no," Lakesh said. "Not at all. Indeed, that is much
too close at hand."

"Surely not Mars," Brigid said.

Smiling, Lakesh shook his head. "Again, not far enough
to ensure the requisite degree of safety."

"Dr Lakesh," Sally Wright said earnestly. Not that she
said anything other than earnestly, except when she was
being diffident. "Do you think it's really a good idea to
go on tantalizing them like this?"

"She's right," Kane said, showing teeth. Of all the Cerberus operators he seemed to have the closest thing to an
easy and natural relationship with the analyst—also an

erstwhile archivist in baronial service—whom he and the others had helped escape from Snakefishville on the Cific coast. Although she had been brought in as assistant and complement to Brigid, her relationship with the taller and emphatically feminine redheaded woman was formal at best. She seemed awed and intimidated by Brigid—and Kane suspected she was half in love with her, as well. "It's not safe. So give—or even Baptiste will jump for your throat."

"Ha-ha." Lakesh's laugh came in a nervous titter, shriller even than his usual. "Surely you are mistaken. Our gentle Brigid—"

"Don't count on it, Doctor," Brigid said.

Lakesh blinked his startlingly blue eyes. They were very large behind his own round-rimmed spectacles. "Very well," he said, deflating slightly. "The only suitable sanctuary, so I have decided, would be one not only not of this Earth, but not of this dimension."

"Many worlds again," Grant said.

"That's brilliant thinking," Kane said. "Which casement? Mankind goes for the stars? The Nazis win? Those are some swell places to go for some rest and recreation."

"As long as we're only sending our minds," Grant added.

"Oh, not those places at all, my friends. Nor am I speaking merely of projecting your—our—consciousnesses there. I speak of a new set of worlds entirely. One to which we can move bodily."

"How?" Grant asked.

It was Brigid who answered, "Mat-trans chamber, of

course It stands to reason that, should alternate universes exist—and we know for a fact they do, unless we have experienced shared hallucinations of extraordinary degrees of detail—a gateway might be so tuned as to project humans there. Given the presence of a geomagnetic node or equivalent to act as a receiving station."

Lakesh applauded softly. "Elegantly and eloquently put, my dear. You do me proud."

A flush, not altogether of pleasure, came to Brigid's high cheekbones. As an archivist she had been his protégée when he was an important figure in the Cobaltville hierarchy, as well as among the baronies in general. It had been Lakesh who, impersonating members of a nonexistent resistance movement, guided her onto the path that would end in her shivering naked in a cell awaiting execution of a termination warrant—and thence to perpetual exile in Cerberus. She had never forgiven him fully for setting her up.

"And now we get to the black, rotten heart of the matter," Kane said. "You've found a prospective alternate world. And you want us to go explore it for you."

Lakesh beamed and nodded. "Precisely."

Chapter 2

"I hate to admit it," Grant said, turning slowly in place to survey the countryside around them, "but Lakesh seems to be right. Looks like this place won't kill us all right off the bat, after all."

They had materialized on a sort of ledge, overlooking a gentle green valley, midway between the hilltop and a creek gurgling below. They were relatively sheltered from observation from any distance, but enjoyed good all-around visibility. The sun stood about halfway up to the zenith. It seemed to be late summer here, as it was back at Cerberus.

Kane pointed to the top of the rise. "Let's go get a better look at the wider world that awaits us."

"Smells nice," Domi commented, producing an apple from her backpack.

"That's the sweet smell of spring in the Midwest," Kane said, "where they actually get rain occasionally."

"Wait'll it gets hot, as well as humid," Grant said. "Won't smell half so sweet then."

Kane shook his head and clucked mock-reprovingly. "Always so negative, Grant." The big man glared at him.

They marched up to the hilltop, each bowed beneath the weight of a well-stuffed pack. Lacking a clear idea of what they might expect, they hauled around supplies for days on their backs.

Grant had paced a few yards off. "Lot of dead ground hereabouts," he commented. "I don't like it."

"I thought all that warrior philosophy Shizuka's been teaching you emphasized the need to appreciate beauty, as well as swing a mean *katana*," Kane said. "It's lovely country. Wildflowers. Creeks. Scattered woods. Green rolling hills."

"What I said," Grant said. "Dead ground. Nothing about Bushido says I have to like terrain that makes it easy for an enemy to sneak up on me."

"What enemy?" Brigid said. "There's no one for miles around."

They were near the confluence of the Missouri and Mississippi rivers which held a high probability of a population concentration nearby, having attracted major ones at least twice in their world's history: the great pre-European Cahokian civilization and St. Louis/St. Charles west across the Mississippi from the old Indian site with its famous earthen mound. In their home world it was now a hellzone, having been comprehensively nuked during the brief but enthusiastic Third World War.

Lakesh had, he assured them, discovered through his mathematical calculation of chronon flux a world similar to their own, but not too similar. What that meant exactly he couldn't tell them, or anyway didn't. But in all events, they had arrived safely, in an unpopulated spot, with nothing at all to suggest the proximity of a hellzone, or indeed anything remotely unpleasant.

Still....

Grant made a growling noise, deep in the vast cavern of his chest. "You should know better than ever to say a thing like that, Brigid," he said.

"There's *always* enemies," Domi said.

Facing west, Kane stiffened. "Now, that's odd," he said, staring fixedly into the sky a bit above the world's edge. He raised his microbinocs to his eyes.

Grant was at his shoulder. "What do you got?" the big man asked.

Kane exhaled dissatisfaction. "Something in the air off that way. Still pretty far."

"Sure it's not just clouds?" The overhead blue stretched mostly unbroken, but fluffy white cumulus clouds piled up above the horizons north and west.

"Nope." Kane lowered the binocs. He kept staring into the western sky. "Then again, we're not sure about anything about this world yet."

"Could that be a sign of some kind of settlement to the south of us?" Brigid asked.

The men turned. Brigid stood a bit apart, pointing south. She wore khaki pants with cargo pockets, hiking boots and a light green blouse. All were dressed in what on their world would be unobtrusive fashion, no bright colors to attract the eye, and durable. The two men wore long shirts with the sleeves rolled down to conceal shadow suits, which the women had declined to wear.

Smoke lay like a sky island over distant hills, slightly west of due south from where they stood. It was a dirty white with a smutty yellow core.

"Could be a forest fire," Grant said.

"Mebbe so," Kane said. "It's getting bigger. Mebbe just got started."

"How?" Domi asked.

"What do you mean?" Kane asked.

"What started it?" She shrugged and bit her apple. "See any lightning? Hear any thunder? See any thunderheads anywhere?"

"Lightning can strike at enormous distance from visible clouds," Brigid said didactically. "Even over the horizon. And perhaps it hit too far away to see or hear."

"You can see lightning pretty far off, though," Kane said, the lines around his eyes and mouth tightening.

Domi stiffened.

"What?" Kane said quietly. He didn't turn his head.

"Something."

Brigid tossed her head with annoyance, started to speak. Kane held up a hand. The tall redhead looked capable of tossing some lightning bolts herself at being commanded, implicitly or not. But she stifled whatever commentary she had intended on Domi's vagueness.

Faint sounds teased the edge of his awareness: soft impacts. A kind of jingle. The breeze was freshening; they might have been tricks of it, of dried leaves left over from last fall clattering against branches in a nearby wood, a woodpecker excavating for bark-boring grubs.

Then came a whicker. Kane knew damned little about horses, which was just the way he wanted to keep it. But he'd knocked around the Outlands enough, where they were a leading mode of transport, to know that sound.

"Get ready for company," he said quietly but urgently.

Grant raised his right hand. A clench of its muscles would pop his Sin Eater out through a bulky sleeve, secured with a couple token stitches, and into his fist, ready for action.

"No," Brigid said. "We're supposed to be friendly."

"Nothing like a little show of firepower," Grant said, "to make sure things stay on a nice, friendly footing." But the big handblaster stayed in its forearm power holster.

"There," Domi said, pointing. A hill slightly lower than theirs stood about a hundred yards northeast, topped with a brush cut of trees still richly leafed-out and green. From it suddenly broke a dozen riders, more, at the canter.

"What the fuck, over?" Grant said, so softly he might not have realized he spoke the words aloud.

Kane's brain could only echo the sentiment although he said nothing. The riders wore armor, glinting bright in the midmorning sun. Not full body armor but mirror polished breast and backplates worn over tunics of strident red, weird billed caps that widened at the top. Their trousers were pink with powder-blue stripes. Their knee high boots gleamed like obsidian.

Each carried a lance with a pennon fluttering from behind its head, except for what seemed to be the leader. He held a glistening saber in a white-gloved hand.

More riders streamed out to either side of the stand of trees. As the first set trotted straight toward their group, the newcomers loped gently down the slope at diverging angles.

"Flanking us," Grant said. "Damn."

"They're already all around us," Domi said matter-of-factly.

Kane spun. Another party of cavalry swirled at the foot of their hill's southern slope, gaudy as a flock of exotic birds. The lancers rode in contrarotating groups about the hill on which the four stood—some clockwise, some widdershins—at a contemptuously easy pace.

"They're messing with us," Grant said.

"Tell me something I don't know," Kane said. He was getting dizzy from revolving in place trying to keep track of the riders. "I make it forty, fifty. All this riding in circles makes it hard to tell for sure."

"Might be more of them in the woods or behind the hills," Domi said. Kane nodded.

"See?" Grant muttered. "I told you this was a bad spot."

Kane laughed crisply. "We came here to make contact with the locals," he said. "They've just saved us a wait. If we really strike an ace in the line, we might get to ride instead of humping it."

"How do we know they're friendly?" Brigid asked.

"They haven't chilled us yet."

He stepped a bit down the north side of the hill, away from the others, and waved his arms above his head. "Hey!" he shouted "Hello, there! We come in peace! Friends! No trouble."

"Are we sure we want him for group spokesman?" Grant asked.

A fresh quartet of riders appeared from the small copse on the next hill north. Three of them were caparisoned like the rest: bright uniforms, cuirasses, wide-topped caps and, of course, black-shafted lances. The fourth wore what appeared to be the same tunic, trousers and boots as the rest. But he wore no armor—no visible armor, Kane amended mentally, thinking of himself and his partner. His head, sporting heavy, wavy, dark-blond hair, was bare. A long, thin black cigar protruded from a classically handsome face, beneath a luxuriant mustache of a redder hue than the hair on his head.

The four rode straight through the circling lancers, looking neither left nor right and not hesitating, forcing the others to change course to avoid blundering into them. Straight up the near slope they loped, to halt scarcely three yards from Kane.

The blond man let his looped reins hang on the neck of his handsome blood bay horse, slipped his right boot from its stirrup and cocked it over the front of his saddle, tipped up the cheroot between flawless white-gleaming teeth and emitted a jet of bluish smoke.

"Well, well," he said in English. "What have we here?" His accent was largely upper-class English—one Kane was uncomfortably familiar with from some of the most supercilious Manitius refugees—tinged with what Kane took for Scots. His voice was a clear tenor. Like his whole manner, its tone suggested confidence that nothing on Earth might shake.

Great, Kane thought, an arrogant bastard. Still, he was a bastard who talked before he ordered his horsemen to skewer the intruders with their pig-stickers—or before unlimbering the two heavy-looking revolvers riding in flapped leather holsters on either hip.

Kane held up his hands before his shoulders in what he hoped was a peaceful gesture short of abject surrender. "We are strangers from far away," he said. Beside him Brigid covered her eyes with a hand at his gaucherie. "We need to talk to your leaders."

The blond man looked down on Kane a moment with eyebrows raised. Then his eyes flicked restlessly among the others. His eyes were greenish blue, a very intense color, and seemed to glow from some wild, internal light that belied his controlled and casual demeanor.

"Hear that, chaps?" he called to his lancers. They had stopped riding in their show-ground circles. A number had ridden up to stand, entirely surrounding the outlanders at only a little greater distance than the bareheaded man had halted. Others remained in clumps at the hill's foot, evidently pulling security. "They say they've come from far away."

The lancers laughed at this as if it were the greatest joke ever. Kane fought the natural tendency of his own face, which was to settle into an angry frown. *What does this clown think is so funny?*

"What *I* say," Blondie said, swinging his laughing blue-green gaze back to Kane's smoldering gray one, "is that you are trespassers—strangers from another world. Why the surprised looks? Our science, which is most advanced, foretold your coming with some accuracy.

"So, to business. I hereby arrest your persons in the name of Her Benevolent Majesty Queen Fiona I, Hegemon of Canada, Imperatrix of the Americas and Protectress of the Human Race. Take them, boys!"

Several lancers parked their lances in holders like leather tennis-ball cans slung to their saddles, dismounted and advanced on the Cerberus four.

"But where are my manners?" the bareheaded horseman asked. "I am Rafael Mackenzie, Lieutenant Colonel, Royal Hegemonic Mounted Police." He said the word *leftenant*. "You have the honor of being taken prisoner by a squadron of the Eleventh Hussars, the Hegemon's Own, albeit vulgarly known as the Cherrypickers."

"I'm Kane. You don't have to do this, you know."

"Ah, but I do, I have my orders, from my sovereign Herself. And I've but one question for you—is that black-amoor there your slave, or are the rest of you his?"

With a growl of rage Grant brought up his right arm. His Sin Eater tore out of his deliberately weakened sleeve and slammed into his hand. His forefinger, already curled, instantly pressed the guardless trigger.

Nothing happened.

Multiple impacts slammed the big man to the ground as a volley of shots cracked out from the line of horsemen.

Chapter 3

"Grant!" Brigid knelt instantly by the big man's side.

Pale lips drawing back from paler teeth in a snarl of feral rage, Domi leaped at the Hussars' blond leader. Mackenzie held a bulky revolver in his right hand. Gray smoke drifted from its muzzle. He kept the barrel tipped skyward, and, laughing, warded off the furious albino girl with the sole of his boot. She fell on her rump on the ground.

Before she could spring again, a pair of dismounted Hussars were on her, pinning her arms behind her and hauling her to her feet. Another pair moved toward Brigid.

Through all this Kane simply stood, hands foolishly raised, face frozen.

Troopers surrounded Kane. He saw now that some of them at least carried bolt-action carbines. Two of these were leveled at him now. Their bores seemed enormous.

"Check that one's forearm," Mackenzie called out almost gaily. "He might harbor a concealed sting, as well. And speaking of which—"

He had holstered his revolver and now turned Domi's big knife ruminatively over in his hands, which were long and slim and pale. He looked at the albino woman, barely restrained by a pair of husky Hussars as she kicked and thrashed and cursed and spit at the colonel.

"Quite the display for such a fair maiden," he said. "You all seem quite the bundle of surprises. Then again, what else, I suppose, is one to expect from visitors from another world?"

"Why do you keep calling us that?" Brigid said. She stood with such angry dignity that no trooper had yet laid hands on her, although she was hemmed in by dismounted riders with carbines aimed at her.

A burly sergeant laid the tip of his saber at Kane's throat while a trooper skinned down his right sleeve. The red-faced noncom whistled beneath his own mustache, which blended seamlessly into great brown muttonchops.

"Lookee 'ere," he said. "That's a fancy bit of work, this."

The trooper gingerly unstrapped the holster and, at a nod from his sergeant, carried it to Mackenzie. The lieutenant colonel accepted it with interest. Domi herself had been tied now, with a handkerchief stuffed in her mouth for good measure. She still struggled with barely diminished fury.

"You ask us that question, fair lady," Mackenzie said to Brigid, "while your escorts are burdened with such otherworldly contrivances? I don't doubt your packs are full of similar artifacts that were never made upon our Earth."

He shrugged. "And in common with the weapon wielded by your unfortunate companion, you'll find that precious few of them work here."

Kane's pack was taken from his back and his hands

roughly tied behind him. "You seem to possess a judgment more reasoned than your comrades," Mackenzie said to Brigid with a bow. "If you give me your parole, milady, you shall not be bound."

"Treat me the way you treat my friends!" she said. "I won't promise you a thing."

"As you wish." At a gesture Brigid was secured. She was not searched, Kane observed—meaning that the 9 mm Heckler & Koch Universal Service Pistol in an inside-the-waistband holster hidden by the tail of the lime-green man's shirt she wore went undiscovered. But with her hands tied behind her, the pistol would be of limited utility.

If *any*. Grant's handblaster hadn't functioned. The smugly handsome Mackenzie seemed not at all surprised it had not. So her USP was probably as inert as Kane's own Sin Eater.

"Lieutenant Colonel!" The cry came from a pair of riders spurring their mounts through the little creek where it ran west of the hill, throwing up sprays of water that broke the sunlight like a thousand tiny prisms. They were pointing up and behind them.

It wasn't hard to see what they were pointing at. Kane realized that if his friends and their captors hadn't been so fixated on one another they all would have seen them before.

A great bloated cigar shape emerged from a cloud, with fluffy wisps clinging briefly to its great blunt snout before relinquishing it. To left and right another appeared, and another. Great gondolas with baskets gleaming like metal plates slung beneath them. Great barrel-like housings, presumably holding propellers, thrust from the gondolas' sides on flimsy-looking structures of metal spars and guy wires. Spines like sticklebacks thrust up through the tops of the gasbags, four on the lead vessel, three on its wingmen. Kane realized they were smokestacks, belching smoke that looked dark against the cloud and the brilliant sky beyond.

"A blimp?" Kane asked in disbelief.

"A dirigible," Brigid said. "A rigid airship. A blimp is merely a balloon, without internal structure—"

"Balloon, hell!" shouted a Hussar. "Them's Aero-Dreadnoughts!"

A flash appeared at the prow of the lead craft's gondola. A tiny cotton swab of smoke was plucked quickly apart by the breeze. Kane didn't see where the shot fell, but a moment later the report reached his ears, like the slam of a distant door.

"Mount up, gentlemen!" Mackenzie cried, tossing Kane's holstered Sin Eater to a subordinate and swinging his cocked leg back over his saddle. "Our erstwhile allies have decided to stick their interfering noses in Her Majesty's business, it appears."

A trumpeter was blowing a call. Like the activity that had broken out all around, it was fast but not hurried. Gaudy as birds of paradise they might be, but these Hussars were unmistakably veterans: coldhearts for true, and no strangers to death from either end of the transaction.

Kane was bodily picked up and plopped into the saddle of a light gray horse. "There ye go," the sergeant said.

"And thank your heathen stars it's us as got you first, and not the bloody Lizards!"

As hands strong and impersonally harsh lashed Kane fast to the saddle he saw first Domi and then Brigid treated the same way. It struck him that these Hussars must have been expecting their arrival in all truth: they had brought several riderless horses for their captives.

More riders came pelting up from the south. "Lieutenant Colonel Mackenzie! Corporal Ponsonby's compliments, and he begs leave to report cavalry and a force of land ironclads approaching from the south."

The sergeant showed Kane a gap-toothed grin. "See?" he said. A trooper snatched the reins of Kane's mount and spurred away. The sergeant leaned forward to swat the gray's rump with the flat of his saber. Kane's head whiplashed cruelly on his neck as the beast rolled its eyes and launched itself like an enormous jackrabbit in the wake of the trooper who held its reins.

The sound of cannonshots fell like hail. Kane saw a geyser of water thrown five yards in the air as a shell struck in the midst of the little stream. Another cracked off among the trees on the next hilltop with a red flash, evoking shrill screams from wounded horses and, Kane thought hopefully, from men.

As his horse was led pell-mell down the hill to the north, each fall of its hooves sending a sympathetic slam like a hammerblow to Kane's coccyx, he took a last look over his shoulder at his friend. Grant lay on his back, spread-eagled, staring at the sky. His pack lay beside him, and his Sin Eater was still futilely clasped in his right hand. The arrival of the Aero-Dreadnoughts had interrupted the looting of his corpse.

There was nothing to say, and Kane could have made no gesture had he been able to think of a fitting one. So he turned his face away from his old friend and comrade, and because he had no choice, rode where fate and his captors carried him.

BRIGID'S THOUGHTS were a fragmented whirl. She had lived through terrible surprises before, and unforeseen circumstances had been a near-constant companion since first a drunken Magistrate forced his way into her quarters in the Cobaltville Enclaves to insist that she decipher a purloined computer disk.

Yet she couldn't remember a time or a circumstance in which everything had gone to pieces so quickly and so strangely.

Despite her haughty—and she now realized, somewhat rash—demand to be treated the same as her companions, their captors had handled her with the utmost gentleness, albeit not one that brooked the least resistance. They were strong men used to using their strength, but obviously they subscribed to notions of male gallantry that, while intrinsically chauvinist, obviously worked to Brigid's advantage.

Of course, their patience had its limits, as the brusque way they handled Domi proved. Still, they weren't the first people to lose patience with the albino wild child—and many had done so without as great a provocation as her attempting to gut their commanding officer like a fish.

Her captors didn't run their horses downhill; Brigid had

read somewhere once it was bad for them, and naturally she retained it. Still they moved at a brisk clip as they led her down into the little valley and then around the base of the next hill. Thunder crashed all around as the huge airships overhead bombarded them. Their aim didn't seem very good; few if any of the shells fell closer than a hundred yards.

She glanced up. For a moment she frowned. It looked as if the vast elongated shapes were shedding seeds like dandelions.

Then one of her captors shouted, "Parasails! Damn." Almost at once he added, "Begging your pardon, marm."

She realized it was true: the dirigibles were seeding the sky with airfoil parachutes. She heard a cracking almost overhead, looked up to see a man wearing a green tunic and brown trousers scarcely fifteen yards up beneath a white-and-yellow canopy. He was firing a carbine from the hip as fast as he could work the bolt. Big ribbons of smoke streamed back from the weapon's muzzle.

A Hussar ahead and to Brigid's left cried out and reeled in his saddle, dropping his lance and clutching his left shoulder. Some of his comrades fired at the descending airborne trooper with their own carbines. Whether they hit or not, Brigid couldn't tell; she had the impression not, as the man swept low and trotted to a halt before the column and to the right.

He struck something on his chest—probably a quick-release catch to shed the canopy billowing and flapping behind. Unfortunately he didn't act quickly enough—or maybe he never had a chance. A Cherrypicker, bent low over the neck of a black horse, galloped up and thrust the man through the body with his lance. Brigid winced as she heard a sound like cloth tearing. The parasail soldier fell without a sound—nor did he stir or speak as half a dozen of Brigid's escorts rode their mounts over his prone body.

As HIS HORSE loped up and down ridges and splashed through streams in the midst of a thunder of hooves, Kane struggled against a debilitating combination of lassitude and confusion. There was the normal disassociation caused by a jump—ironically, less severe this time than on many other occasions.

A storm of gunfire broke out nearby. Rudely lashed to the saddle as he was, his hands tied behind him, Kane felt a vulnerability so intense it sickened him. Facing danger was one thing. This sense of total helplessness—strapped to a living creature that had a mind of its own and was none too happy with its circumstances itself, the way its eyes were rolling—was uniquely unnerving.

Horsemen plunged in among Kane's escorts from the left. His guards' mounts snorted and reared. Pretty damn careless, riding into their own buddies like that, he thought.

Then he realized the new riders weren't wearing red, nor was any armor visible. Instead they wore green tunics and brown trousers with red stripes down the sides; and brown slouch hats.

Sabers flashed. Pistols barked. Men cursed and horses screamed. Caught from the flank and apparently by surprise, the Cherrypickers were unable to use their lances effectively. Their opponents, who had been on the charge, had no such difficulty.

Kane saw a red-jacket go down with a lance thrust through the armpit hole of his cuirass. The rider pulling the reins of Kane's mount turned around in his saddle.

Kane's heart went into freefall as the man raised a revolver with a gigantic cylinder and highway-tunnel bore, right toward Kane's face.

"No! Alive, damn you!" he heard Lieutenant Colonel Mackenzie's voice bellow from somewhere in the melee swirling ahead.

Scowling over his grandiose black mustache, the trooper lowered his hog's-leg. A moment later his face vanished as blood and bone exploded out to the sides beneath his gleaming helmet.

Only by the ringing of his ears was Kane even aware a firearm had gone off near his head. He had a moment's further desperate realization that his mount was now under no one's control, not even its own. Then a rider laid his mount alongside Kane's. Letting a double-barreled sawed-off shotgun dangle from his wrist by a braided rawhide lanyard, the greencoat leaned down to grab the reins of Kane's horse.

A dark face grinned with startling white teeth that seemed mere inches from Kane's.

"Not a very sporting weapon, is it?" the bluecoat asked. He straightened in the saddle, pulling the reins to steer Kane's horse to the left.

With a hoarse yell, a Hussar rode toward Kane's new captor, saber raised. The man coolly drew his revolver with his left hand and shot the saber man through the throat. Blood fountained from a huge hole. The ball apparently smashed the cervical spine; the man went instantly limp and sprawled from his saddle onto the green turf.

"Forgive my manners," the bluecoat said. Other similarly clad riders had fallen into formation to either side and were fending off redcoats. The effort seemed halfhearted. The Hussars seemed more interested in bearing their female captives away than in trying to recover Kane. "I apologize for my brisk manner of liberating you. But freed you are—and I assure you that you'll find our company more salubrious than that of your captors. I'm Colonel Randall Rodríguez-Satterfield, Republic of Cíbola Militia, at your service."

"Kane," Kane shouted back. "What about my friends?"

Rodríguez-Satterfield shook his head. "No time. The hegemonic sky fleet has arrived overhead—"

He jerked his chin upward. Kane's glance followed the gesture. Almost literally over their heads two vast airships floated beam to beam, a Canadian vessel's sponson-mounted propellers almost touching the fan ducts of the Cíbolan ship, as they slammed broadside into each other's armor-plated flanks. Kite shapes drifted around them, dwarfed by the monsters, swirling and swooping upon one another and the aerial behemoths. War gliders? Kane wondered.

"And our friends from the south draw near in force quicker than anyone anticipated, which will render our poor human rivalries moot if we don't soon make good our escape."

Kane looked back, though it made him feel dizzy, lurching with hands tied behind him on the back of an unfamiliar beast as he was. A vehicle seemingly not too much smaller than one of the Aero-Dreadnought's gondolas had mounted a ridge not a mile distant—just south of the hill they had first climbed. It was a long construction with sides sloping to a flat upper deck, from which smokestacks protruded—and turrets. Both belched smoke. It rode upon several sets of tracks.

Beside it crawled a far smaller vehicle with what looked like great cleated tires, possibly of steel. This machine resembled a steam tractor in a sort of iron tent far more than any armored fighting vehicles Kane had ever seen in pictures or in person. In the sky above the land crawlers the dark mobile clouds of more Aero-Dreadnoughts could be seen.

As he spoke, Rodríguez-Satterfield broke open his shotgun, ejected the empties and stuffed a pair of cartridges of what looked like brown waxed paper with brass bases into it, then locked it up again. Gripping its narrow wrist with the hand that held the reins of Kane's mount, he reached into a tunic pocket and produced a palm-sized object that Kane couldn't see, and he held up before him as he and their dozen or so escorting riders bent dead west.

A tiny but bright white light from the armored prow of one of the lesser giant airships not yet engaged in close battle with enemy vessels, flashed. Kane realized it was a mirror reflecting sunlight: a heliograph. Apparently that was Rodríguez-Satterfield's means of communicating with the aircraft, as well. No radio, he thought.

Tilting great vanes at its stern, the airship began to descend toward them. "Is that thing going to land?" Kane shouted to his escort over the tumult of land and air battle.

Rodríguez-Satterfield showed him another bright grin. "Not precisely. Now, do your best to keep your seat, friend Kane. We've got to ride like the wind!"

Kane gritted his teeth and leaned forward in hope of reducing the wind resistance of his body. He clamped his knees as tightly as possible to the barrel of his mount. As they drew away from the general roaring exchange of gunfire and artillery, Kane was torn between fear of falling off and fear of pulping his balls against the saddle's frontal structure.

Shells began to boom off ahead. Kane looked up to see a strange contrivance, like a fat winged bomb or a streamlined bathtub with stub wings, flying, seemingly, straight for him. He bared his teeth, thinking it some kind of missile aimed at him. Then he saw, almost invisibly fine even at a hundred yards, the hawser leading upward to a dirigible blotting the sky like a great dark cloud.

Chapter 4

"You have got to be shitting me!" Kane shouted.

His liberator—self-proclaimed, anyway—laughed hugely. He had lost his hat in the fighting, or maybe the wild ride. He had a brush of glossy black hair.

"You've made the leap from a whole different world!" he called. "This should be child's play."

"Everybody seems to know more about this world-hopping stuff than we do ourselves," Kane said, more to himself than to his new companion. "How the hell do people who ride horses and use black powder blasters get so damned blasé about dimensional travel?"

"It's a long story." Putting himself knee to knee with Kane, the colonel transferred the reins of Kane's horse to his left hand. With his right he drew a bowie blade, more short-sword than knife.

"We have to do this on the run," he told Kane, "so please forgive a little blood."

"You're not—" Kane said. Then of course the colonel did. Kane felt a sting on the skin inside his right wrist. Then he felt the cords that bound his wrists drop away.

"The reins!" Rodríguez-Satterfield tossed them to Kane, who caught them. "Now, ride like wind itself. We've got to catch the sky car on the fly."

Before Kane could object that he had no idea what the colonel was talking about, the car had swooped past them going the other way. Rodríguez-Satterfield wheeled his mount and galloped in pursuit.

At least nobody was shooting at them. Kane hauled the reins around to the right. The horse obediently turned. It was tossing its head, rolling its eyes, and its nostrils were flared.

"Don't dump me on my ass, here, horse," Kane said, patting the beast on the neck. "And we'll be rid of each other forever in no time at all!"

He booted the horse in its sides. It rabbited away after Rodríguez-Satterfield. The colonel looked over his shoulder and called encouragement to Kane. Kane couldn't hear for the din of battle and the roaring of blood in his ears.

The colonel had been holding back. Now he touched his own mount's sides with his spurs and it spurted ahead in pursuit of the sky car, which was still moving away faster than a man could walk. Kane's horse, well charged with adrenaline and not so much being steered as following its herd-mate, ran flat-out and had actually closed the distance when Rodríguez-Satterfield dropped his reins, stood up on his saddle like a trick rider, caught the sky car and hauled himself aboard.

"I am *not* doing that shit!" Kane shouted. His horse ran beneath the car, still doggedly following the colonel's mount, which had accelerated once shut of the tall man's not-inconsiderable weight. Kane stretched his hands up, felt them hit wood, grabbed, pulled for all he was worth and tried his damnedest to levitate.

One way or another he got enough of a grip to be plucked from the saddle. Legs bicycling in the air he was borne away, higher and higher. As the ground dropped away, he adjusted his grip on the right wing of the sky car, facing its tail.

But his grip wasn't good enough. The fingers of his right hand slipped off smooth laminated wood. He found himself dangling by one hand as the dirigible climbed— and the sky car itself was winched upward toward the gray armored belly of the gondola slung beneath it. Below him toy soldiers fought and fell and some lay still. It was very lifelike.

A strong hand clamped on his wrist. "Don't worry, amigo," the colonel shouted. "After all we went through to get you, I'm not going to allow you to slip away so easily."

Kane looked up into his grin. "Good," he grunted.

With Rodríguez-Satterfield's stabilizing grip on his wrist, Kane was able to resume a hold with his right hand. The colonel's wiry strength was substantial; combining their efforts reeled Kane quickly into the sky car's cockpit, where he fell in a boneless heap and lay panting.

To allow his guest at least a little room to sprawl, Rodríguez-Satterfield stood on the rounded fuselage aft of the open cockpit, holding to the cable with one hand. He looked like a Mexican Errol Flynn in some unlikely vid from the early twentieth century.

"I wish I could allow you more of a rest," the colonel called, his voice pitched to cut across the wind—and the unceasing clatter of rifle fire from below and the booms of cannons and shells going off overhead, where an aerial battle still raged unabated. "But I fear I must ask your assistance."

Kane looked up. With the hand that wasn't holding the hawser, Rodríguez-Satterfield proffered a huge, ungainly double-action revolver, butt first. "You can shoot?"

Bracing himself into a spraddle-legged half stand in the swaying cockpit, Kane accepted the piece, sighted experimentally along the top. It had a conventional Patridge sight with a square notch in the fixed rear sight and a square-topped post for a front, like the iron sights of a handblaster from his own world—he had to override a tendency to think *time*. He had expected something crude, like the groove down the top-strap as with certain old-time single-action handguns still in use in the Outlands.

"I think so," he said.

"Good," Rodríguez-Satterfield said. "Because I fear with such small weapons, the both of us won't be too many to keep ourselves alive!"

As the colonel spoke, Kane became aware of an odd grinding sound, which he hoped wasn't the mechanism cranking them up to the dirigible giving up the ghost. Then he started hearing strange moaning whispers that seemed to whip by on the wind of their passage.

Then he realized someone was shooting at him. He looked out ahead of the sky car to see a remarkable sight: something like an ultralight he'd seen pictures of once in an old book on flight. Its high single wing was attached to a sort of cagework of what looked like wood. A tiny engine turned a propeller at the cage's rear; booms ran back to either side of it to meet and support a tail assembly.

It all looked more like a box-kite than an aircraft—even more precarious and rickety than the crates they flew in World War I. A man sat in a chair in the cage in front of the engine, dressed in flying leathers, cap and goggles, hunched forward into the wind.

And, oh, yes, he was busily cranking the handle of a Gatling gun with his right hand while he steered with a tillerlike stick in his left.

A yellow flame flickered from each barrel as it rotated in turn to the top. Smoke streamed back continuously, making the craft appear to be afire. Kane caught an impression of a bulky metal box, possibly a feed bin, clamped to the weapon's side.

The sky car's wooden hull vibrated under Kane's feet and against his knees, braced against the cockpit's sides. A couple of holes appeared in the stubby wing no more than a yard from him. The enemy flyer whipped past, trailing an almost inaudible acid-mosquito whine as well as smoke from its now quiescent gun barrels.

Kane saw a red circle painted on the vertical stabilizer, with a red maple leaf within. A big hole appeared off center in the rondel as Rodríguez-Satterfield discharged his scattergun with a boom.

"Meant to hit something vital," he called down to Kane. "But that was symbolically appropriate, anyway. Look alive—the bastard's not alone!"

A rocket whipped by with a whoosh and a plume of yellow sparks. One stung Kane's bearded cheek like a hornet. The cockpit of the sky car—which still reminded Kane of a toy a child might have carved, possibly of soap—filled with smoke. He brushed furiously at embers that had landed on his sleeve and the chest of the shirt he wore over his shadow suit.

A red-and-white glider was swooping in on them. More rockets hung from brackets beneath its long, slender wings. Kane raised his borrowed revolver with both hands, mindful that the big bore might translate to a big recoil. With small need to lead since the craft was basically flying straight at him, he lined up the sights on the windscreen of the bulbous enclosed cockpit and squeezed off a round.

The boom and recoil weren't as imposing as Kane feared. Nonetheless he fell back in the bathtublike cockpit and almost dropped the weapon in surprise. The whole upper works—hammer, frame and cylinder—slammed straight back toward his face on rails set in the frame. Then it snapped forward again, leaving the hammer cocked above a fresh cylinder.

"Sumbitch!" Kane yelled. "It's semiauto!"

Another boom. The glider's windscreen crazed and turned white as buckshot sprayed it. The unpowered aircraft banked quickly right and whipped away.

"Good shot," Kane said.

"Not too hard with a sawn-off. I get the impression you're not familiar with the automatic revolver?"

"No."

"Handy things. Magazine revolvers are all the rage back home, but I've a certain fondness for my Taliaferro. Watch out!"

The buzzing pusher-plane was back, curving in from Kane's right. The pilot was cranking his Gatling like a hypercaffeinated organ-grinder's monkey. Kane pushed the blaster out before him with both hands. It still felt heavy, although the effect was probably psychological, since it almost certainly weighed less than his Sin Eater. He began firing systematically in return.

He didn't seem to be hitting anything. Fortunately, neither did the Canadian airman. Then the pilot jerked and slumped forward.

A white shape flashed noiselessly past overhead: another war glider, this one showing a green-and-gold rondel. Blue smoke trailed back along its spermlike fuselage; Kane realized a line of holes had walked across the top of the attacking ultralight's port wing, right across the cagelike cockpit and the pilot's body. This new flier was a friend. But now—

"Hang on!" Rodríguez-Satterfield yelled. The pilotless plane came straight for their sky car. Once more letting his shotgun hang, he began to scale the cable like a monkey.

Kane stood up in the cockpit and tried to emulate him, still holding on to the revolver. He didn't have enough time anyway—

Whether the pilot's dead or dying hand had pushed the tiller forward, or the weight on the snout had caused it to dip without the pilot's constant attention to trim control, the ultralight warplane nosed down and dived. Its fragile vertical stabilizer splintered on the sky car's fat belly.

Kane quit trying to grab the cable and started glaring

around mad-eyed for more targets. A brisk dogfight swirled about them as gliders and a few powered craft showing red-and-white Hegemonic rondels mixed it up with a similar mix of fliers showing two different sets of insignia, who seemed allied to one another.

The car rocked as Rodríguez-Satterfield slid back down to let his boots thump on the fuselage again. He crouched into a relaxed posture, not a defensive one. Kane realized he found the sky car's motion quite alarming, now that surprise, disorientation and the adrenal buzz of immediate mortal danger had all begun to fade into background.

"Our Kai-Gwe friends have put in a timely appearance," Rodríguez-Satterfield said. Kane guessed he referred to the aircraft sporting the red, blue and gold third-party insignia. "I think the Canadians are about done with us now. The gunners in the *Rocky Mountain Angel* have us covered pretty well."

He bobbed his head upward. Kane's eyes followed. He cringed reflexively: the airship's gondola was as big as a building—a building about to land on their heads.

He forced himself to relax. The airship wasn't falling on them. Indeed it seemed to be climbing at a gentle angle, driven by its ducted fans. The sky car was being pulled up into it through a black oblong hole toward the great vessel's stern. The steady crackle of Gatling fire surrounded them like rain, though Kane couldn't see the gondola gunners.

"A wise man never likes to tempt the Devil," Rodríguez-Satterfield said, "but I'd say we're about home free."

He pointed back toward the hill on which Kane and his friends had been captured. It now lay at about forty-five degrees off the dirigible's starboard bow. The great airship was evidently turning as it climbed—no great feat, the combat aviator in Kane realized, when its primary lift came not from airfoils but a big bag of buoyant gas. Which he hoped with sudden fervor wasn't highly combustible hydrogen, ready at the strike of a random spark to light off like so much gasoline and descend in a great mass of flame on his head.

At least a dozen other airships swam like a pod of whales. Mostly were higher than the *Angel*, which had descended to scoop up the escapees. Even at almost a mile's range Kane could see some were pretty ripped up, with gray smoke drooling out through rents in their armor and flapping-edged tears in their gas bags. None was actively ablaze, a good sign in his estimation: it indicated the envelopes were filled with nice, neutral helium.

Still, one of the vessels that had swung to follow the *Rocky Mountain Angel* seemed to lose altitude slowly. Kane wondered why the others with badly ripped envelopes weren't.

At any event the airships with huge red-and-white pennons whipping behind them had turned north and showed no inclination to pursue.

"Home free," Kane echoed, "for the moment."

Rodríguez-Satterfield flashed him that brilliant grin. Sumbitch could model a twentieth century toothpaste ad.

"So you're a realist, Kane."

Kane laughed a hoarse, short laugh. "In a pretty unreal situation."

Suddenly poles with padded tips were prodding down from above, wielded by airship crew to prevent the sky car banging off the *Angel's* hull as it was reeled inside. Cool dimness swallowed them like birthing in reverse.

SLOWLY GRANT RETURNED to a whole-body ache that seemed to throb to the beat of his heart.

I hurt, he thought. Therefore I'm not chilled yet.

He wasn't sure if that was a good thing or not.

He recalled being surrounded by a lot of low-tech slag-jackers in gaudy outfits. With spears. He remembered losing his temper and drawing down on them—and the giant, thunderous, echoing silence produced by his faithful Sin Eater. Then he remembered a whole lot of yellow flashes, a world of pain, then nothing at all.

His shadow suit had stopped the horsemen's bullets. But it hadn't stopped them from throwing him an almighty beating. From the way pain lanced through his chest and down his spine at every inhalation, he knew he must have some heavily bruised ribs at the least.

He grew aware of a tugging at his right arm. Gradually he opened his eyes to slits.

A thrill shot through him like cold lightning, branching through every vein: an inhuman creature crouched over his outflung right forearm. It was assiduously trying to unfasten the power holster strapped beneath his ruptured sleeve.

Its face was partially obscured by shadow from its low-slung, angular coal-scoop helmet. What Grant could see had a rounded muzzle, near lidless mouth, narrow nostrils.

Its eyes and ears, if any, were hidden. The body was held parallel to the ground by a pair of sturdy legs, jointed like an animal's, and counterbalanced by a tail that tapered to a blunt tip.

The tail stuck incongruously out the seat of what otherwise resembled forest-pattern camou trousers.

The hands fiddling with the Sin Eater's holster were not too different from human, if you overlooked the sharp slate-gray talons springing from the fingertips. The hands were longer, slimmer, with bones and sinews more in evidence than in a human's. The skin was yellowish-brown and supple, not at all scaly in appearance. But something still yammered in Grant's mind: *lizard*!

It had been a human who had infuriated Grant and provoked him into the act that had got him shot down to die like a dog. The same humans who had shot him had doubtless made off with his friends, who just as certainly now mourned him for dead. But there were no humans in bright red coats and shiny metal lobster-shells to take out his anger on. Just the lizard trooper rolling him for his power holster, and several similar shapes glimpsed dimly around him through slitted eyes.

He'd long since had more than a bellyful of aliens, inhumans and quasi-humans having their way with poor old humans in general and him in particular. Time for some payback.

By imperceptible degrees his left hand slipped to the hilt of his big Magistrate Division combat knife. His thumb silently undid the catch. Then he whipped the big blade free and, roaring, lunged to slash the throat of the lizard unfastening his holster.

It occurred to him as he rolled off the ground that he had no idea what kind of reflexes these reptiles had.

But he didn't find out then. Because the violence of his lunge crashed broken ribs together like rocket freighters filled with pain. Nova agony exploded through his chest and drove the breath from his body, and his mind from consciousness.

Chapter 5

"DR. BAPTISTE?" a voice called through the stateroom door. It appeared to be solid oak. Brigid wondered how there could be such a thing aboard what was, after all, a gondola slung from a balloon. Granted, it was an armored gondola, plated in steel. So much more reason to conserve on weight with interior appointments.

At a muffled exclamation she turned and glanced at the divan built out from the wall beneath the porthole. Since they had lifted off and flown north, away from danger, the armored shutters had been opened to admit bright afternoon sunshine. Which illuminated a glowering Domi, her hands trussed behind her in the same manner as Brigid's.

"Yes, who is it?" Brigid called. From their formality—not to mention their love of archaic display—she guessed these people put great stock in titles. She doubted her ability to counterfeit some kind of nobility, especially among people with intimate daily acquaintance of the real thing. So she styled herself a doctor. Although she had never been granted a formal degree, since the baronies didn't bother with that kind of thing, it wasn't really a lie: her education and many years' experience as a senior archivist in Cobaltville would easily have qualified her for multiple Ph.D.s.

"Lieutenant Barrows, ma'am." The voice, a clear and painfully young tenor, said the word *leftenant*. "The captain wishes me to inform you that he requests the pleasure of your company upon the bridge at your convenience."

The lieutenant opened the door. He was a fresh-faced young man in scarlet tunic and high, narrow white collar, with wavy brown hair and sideburns sprouting from his head. He blinked nervous blue eyes and smiled.

"I'll be happy to accompany you to the bridge. but only if you release my companion." Brigid nodded in Domi's direction.

The lieutenant looked skeptical.

"Leave us both tied up or free us both," Brigid insisted. "You can guard her yourself if you like."

The lieutenant disappeared for a moment, then reappeared with another soldier who watched warily as the two captives' wrists were untied and Brigid was escorted out of the staterooms.

"IT SEEMS TO ME I see a question in your eyes, Dr. Baptiste," Captain Sir Ramsey Harrowgate, master and commander of Her Majesty's dirigible *Adamant*, said. He was a short man whose sturdy frame was wrapped in a blue tunic and white trousers, over shoes, not boots. His hair and extravagant sweeping sideburns were white, his face pink and jovial. The whole outfit was topped off with a black cocked hat with a trim of white feathers.

Brigid smiled. "If you just see one there's quite a queue behind it, Captain. But the first one that comes to mind is the view."

"Ah, yes," the captain said. "Splendid, isn't it."

To say the least, Brigid thought, impressed despite her resolve not to be, given her state as a kidnapped captive. Still, since being winched with a tied-up Domi and several captors, including Colonel Mackenzie, into the underbelly of an airship hovering twenty yards above a hilltop, on a platform with brass safety rails, Brigid had been rethinking her initial assessment of her captors.

The verdant panorama outside was enough to overcome, or at least dampen, most of her scruples. They had long since left the Mississippi behind, flying northeast over what Brigid thought would have been northern Illinois in her own world—once upon a day. The land undulated gently below. It was given largely to fields planted in a dozen shades of green, with here and there the brown of a fallow field. Areas of cultivation were punctuated by myriad streams, shining in the light of the sun sinking toward the horizon, tree-tufted hills, forest expanses far greater than she would have expected.

She was not especially familiar with this part of her own world, and had certainly never seen it from this altitude. She had the impression that the land beneath was less populated than it must have been in the waning days of the twentieth century, before the nukecaust and skydark. She wondered what had happened here—and what the year was. Might we have traveled backward in time three centuries as across dimensions?

She shook her head, pulled herself back to the present. "And that's precisely what puzzles me. This is a war airship, a war dirigible—I don't know precisely what to call it. But it's meant to fight, is it not?"

"Indeed it is, my lady. As it did during your rescue a few short hours ago. And while both the terms you used are quite and appropriate, technically our *Adamant* rejoices in the class name of Aero-Dreadnought."

Brigid's mouth tightened at the use of the word *rescue*. She made no other response. Despite what she could only think of as Grant's murder—he had drawn his weapon, of course, but only in response to Mackenzie's obscene provocation—she had begun to revise her opinion of the Hegemony of Canada overall. Her reception and treatment aboard *Adamant* had been courteous, so at odds with the casual cruelty of Grant's death.

These elegant and courteous officers surrounding her seemed utterly disconnected from such random, brutal violence, as if they, too, were recent arrivals from a separate universe.

"These windows—" she gestured at the several panels that swept around the front of the bridge, to provide a view of at least 120 degrees—"they seem incredibly large, unless they're of—" She hesitated, realizing her hosts would not likely know the term *armaglass*. "Unless they're bulletproof."

"Oh, they are, to be sure, Dr. Baptiste," Harrowgate said. "Synthetic gum. The very latest, don't you know. But while they'll shed rifle balls like water from a duck's back, as you discern, they'd never suffice to turn a solid shot from a modern rifled gun."

She realized the captain used *gun* in the technical sense

of an artillery piece. "We've shutters, just as your cabin does, ma'am," Harrowgate said. "Great armor plates which we winch into position going into action. Then we see using a combination of much smaller ports and clever arrangements of prisms and mirrors. I'd demonstrate, but the truth is they're a deuced lot of trouble to get into position and then out again."

"It's quite all right, Captain," she said. She found herself smiling.

"My apologies again for the rude manner in which you were handled on arrival," said the big, bluff man who stood beside the captain. His red coat sported a super abundance of gold braid on the shoulders and collar. He towered a head above the short, wide Harrowgate. He had dark blond hair, well grayed at the temples, and an impressive mustache. He had been introduced as Brigadier Stanley Smythe-George of the Fourth Cavalry Regiment. "I…should have preferred to see it handled differently, Doctor."

"What he means, but is too loyal to Her Majesty's army to say," said Harrowgate, "is that the Eleventh Hussars tend to be a law to themselves."

"And so much more the Royal Hegemonic Mounted Police," the brigadier said with a shrug.

Then he looked sharply at Lieutenant Barrows, who stood attentively by. "Eh? What's that you say, Lieutenant? Speak up clearly now—don't mumble. It's undignified."

"I said, 'And more so, still, the Devil Mackenzie,' sir," the young officer said, cheeks burning pink. "Begging your pardon, Brigadier."

"Yas, hmph." Smythe-George gave the boy a freezing glare. Barrows wilted appropriately. Still, Brigid noted just a hint of mischief twinkling in his eye. It would take more than a superior's transient ire to repress the irrepressible youngster, it seemed.

"It's true enough," Captain Harrowgate said. "I'd clap him in irons for the duration of the voyage on general principles, if I could."

Brigid turned to face him fully. "Do I understand that you, as a representative of Her Majesty's government, are formally disavowing responsibility for the death of my associate—my friend?"

The two officers exchanged glances. "You are a most formidable woman, Dr. Baptiste," the brigadier said.

"Thank you," Brigid said. She continued to gaze at Harrowgate with emerald intensity.

"It is out of my hands, ma'am," the captain said. "Perhaps that sounds like an evasion of responsibility. Nonetheless, it's true. What I can do, and I have full confidence that I speak for Brigadier Smythe-George, as well, is insure that a full board of inquiry takes the events leading up to your rescue under the closest examination."

Smythe-George nodded vigorously. "Quite right, Sir Ramsey. The orders were most explicit. All—visitors— were to be taken into protective custody in the best possible condition and returned to Gloriana for consultation with our sovereign—and, of course, Dr. Miles-Burnham. 'Dead' is deuced hard to construe as 'best possible condition,' I'm bound."

"While I agree, Brigadier, I can construct a simple log-

ical argument whereby it is so construed," Brigid said
coolly. "If this—*Lieutenant Colonel*—Mackenzie is as resourceful as his reputation hints, he should be able to
come up with it at least as readily as I."

Smythe-George blinked at her several times. Then his
eyebrows rose. "Ah! I see. Confound me for a plodding
old fool." He glanced to Harrowgate. "Formidable, I said,
and formidable, I maintain!"

"I shan't argue, Stanley. Yet I offer my word of honor
as an officer and a gentleman of many years' service, to
Her Majesty Queen Fiona and her late lamented father
King Brian before, that no effort shall be spared to get to
the bottom of what happened, and how your friend came
to die in the process of being 'rescued'!"

"With all respect, gentlemen," Brigid said, "you've repeatedly used the word 'rescue.' Given our actual experiences, you'll perhaps appreciate that it seemed far more
reminiscent of a kidnapping. At the very least, what were
we being rescued *from*?"

Smythe-George's expression of confusion was almost
parodic. "You don't know?"

"Of course she doesn't know, Stanley, you great twit,"
Captain Harrowgate said. "She's from another dimension.
An alternate universe."

"Oh." The brigadier puffed his impressively sideburned
cheeks. "Quite. Forgive it, ma'am."

"Only if someone will answer my question!"

"Quite so," Harrowgate said. "We rescued you from the
Reptoids. Beastly fellows, really."

"Invaders from another world," Smythe-George said,

bobbing on the balls of his booted feet with hands clasped behind his back. "Aliens, that is."

"CARE FOR MORE BRANDY in that coffee, Kane?" Colonel Randall Rodríguez-Satterfield asked.

"Yes!" Looking out an oblong viewport over the hills of what had been the barony of Mandeville in his own world, Kane tossed off the contents of his lightweight spun-metal mug and held it out.

"Fill it up with everything while you're at it. Did you say, 'Invaders from another world'?"

"I most certainly did," Rodríguez-Satterfield said. He spoke with a Southwestern accent tinged with Spanish. It was clear he was well educated, occasional colorful flashes of slang notwithstanding. The two men were alone in the small compartment, which seemed to be a break or ready room. If a damned plush one, with burgundy carpet and what looked like stained-walnut panel walls. The colonel brought an engraved silver coffeepot from a sideboard, poured Kane's mug full of steaming black liquid, put back the pot and brought a decanter of brandy.

"You act as if there's something extraordinary about that," the colonel said, pouring the cordial with a liberal hand. "You're from another world, too, comes to that. Aren't you?"

Kane shook his head and dropped into a chair of muted red plush. "Yeah. And everybody acts as if they know all about it."

Rodríguez-Satterfield perched his skinny butt on the edge of the sideboard and let a booted foot swing. "By 'everybody,' you mean…?" he prompted, lighting a slim black cigar. Kane noticed that no more than a pleasant waft of scent reached his nostrils. Evidently they had good ventilation aboard this gas bag—but he didn't feel a draft.

"I mean the guys in the red coats. You." He bolted another shot of supercharged coffee and shook his head again. "Who are you? Who are the redcoats in the tin vests? And what's with the guys in the green-and-red uniforms with the war paint? And finally, you got a spare cigar anywhere handy?"

The colonel laughed. "Last question first—the humidor on the sideboard. Help yourself—you're an honored guest."

Kane did as he was told, finding an assortment of smokes wrapped in plastic—an odd touch in these brass-and-oak surroundings. He selected a nice thick Havana, accepted a light from Rodríguez-Satterfield and resumed his seat.

"Since you know who I am, I presume you meant 'you' collectively," the colonel said. "Forgive me not explaining sooner. I am a proud citizen-soldier of the Republic of Cíbola—basically the central and southern Rocky Mountains, and assorted surrounding plains and desert. The gentlemen in the green and brown are warriors of the Kai-Gwe Republic, our neighbors to the east, and our allies for a generation or so—near an eternity, in this turbulent modern world of ours. The fellows in red coats and pink pants are Hussars from the Benevolent Hegemony of Canada. They were our allies, too, of considerably more recent vintage."

"I could tell by the way you were sabering and shooting each other."

Rodríguez-Satterfield laughed again. "The alliance didn't exactly last. It was always fool's gold, far as I saw. I voted against the whole damned enterprise, but when the senate passed it, I chose to follow its dictates rather than hand over my commission and go back to my family hacienda."

"What was the alliance about?"

"Fighting the Reptoids. St. Louis was the first place they managed to capture, on their third attempt at landing. That was twenty years ago. They've been consolidating their foothold and trying to expand ever since. Actually, they've been expanding and getting beaten back, expanding and getting beaten back, for years. That's here—they've had a lot better luck other places, such as Europe."

"Europe," Kane echoed.

Rodríguez-Satterfield blew out greenish smoke. "We had hopes of beating them for good, at least breaking their stranglehold on the middle Mississippi. Their human subjects outnumber 'em a hundred to one. If we could hand them a brisk enough beating, the men might remember that they were, and rise up to help us overthrow them. So the thinking ran. But we'd barely assembled—and I won't bore you with how it came about that we consented to do any such damn fool thing as hook up with the redcoats north of St. Louis, instead of attacking in a pincers movement from the north and west—when the alliance went to hell.

"And at that juncture—" he sent a smoke ring toward the ceiling "—you and your friends dropped in right between four armies in three hostile camps. Tough bit of luck there, amigo."

"About standard," Kane said, "for us."

Chapter 6

"Deuced bad luck on the part of you and your friends," Brigadier Stanley Smythe-George said, "dropping right into no-man's-land, to coin a phrase."

"What caused the alliance to fail, Brigadier?" Brigid asked, leaning forward with her elbows on the table, cupping her hands around what appeared to be a clear glass mug of green tea. It wasn't glass; she knew that from its weight, or lack of it, when she picked it up before it was filled. Although the tea was so hot it steamed visibly into the pleasantly cool air of the wardroom, the mug was barely warm to her palms.

The florid-faced officer shrugged. "Doomed from the inception, don't you know. The Kai-Gwe at core are reactionaries, trying to cling to their tribal ways in the face of progress. Not that I blame them, to be sure. Still, it's mostly traditions such as raiding and plunder they're eager to retain. As for the Cíbolans, they're bandits, the next thing to anarchists, ruled by soulless plutocrats, I shouldn't wonder if they made your friend Kane a slave to pay his way, or turned him to a carnival curiosity, if it's true he had the ill fortune to fall into their hands."

Brigid felt her mouth tighten. Outside, the light thrown against the clouds was growing butter-colored with the decline of the day. They had flown mostly north, as far as she could tell, for hours now, driven by the great steam-turbine-powered propellers. She could feel the engines' pulse, vibrating through the floor, in the bulkheads, the air, her bones.

"There is a great deal here I don't understand," Brigid said, choosing each word precisely.

Smythe-George bobbed his head. "Naturally enough."

"One thing puzzles me deeply—why is it that everyone knows we come from another universe and not just takes it in stride, but seems to have been *expecting* us."

"We were advised, of course."

Without words for the moment, Brigid let an arched eyebrow ask the question.

"By scientific instruments placed at the order of Professor Nigel Miles-Burnham, late of Oxford and the Royal Astronomical Society. Late of Britannia, too, for that matter—the dear mother country having, tragically, herself joined the category of 'late' these past few months."

The brigadier waited expectantly. "And who might he be?" Brigid asked.

Smythe-George's eyebrows shot up. "You really *are* from another world, aren't you?" When Brigid continued to look at him levelly, he said, "Ah, but of course you are! But truly this tears it, if there was any doubt. For Dr. Nigel is the world's greatest scientist—and quite possibly the most famous man in the world!"

"SPIES," Rodríguez-Satterfield said.

Kane gave him a quizzical look. They stood on the

afterdeck of the great airship's gondola, with the gas bag itself looming above them like a football-shaped mountain. The sun had vanished behind an ominous line of thunderheads ahead like a dark parapet across the western horizon. Silver shafts of sunlight shot out from the top of it; the light across the rigging and polished wooden deck threw everything into sharp relief. It was chill, and the wind whipped by; the airship moved at what Kane judged was over a hundred miles per hour at an altitude of almost three thousand yards height.

"We have them. Everybody has them. In both directions."

Kane barked a laugh. It was all but swept away down their wind of passage. A decorative handrail of what appeared to be polished brass ran around the deck. Gatling guns, but a token few crewed, were mounted at intervals around the rail for air defense. The four great stacks marched in line from fore to aft, rising to pierce the gravid belly of the bag. Hatches were protected forward by windbreaks of what looked like laminated wood, which looked more like stylized snowplow blades than anything else.

"So your security's lousy."

Rodríguez-Satterfield hunched a shrug. "True enough, my friend. But there's only so much any of us—even the Canadians—will give up by way of personal autonomy in the name of security. Besides, tell me true, when have you seen even the strictest security measures work as advertised?"

"Damned seldom," Kane admitted, remembering how often as a Mag he'd heard what were closely held secrets in Cobaltville's Monolith dropped as careless scraps of gossip in its Tartarus Pits below. "But does that mean the lizard men, as well?"

"The Reptoids." Rodríguez-Satterfield nodded. "Just for information—we call them lizards, and snakes, and plenty worse things, too. But they're not reptiles the way a chuckwalla or a Gila monster or a sidewinder is. They're warm-blooded, like dinosaurs."

"Okay. Same question—how do humans like you spy on them? Have a damned hard time passing in any disguise I can imagine, unless the bastards have bad eyesight. Come to think of it, the same problem comes back the other direction—how do they spy on you?"

"First and most obviously, embassies and the like. We—that's the human nation-states of North America—send them delegates, and they send theirs to us. Everybody sends delegates everywhere. Hell's fire, even our backwater little capital of Auraria has its ambassadors from Zulu and the Deccan, and they've got ours. It's a toss-up which we of the modern world love the more—diplomacy or war. They seem to be the things we generate the most of. And that's despite the fact that, claims of their proponents to the contrary, neither of those things seems to diminish the amount we do of the other much."

"That'd seem easy enough to deal with," Kane said. "Just don't show the grand ambassador from Mumbo-Jumbo your secret war plans for invading his homeland, you're all set."

Rodríguez-Satterfield laughed. It seemed a common response of his to life. His laugh as always rang hearty and

sincere, nothing was forced or phony about it. Or any part
of him that Kane had yet discerned.

"If only it were that simple! And at that, I could tell you
stories, but why bore you, when there's plenty of juicy
tales to tell? I must warn you, amigo—we Cíbolans are
champion tale-spinners. We love nothing more than the
sound of our own voices, and they ring sweetest to our ears
when they're telling yarns. The taller, the better."

"Forgive me if I get the feeling," Kane said, walking to
the rail and peering down at landscape now blurring into
indistinguishability as shadow below outraced night
above, "that where I'm concerned the truth's the tallest tale
of 'em all."

Rodríguez-Satterfield showed white teeth in his dark
handsome face. The way dusk and cloud had bleached the
light rendered the contrast starker. "Precisely."

Kane swallowed and stepped back from the rail. As a
seasoned veteran of the Cobaltville Magistrate Divisions
Deathbird attack helicopters, Kane thought himself inured to heights. Especially given some of the physics-de-
fying maneuvers Grant had put their heavily modified
Apache through. And he'd done some time pretty high up
some pretty sheer cliffs.

Yet a glance over the rail at the Great Plains now starting to unwind below made him queasy and unsure of his
footing. Unlike a Deathbird, this aerial battlewagon wasn't
enclosed—unless you counted that shiny rail, which neither Kane's brain nor his inner ear did. And unlike the av-
erage mountain peak, the Aero-Dreadnought was rushing
ahead at a good clip. And for all its enormous mass, as

Kane became acutely aware the instant he looked down, the gondola swayed beneath his feet and bounced slightly in response to vagaries of the airflow around the craft.

Rodríguez-Satterfield didn't seem to notice. Perhaps he was too polite to. After studying his cheroot for a moment, he went on. "But the greater answer as to how we and our scaly friends manage to spy on each other is the same in both cases—human collaborators."

Kane turned toward him, glad of the distraction. "Quislings?"

Rodríguez-Satterfield shook his head. "Don't know the word."

Kane grunted. "Guess not. Means *traitors*. Some kind of historical thing—Baptiste'd know."

"Baptiste? Ah, one of your female companions. Yes, our histories clearly diverged some time ago. I'm eager to hear of your universe, as well. But I've promised to tell you of ours first, since that's more urgent for you than learning of yours is for me.

"Yes, some humans serve the Reptoids. Some are hirelings, but others do so out of a sense of duty, no matter how perverted that might strike you. The Reptoids have been on Earth for a generation. In their Mississippi holdings alone they control a population of several hundred thousand human souls, perhaps in excess of a million. A good number of those don't remember a time when the lizards didn't rule."

"The new generation doesn't hate them as occupiers?"

"Some do. Not all, by any means. And it's not just those born since the conquest who serve willingly, by any stretch. There are those who were adults when the Reptoids landed, some who actually fought them at first, who serve them willingly now. And not only for self-interest—or so they claim, since in my experience what any human, or any other creature, does is *always* in its self-interest, to the best of its judgment."

"Yeah. But how can they tell themselves that? I guess the lizards don't, what? Eat people."

The colonel laughed. "The notion would horrify them as much as it would you, if I told you we ate babies captured from our human rivals in the Silver Kingdom or the Dominion of Kali. As we don't, I'll add, just for the record. No, the Reptoids claim their only aim is to help us, for a fact."

He shrugged. "That's something human nations say, too, when they set out to conquer one another, isn't it? It's always for the good of the conqueree.

"And truth to tell—since we're brave comrades who've faced down danger together, and all that heroic buffalo flop—they're not that bad, the Reptoids. They aren't looking to exterminate or replace us. They're not even looking to enslave us."

Kane gave him a skeptical look.

"I tell you true. They want to rule us. Their rule isn't even all that odious. The Kali worshippers are palpably worse, the Minnetonkans no better, and just between you and me and—" with his cigar clipped between his first two fingers he swept his hand around the horizon "—the wide, wide world, our erstwhile allies the Canadians aren't an unqualified improvement, with their obsessive desire to control the lives of all their citizens in minute detail. And, ultimately, everybody else's life, too."

"Cali worshippers? They worship the late, great state of California?"

"It became a state in your world? Fascinating. Never got the chance in ours. No, the goddess. Kali. The Black Mother. Real nice lady. Although the Dominion does occupy the northern part of the former U.S. Territory of California. Between the Silver Kingdom and New Russia."

He made a grand flourish of his cheroot. It was dim enough now that the ember glow was clearly visible, a small red eye. It drew an afterimage arabesque across Kane's retinas.

"But later for geography. There are those humans, not solely to be found within the areas ruled by the Reptoids, who believe their ways are better for us than our own. So they serve the invaders out of idealism. Then, as said, there are always those who will do anything you can imagine—and a few things perhaps you can't—for gain."

"I track you there," Kane said, "except mebbe the part about what I can imagine. Not so much a matter of what I can imagine as what I can remember." Not all of which, he thought but did not say, was done by other people. Or even things. "But then, how do you spy on them back? People who buy into the Reptoid line'd hardly help you fight them."

"Aside from our own subornees? The Reptoids, as I said, are colonialists. They also reproduce fairly slowly, at least here on Earth's surface—makes you wonder what it actually is that drives them forth in search of other people's star systems to subdue. And as I think I also thought to mention, they're a distinct minority everywhere in their own holdings, except a few small enclaves more probably describable as forts or strongholds."

"Which means that humans do most of the work for them."

Rodríguez-Satterfield nodded. "Which also means, not just hewing wood and hauling water. But indeed, in positions of high authority—top bureaucrats, or top deputies to lizard bosses. Or right up close to top Reptoids. Think, servants."

"That'd still seem to leave you holding the short end," Kane said, "if the Reps are smart enough to keep all humans, even their butlers, out of their most secret councils."

"Most perceptive, amigo. And totally correct. But that's the game, isn't it? If we held all the cards the only Reptoids left on Earth would be in zoos, and their comrades could only look down from the Moon and gnash their teeth in despair."

"The Moon." Kane shook his head. The idea of a base on the Moon didn't phase him. He'd *been* to a base on the Moon. But the disconnect between this steam-engine technology and all the blithe and knowledgeable talk about other worlds made his mind clang like a bell.

He dared a glance over the side again. The very ground seemed to be roiling beneath them. He drew back again, afraid he was experiencing some new and horrible form of airsickness. Then he glanced over again and realized that, no, what looked like some kind of dark fur or mold was indeed seething around down there with motion ill-defined but unmistakable in the dense twilight.

Rodríguez-Satterfield came up beside him. "Ah. Buffalo herd. Decent sized one, perhaps a million."

"We got 'em back home, too," Kane said, "but not that thick."

The colonel clapped him on the shoulder. "Come on, friend Kane. Let's get below and around a fine meal and some finer brandy. It's going to be damp out on deck before too much more time passes—not to mention a bumpy ride."

Kane pointed ahead to the anvil-headed cumulonimbus wall, looming much higher and blacker than before. As if on cue, blue-white lightning veined the cloud for thirty degrees of arc, lighting the looming brutal mass like a nuke-blast.

"You don't mean," he said, "we're flying into *that*."

Rodríguez-Satterfield firmed his grip on Kane's shoulder. "Since we can't fly over it, and don't want to take time to fly around," he said, "it means that dead center. And anyway, what of it? We faced down danger together already today. Only then we didn't have brandy and fine cigars. Makes a difference, does it not?"

"It does," Kane agreed, and followed him belowdecks.

A SOUND OF THUNDER interrupted Brigid's dinner. The other diners in *Adamant*'s captain's mess continued eating without sign they noticed.

She stirred her London broil, peas and mashed potatoes a little with her fork to enhance a polite dissimulation that she'd been eating. Beyond a few nibbles of the soup and fish course she'd taken almost nothing. Usually her appetite was healthy enough, especially after vigorous activity. But tonight she was disturbed. She mourned Grant and worried about Kane, although she knew he was capable of taking care of himself. But so was Grant, she thought. And then, there was the question of her status and Domi's, as yet far from certain, despite their gentle and genteel treatment aboard the Aero-Dreadnought.

"Aren't severe storm cells dangerous to airships?" she asked.

The white-haired captain looked up, glanced at Brigadier Smythe-George and smiled. "They can be altogether lethal, Dr. Baptiste," Harrowgate said with an indulgent smile. "Especially when they're filled with hydrogen, which, thank heaven, we are not."

"That's not thunder, Dr. Baptiste," said the eager young Lieutenant Barrows. He had been permitted to join his seniors at table, apparently because he had been assigned as Brigid's minder. He seemed quite overwhelmed at the rarefied company—but not sufficiently to keep his natural ebullience in check for long.

He did clamp his mouth and duck his head down into his stock collar as his superiors turned stern gazes on him. He mumbled an apology and concentrated on chasing a last pea around his plate with a fork. His plate, like the others, was of some lightweight ceramic or synthetic, with a steel plate in the bottom and a magnet hidden beneath the spotless white tablecloth to clamp it down in lieu of mass. As Brigid suspected from the outset, the designers and crew of an Aero-Dreadnought compromised with the need to clad themselves in massive plates of armor by economizing on weight whenever possible.

"What is it, then, Lieutenant?" she asked.

He blushed, turned eyes to the brigadier. Smythe-George nodded. Reluctantly.

"That's gunfire, ma'am," the subaltern said. "Naval gunfire, if I might hazard a guess."

"The lad strives mightily to impress, Dr. Baptiste," Harrowgate said. "The fact is, we're over Lake Michigan. To hear land-based artillery out here would be quite remarkable."

"Naval gunfire," she repeated. Without excusing herself she rose and went to the quarter porthole. She wasn't sure what impelled her to move with such alacrity, whether simple curiosity or fear that the shells might reach the *Adamant*.

The sun was still visible, halved by the water horizon, just off the starboard quarter, beyond a great propeller on its sponson. Surely it was fully set from the vantage of those on the lake surface, three thousand yards below. But a red glow fell across the scene like luminous blood.

Ships fought down there. Ironclads, Brigid guessed, remembering pictorial histories from the American Civil War. If that had even happened in this universe.

Naval design must have evolved in the intervening two and a half centuries. But in the gloom the combatant vessels looked the way she envisioned the *Monitor* and the *Virginia* might have, viewed from high above. From the sporadic orange stabs of flame she gathered that at least a dozen vessels contended on the lake's uneasy surface.

The smoke from their stacks and that from their guns surged upward, gradually shrouding the dark, low-slung forms from her sight as she watched. The cannon flashes lit the artificial fogbank like lightning a distant cloud.

"Who's fighting?" she asked.

"Our lot, I shouldn't doubt," Captain Harrowgate said, downing silver to announce the meal was done, and dabbing his mouth fastidiously with a napkin. "Battling the Minnetonkans. We're taking the risk of overflying contested territory. Exigencies of speed, don't you know."

"You don't hold Chicago?" she asked, pressing a hand against the glass of the port. She seemed unable to look away from those mysterious-seeming flashes.

"'Chicago'?" Smythe-George repeated blankly.

"An old name for Fort Dearborn, Stanley," the captain said. "The Minnetonkans call it Tikamthe, Doctor. And no. That's one reason we've taken a considerable detour to the northwest, to avoid Fort Dearborn's considerable aerial defenses. That and the winds."

A white flash below, momentarily sun-bright, though smoke completely obscured its origin. Brigid's eyebrows rose as the glow expanded, became yellow, then orange, then persisted in angry red. Several seconds later she heard a slamming sound, and it seemed the gondola shook slightly as though buffeted by a blast of wind despite its armored mass.

"Magazine explosion," Harrowgate said. "God send it was one of theirs."

Tight-lipped, Brigid turned away from the port.

Chapter 7

Grant raised his head off his chest as the door of the white womb opened.

It took heartbeats for his eyes to resolve an image: *white* was an understatement. The cell's walls and floor and ceiling were so bright and featureless that it became all but impossible to tell where one ended and others began. Sourceless white light glared so dazzlingly that even walls, floor and ceiling could only be guessed at. The only object in the cell not blinding white was his own scarred and naked body, bound to a chair in the middle of it. As he had been for hours.

As he squinted at the figure in the doorway, he heard what he presumed to be it speaking to someone outside the cell. To his surprise his lizard-men captors' language didn't consist of hisses, but of gutturals, snarls and explosive plosives. More what he might have expected of a wolf than a lizard.

He chuckled. The vibration sent bright blue-white stabs of agony through the red-and-black ache that was his rib cage.

"Dunno what you're sayin'," he made himself say,

though words were knives in his throat. "But it sounds as if someone's getting his ass well and truly ranked-out to me."

"LITTER-MATE OF DRONES!" snarled Chief Egg Inspector Zirak of the Central Intelligence Directorate at the head jailer of First Field Army's forward military-intelligence headquarters, north of the suburb of St. Charles. The jailer tipped his torso to lower his head and elevate his stumpy tail in submission. "This man is a source of potentially priceless information. Why do you mistreat him? Have you no more wit than a female?"

"But, Chief Inspector," the wretched army jailer whined, "it is standard procedure for the softening-up of barbarian captives!"

"Again proving 'military intelligence' to be an oxymoron," snapped Zirak.

The jailer, who didn't know what "oxymoron" meant but presumed—not altogether incorrectly—that his own intelligence was being impugned, could only grovel lower, making clucking noises to signify abject self-abasement. In theory, CID was a civilian agency, with no power over the Talon, as the collective military of the True People was known.

In theory. The fact was significantly otherwise. And hierarchical instinct, not to mention that of self-preservation, superseded the nominal chain of command. A person who failed to behave with sufficient meekness to a male as senior as a CID chief inspector risked finding himself mucking crèches and dodging the snapping jaws of immense nonsapient queens defending their equally toothy and surly broods.

"Correct this worthless one, O master!" the jailer said, staring fixedly at the toe claws of the furious chief inspector. They were dull in both sheen and tip, cracked and faded in fact, more like the claws of a common laborer than a true hunter of the Nest. Then again, that had small bearing on this disreputable-looking specimen's ability to relegate the hapless jailer to baby-shit patrol for the rest of his miserable life, and that likely to be brief. "This I beg."

"I'll speak to him and soothe him," Zirak said. "Then get him out, give him anesthetic and turn him over to my men."

"But, Chief Inspector, the alien animal is dangerous!" the jailer said. "He was carrying an unknown weapon no softskin should have had, and wearing marvelous lightweight armor even the people could not replicate."

Zirak pivoted on his strong back legs. Everting the crimson ruff that normally lay almost imperceptibly around the base of his powerful neck, he opened his mouth to show an equally bloody-looking gape. His white teeth were surprisingly similar to a human's despite being set in a most inhuman blunt, round muzzle: incisors, canines, a few more incisors, then broad flattish molars. An omnivore's bite—but evocative enough of the people's pack-hunter ancestry to take off the jailer's forearm at one great snap.

"Fool!" Zirak said, and this time he did hiss. "So you think me a drone, then? Am I not a hunter? What have I to fear from a naked one?"

The jailer fell over and groveled on the floor, pissing the tile in panic. The uniform trunks of lightweight flexible material he wore left his subcaudal excretory orifices open along with the tail itself. Too bad, thought Zirak. If he wore full-seated trousers like a softskin, my feet would not be befouled now.

He turned to gaze into the cell. Though he carefully kept it from showing in his face or posture, his pulse sang with excitement: imagine, a captive human from a world in which their technology exceeded the people's! Far from feeling chagrined, he was like a lepidopterist presented with a beautiful butterfly from another planet.

He was a lizard who loved his work.

"Pull yourself together and do as I have said," he said with mild matter-of-factness the jailer took to be more menacing than the bared teeth. The jailer was not a particularly perceptive Reptoid. But as it happened, he was right again.

THOUGH HIS EYELIDS hung like lead shutters, Grant had watched the exchange with keen interest. Between the glare, the intervening bulk of this new lizard dressed in what look like mufti to Grant's eye, and the fact the jailer was out in the hall, meant he couldn't see many details. But he got the essentials of the transaction, especially the rustle, nail-scrape and sodden thump when the civvie turned around quickly and made the jailer fall right on his ass.

Grant laughed and laughed. It hurt like Billy Jesus. But it was funny. And Grant desperately needed something to laugh about.

The newcomer approached him cautiously, looking at him with head slightly averted. In knocking around the world in the company and influence of the likes of Baptiste and Lakesh, Grant had learned well enough what that meant: one predator politely approaching another.

"I apologize for the rudeness with which you have been treated," the lizard said in flawless Midwestern English, except for a bit of a lisp. For some reason Grant's eyes, blurred though they were, noted that his teeth were sheathed in substantial, flexible lips. "I will help you. Call me Ishmael."

Grant laughed until he passed out.

LIGHTNING LIT the darkened wardroom a garish white. "'Here's a toast to the dead already,'" the airship officers sang as thunder crashed like cannonades and threatened to swamp their words. "'Hurrah for the next man who dies!'"

Kane stared around as if they were mad. He had heard the ancient, defiant airman's toast or song or prayer before. But never under circumstances in which he and his companions seemed so immediately likely of qualifying for the promised accolade.

Lightning flared again, illuminating the faces of the eight men who sat around the table with Kane, swilling from big lightweight pewter-looking mugs. They had to be mad, daring a monster storm like this. The massive gondola rolled and pitched like a kayak in rapids to the fury raging outside.

"Drink up, Kane, 'migo," Rodríguez-Satterfield said.

"How can you booze when a lightning strike or some kind of nasty wind-shear could rip even this big mother out of the sky?"

"How can you not?" asked Josiah Tayson, a tubby man of medium height with sideburns flaring out of his high stock collar. He was the *Angel*'s gunnery officer; this was his domain.

With the armored gun ports open, the wet, ozone-tinged wind whistling through and the lightning strobes casting shadows and shapes like handfuls of distilled good and evil, the gun deck bore a striking resemblance to an agglomeration of the least appealing visions of the afterlife from all the world's cultures. The guns looked like great smooth hunched demons. The blocks and rigging were implements of correction, infernal and eternal.

There were surprisingly few of the gargoyle guns, six in each broadside. Kane had been told the ship mounted several more cannon—rifles, they were generally called—on other decks as stern and bow chasers.

In addition to the quick firers he had seen mounted on the weather deck rail, Gatling blister turrets could be extruded from the gondola's belly to defend against attack from below. These were rotated, he had been proudly informed, by electricity generated by the great steam-turbine engines he could feel purring away on the engine deck, driving the *Angel* on her mad career through the evil heart of a Great Plains supercell.

The men who served the great rifles had been stood down. Tonight the Aero-Dreadnought *Rocky Mountain Angel* faced a foe against which no cannonade would avail.

"Besides," as Tayson had cheerfully explained, "who else'd be fool enough to be up in the very Devil's weather like this?"

Seeing the point to the gunnery officer's question, Kane thrust forward his mug. He was pleased when "Major" Marc Furet, the small and wiry chief ultralight pilot, poured from a bottle of El Dorado Gold Label Whiskey. The alternative was Taos Lightning in white clay jugs. Kane suspected it was at least a little less sinister, or anyway corrosive, than the various distillates called by that name in his own world. But his stomach was in rough enough shape already without finding out firsthand.

Furet's actual rank was captain, but naval tradition held that a ship could hold only one captain, and that was *the* captain; hence the courtesy promotion. He had a cherub's face under a tousle of white-blond curls. His expression was anything but cherubic, however. Of the four powered light aircraft *Angel* carried, only his had made it back to safe landing atop the two-hundred-yard-long gas bag. Before they pulled out of sight of their fellow Aero-Dreadnoughts, which had hung back to screen the *Angel*'s escape, a fellow ship had communicated, by heliograph or perhaps extremely short-range spark-gap telegraph, that it had picked up a second *Angel* pilot.

Furet had joined with gusto in singing the morbid song. Kane knew it for an old fighter jock's hymn. It must have special significance for him this night.

Kane tested his mug cautiously. He thought he'd seen the fighter pilot—if you could call an armed sailplane or a box kite with a mousepower electric engine a fighter—

pour from the bottle with the label. But this wasn't Kane's first drink of the evening—on top of a day he wouldn't wish on a Sharpeville Mag.

He sucked down a long swallow. For some reason the question that had been gnawing in its cage at the back of his mind all day chose that moment to break free.

"Can somebody," he said, wiping his mouth with the back of his hand, "tell me why that bastard Mackenzie asked that question today? About whether Grant was our slave or we were his?"

Silence took the group of men gathered around the table; even the storm's rage seemed to abate for a coincidental moment. None of Kane's companions was black, nor had he seen anyone identifiably black aboard the *Angel*. These eight men were by appearance Anglo, Latino and Indian, and some, like Rodríguez-Satterfield, by appearance as well as name, could be taken for one as another. They struck him, despite their somewhat fancy mode of speech and current jovial inebriation, as basically hard men without a lot to prove.

It was a type he wasn't exactly unfamiliar with.

"Well-l-l," said Trace Chapman, a tall rangy man with heavy straight blue-black hair worn long and gathered in a ponytail and dark craggy features of a Plains Indian, as he took a pull from his mug. He was an infantry officer, commander of a small detail aboard the Aero-Dreadnought. "So you've met the Devil, have you?"

"And lived to tell the tale," Tayson said.

Lightning flared and thunder cracked. The gondola wallowed like a ship caught broadside by a high sea.

Doing his best not to wince, Kane said, "He seems to be almost as well-known as the fact we were coming."

"A man like that tends to have his reputation spread far and wide," said Antonio Romero, the chief engineer. He was a square, solid man of medium size who showed his liquor less than anyone but Rodríguez-Satterfield and looked more Anglo, at least by this light, than anyone but Furet and Kane himself. "Especially by way of the yellow journals."

"Sensational exploits, to be sure," said the voluble Tayson. "The affair of the Lost Battalion of Ashkabad. And of course the seduction of the youthful Duchess of Pomeranz…"

"And her dowager mother," Tayson added from behind his own mug.

The others laughed at that, everyone except for the ship's surgeon, Elton Diggs, a tall, dark, cadaverous man with forehead and hair alike receding from a blade of nose. He stood by the table swaying gently in directions and rhythms that bore no visible resemblance to the motions of the airship; it made Kane dizzy to watch him for any length of time.

"Don't forget the allegations of torture in Maluku," he said, "or the Red River Massacre of '99."

"He's a bad man, for true," said Rodríguez-Satterfield, slamming the contents of his latest mugful and grinning. "Represents all those things the hegemony claims to abhor, and which are really the mainstays of its empire."

"They don't call him the Devil for nothing," said Elias Silva, the brooding, bearlike navigator.

"But to attend to our guest's question," Rodríguez-Satterfield said, "did your world experience the Secession War?"

"Don't think so. Give me a date." He didn't want to admit that his knowledge of his own world's history was sketchy at best. To the extent the Magistrate Division even bothered with that kind of thing, the cadets were taught a version of what all the other Enclave dwellers were: a colored, if not particularly inaccurate, account of how chaotic, and violent the world was before the unification program brought the blessings of strict discipline and expiation to the formerly United States.

The denizens of the Tartarus Pits, of course, were taught only to obey.

"Began with the shelling of Fort Sumter in North Carolina in April of 1861," Tayson said. "Certain Southern states sought to secede from the Union over abusive tariffs and the slavery question."

"Oh, yeah. The Civil War. That's what I always heard it called."

The Cíbolan officer nodded. "In July of 1863 a great battle was fought in Pennsylvania, around a town called Gettysburg. The issue was in some doubt then. During its height, at 1:13 on the afternoon of the second, *something* enormous struck the Earth in western France, in the department of Côte-d'Or, southwest of Dijon. Some twelve and a half minutes later it exploded outward from the Earth from the Bahia Moreno, at the city of Antofagasta, on Chile's Pacific coast."

"It went all the way through the Earth?"

Tayson nodded. "All this was established by various historical and scientific investigations decades later, during the early twentieth century. After the dust settled, so to speak."

The gondola rocked again to the brain-battering roar of a lightning discharge that filled the compartment with arc-welder-blue light from every port. Kane barely noticed.

"What could go *through* a planet?"

"We still wish we knew," said Juan-Diego Wayne, the signals officer, who looked a bit like a shorter, younger Rodríguez-Satterfield.

"The distinguished Britannian scientist Dr. Sir Nigel Miles-Burnham—" Tayson said.

"Now in Canada!" said Wayne.

"Now in Canada, has theorized it was a fragment of the primordial stuff of the universe itself, if I summarize aright. I'm not the scientist Miles-Burnham is, but then no one is. Aside from killing several hundred million people outright, with the great heat and blast and seismic sea waves, the Great Destructor brought the Great Change, which appears to have fundamentally altered the laws of our reality."

"Which is why, Señor Kane," Romero said, "little of your technology functions here. The higher-energy-level interactions are barred from us. Apparently forever."

Kane stared at him through slit eyes. "Lightning still works," he said, "unless you got a hell of a special-effects crew on board this gas buggy."

The engineer nodded. "Such is the mystery of the Great Discontinuity," he said.

"But at least it affects the damned lizards as much as us," Furet added.

Chapter 8

It was long after dark when Brigid was awakened from a blessedly dreamless sleep by an apologetic knock at the door of the cabin she shared with Domi. She realized at once that the Aero-Dreadnought had ceased its forward motion and was descending.

With young Barrows waited a squad of six Hegemonic Marines in scarlet coats, white trousers and shiny steel lobster-tail helmets. "Profuse apologies for the unpleasant necessities, Dr. Baptiste," he said. "You understand, I trust?"

"Am I to be bound again?" she asked. The muscles of her face felt turned to wood.

He shook his head vigorously. "Not at all. Ah, that is if you will give your parole not to attempt escape."

"Of course." She shrugged. "Where would I go?"

"Please," the young officer said, "you must understand that we undertake these measures for your own safety. I hope that you will continue to think of us as friends. And remember that we are, after all, in a war, and must sometimes adopt expedients distasteful to us."

Because of his continuing floppy-puppy sincerity Brigid decided to give him the benefit of the doubt, that he actually believed the boilerplate bureaucratic lie about the armed escort being for *her* safety. They've treated me well, Brigid thought, treated *us* well since our capture. She saw much to admire in the caring, benevolent social order of the hegemony that Harrowgate, Smythe-George and their junior officers had enthusiastically described to her on the bridge and over dinner.

And even the captain's hands were tied, she reminded herself. He had to follow the dictates of distant superiors.

"Begging your pardon, Doctor," Barrows said, "but what of your charming compatriot?"

There was no tincture of irony in his pronunciation of the word *charming*, suggesting he was either even more ingenuous or a far more accomplished liar than Brigid suspected.

Domi refused to answer his question.

"She won't give her parole, Lieutenant," Brigid said. "She has her own code of honor."

Barrows nodded crisply. "Understood, ma'am. Gentlemen?"

He and Brigid stood aside as four of the Marines, stooping low so that the muzzles of their slung rifles didn't clash with the top of the hatchway, entered the cabin. Approaching reluctantly, as if suspecting she was radioactive, two picked up the tiny writhing woman by the arms and bore her out, the second pair following and looking visibly relieved that it seemed unnecessary for them to grasp her windmilling white legs.

The legacy of Queen Victoria was thriving in modern Canada, Brigid reflected. Whether it had resurged or persisted straight through for two centuries.

"Where are we?" Brigid asked Barrows as they followed the Marines and the still struggling Domi down the gangway.

"Landing at the Pelee Island Hegemonic Canadian Naval Station on Lake Ontario, ma'am. It's a most strategically important fortress and coaling point in our conflict with Minnetonka. After you retired we passed south of the substantial industrial port of Windsor, known to the francophones as Cadillac."

She made a quick search of her eidetic memory. "Detroit?" she asked.

"I believe it was once called that, ma'am."

She was disappointed—perhaps irrationally—if not really surprised that neither Captain Harrowgate nor Brigadier Smythe-George appeared to wish her farewell. Instead Lieutenant Barrows led her and the Marines down a lightweight metal gangplank to a concrete apron scoured by a chill, dank wind. Gangs of men were still hauling down on guys that trailed up to the great gondola and far greater envelope above, and fastening them to great rusted eyelets sunk in the concrete, although clearly the major work of drawing down the great airship had been done by a two-story-tall steam-powered winch rising from the landing zone.

At the foot of the ramp Barrows and his men turned the women over to a middle-aged lieutenant of the surface navy and another Marine detachment. By this time Domi had consented to calm down sufficiently to walk on her own two feet, which were liberated for the purpose. She and Brigid were escorted not to the gate through the high inward-sloping concrete walls surrounding what she guessed was the fortress itself but to a dock a half mile away. The journey quickly turned brisk as they moved out of *Adamant*'s weather shadow and a cold, spare but stinging rain began to pelt them from black overcast swept by searchlight beams from within the fort's walls.

A long low shadow-shape lay in the water by the dock. It was a ship—clearly a ship of war, with the few lights showing silhouetting turrets bristling with guns. Its bow, like the fortress walls above it, sloped backward from the waterline, giving it a peculiar look to Brigid's eye.

Yet another lieutenant, younger but by both men's body language senior to the chief of Brigid's and Domi's current escort, greeted them at the foot of a gangplank let down from the vessel to the dock. After accepting charge of the captives, the new officer pivoted and saluted Brigid smartly.

"Dr. Baptiste," he said. "I'm Lieutenant Watts-Dunton. Please permit me to welcome you ladies aboard the pride of Lake Ontario, Her Majesty's turbine ram, RHCN *Tyrannulet.*"

They were escorted aboard with polite firmness by Watts-Dunton and his Marines. Domi walked alongside Brigid in sullen silence.

The vessel didn't strike Brigid as large, as far as ships went: a hundred yards or less in length, dwarfed by the immensity of the dirigible moored nearby. Still, its lines gave it a thrustful, formidable appearance. She wondered if it had been deliberately designed to intimidate.

She and Domi were shown below, into a cabin somewhat utilitarian by the *Adamant*'s standards, although still luxurious for a ship of war: stained wall paneling that looked like real wood, brass fittings, two bunk-style beds, a chair with tables and a brass lamp with green shade. While Brigid took stock of the new surroundings, Domi, still smoldering, moved with compact purpose, doing something Brigid didn't see.

Whatever she did was no more than just in time. After a perfunctory knock, the door swung open to reveal an abashed-looking Watts-Dunton, backed by four redcoat Marines and a pair of grim-faced matrons taller and broader than any of the men. They were dressed in stiff, drab tunics of a greenish tan that was neither olive nor khaki but combined the least appealing elements of both.

"Begging your pardon, ladies," the lieutenant said, "but as we move into the hegemony itself you will find yourselves far more comfortable dressed in more appropriate apparel."

Brigid didn't protest the implicit sexism; this was, after all, a different world—and she understood full well she had experienced its pleasant obverse that afternoon, in the chivalry of Captain Harrowgate and the brigadier. Besides, while it was clear that such archaic gallantry made Watts-Dunton and even his obviously lower-class Marines reluctant to lay hands on a female, the matrons just as clearly felt no such compunction. Sweeping past them into the corridor with such dignity as she could muster, Brigid wondered briefly if burly RHMP matrons were part of the standard complement on Her Majesty's surface ships of war. She decided that was unlikely, and that these must have been ordered in especially to handle her and Domi.

Dressing them "appropriately" meant conveying them to dismal little cubicles, with walls painted in colors not unlike the matrons' tunics, if a touch greener and yellower. There they were stripped naked and thoroughly, if impersonally, searched by the matrons. Then, as promised, they were given garments the Canadians deemed "suitable" for young women of their status.

The undergarments were a pleasant surprise, lighter and less restrictive than Brigid had expected, underpants that were almost trunks and seemed made of real silk; a sort of camisole of the same stuff; and an odd and unpleasantly stiff contrivance of two rounded cones and some straps that she recognized as analogous to a twentieth-century brassiere of her own worldline. It was more restrictive and cumbersome than the sports-type halters she was accustomed to from her own time, but far better than the terrifying steel or whalebone corset she had feared being required to strap on like some medieval penitential device.

As she pulled on the lightweight undershift over the bra and trunks, she heard muffled exclamations from the next cubicle. Then a few wild thumps. And finally the unmistakable sound of a slap by a meaty palm.

She shook her head.

For an overgarment she had a dress of some material she didn't recognize; fabrics lay far afield from her assigned research areas as archivist, and it had never occurred to her to become interested in such trivia. The cloth was a slightly shimmery green, and seemed artfully stiffened so as to prevent it clinging too intimately and revealingly to a woman's curves. But once donned it felt light, cool and comfortable. As did the underwear, even though the boxy contrivance strapped to her chest felt decidedly peculiar. While contemporary mores obviously mandated that a woman's sexuality should be masked even as her gender role was emphasized, fortunately they didn't require she be physically uncomfortable.

They were released into the yellow light of the gangway overheads. Domi was dressed in a blue gingham sundress. It made her look almost painfully young—and cute. Brigid decided not to say so. Nor remark on the sunburnlike patch of red on her left cheek.

Back in their cabin, Brigid slumped on one of the beds, overwhelmed by fatigue. Domi went to the other bed, knelt beside it, rummaged beneath the mattress.

"It's too bad they got your knife," Brigid said, knowing Domi had a somewhat morbid attachment to the weapon.

"Didn't!" the albino woman said, suddenly standing and flourishing the nine-inch blade with the saw-toothed back. "I hid it before those fat secwomen searched us."

Brigid felt a stab of irritation. "You're playing dangerous games," she said. "And I don't believe there's any point. These are fundamentally decent people."

"Just because they're bad at the police-state stuff," Domi said, "doesn't mean they're good."

"You're impossible," Brigid said.

"Thanks," said Domi.

In stony silence the two women removed the garments

they had so recently put on, turned out the gas lights and got into their bunks. By unspoken consent Domi took the upper one.

Throughout the night *Tyrannulet* thrust across the dark waters of Lake Ontario with all the authority of the steam-turbine engines Lieutenant Watts-Dunton was so very proud of. Still, it seemed to Brigid she had only just shut her eyes when pounding on the cabin door roused her. With no ports to outside and relieved of her wrist-chron— and with sour-faced lack of comment, of her inert Heckler & Koch handblaster—by the big, brusque matrons, she had no way of knowing how much time had really passed.

She and Domi dressed without exchanging a word and opened the door. An older, more taciturn lieutenant than Watts-Dunton met them with the obligatory Marine backers and another pair of matrons, apparently to handle ticklish situations. As they were escorted down the corridors Brigid realized the vessel had come to a stop and lay rolling gently in response to the waves of the lake.

Mist hanging low over the water horizon diffused the milky light of dawn. The women were escorted out on deck and down a ramp to a granite pier. The air smelled of dew and hot engine lubricants. A few lights of what was evidently a city, or settlement of some kind, showed through the fog shrouding the land. Nearer to hand the gray weathered walls of what conversation between their escort and seaman on the dock called Fort Lorne Michaels frowned out over the warship.

A plain carriage drawn by a team of four bay horses awaited. Brigid and Domi were handed over to a pair of trim, middle-sized men in long tweed coats with hats pulled low, who were introduced as Cobden and Bright, no titles nor service appended. Notwithstanding the fact she was a seasoned veteran of many battles and more than a few intrigues, Brigid remained somewhat ingenuous; nonetheless, she instantly made them both for coldhearts of the first order.

If she needed confirmation, Domi was quietly if sulkily cooperative as the men, with terse, superficial politeness, escorted them into the carriage and then rode facing them on a road that climbed a rocky slope. Obviously Domi didn't care to provoke their escorts. Brigid regarded the little albino's survival instincts as unimpeachable.

A light rain began to spatter and streak the carriage windows. The carriage smelled of leather and, faintly, of old sweat. At the top of the slope the carriage turned right and rode along the shore of Long Point Bay, unquiet gray beneath a sky slowly fading through indigo to mauve, with tall straight-boled trees on the left. Their journey would have been a walk of but a few minutes; evidently the hegemony preferred to spare its involuntary but invaluable guests the inconvenience of trudging through chilly drizzle.

Or perhaps the hard men who had them in charge wished to spare themselves the walk.

In the yellow glare of gaslights an engine waited and gleamed. It was a glorious thing, its cab and stack black and polished like a Cherrypicker's boot, its great cylindrical main tank a gleaming purple and all trimmed with gold, beneath a nodding white plume of steam. It looked to Brigid's eye like the late-nineteenth-century locomotives of her worldline. But it seemed somehow bigger, more powerful and just streamlined enough to suggest the capability of tremendous speed. Again she thought to see the same kind of arrogance by design she had remarked in the lines of the Great Lakes ram *Tyrannulet*. She wondered if that design philosophy was peculiar to the hegemony, or a trait of this world at large.

Despite its ostensible power, the arrogant engine drew few cars today: coal car, a passenger car, what appeared to be a combination kitchen and dining car, two more passenger cars and a baggage wagon at the rear. The carriage drew to a halt on the cindered roadbed next to the coach right behind the dining car. As Cobden and Bright handed them down with murmured insincere pleasantries, Brigid noted several soldiers in red coats and silvery helmets, with rifles slung, clambering aboard the first of the passenger cars at the front of the train.

"Soldiers in the car behind, too," Domi said out of the corner of her mouth. "They must not want us getting away."

They were squired into a compartment with two well-padded wooden bench-style seats, upholstered in deep green plush that matched the drapes on the windows, facing each other. Their warders withdrew, but Brigid sensed they remained near at hand, and that any move from the compartment would be immediately detected.

The train got under way with a shrill bull-elephant trumpeting of vented steam. Brigid tried to make conversation; Domi opined that the compartment was likely bugged. The suggestion irritated Brigid: Domi's attitude was going past antiauthoritarianism to waywardness, if not obsession. But something in her mind concurred, so they passed the journey in uncomfortable silence.

The weather stayed overcast. The passing landscape rolled like easy green waves. Neat hamlets of a European appearance rose from the midst of tilled fields. Herds of sheep or red or black-and-white-spotted cows grazed on the flanks of hills crowned with trees whose leaves had just begun to turn autumn-colored at the edges.

Almost all the few folk they saw abroad were afoot; once or twice Brigid glimpsed horsemen off in the distance, and occasionally farm wagons waited behind yellow-and-black-striped wood barriers at dirt road crossings, behind teams of wide, placid horses with blinders and hooves the size of dinner plates. All in all, it struck Brigid as a placid, bucolic landscape—which could scarcely have been more different from the tortured, impoverished, violent North America she and her friends had left behind.

Half an hour after the train got under way a peremptory knock roused them out of the lonely half doze each had settled into. Cobden—even Brigid's photographic memory could only distinguish him from his partner because he left the bottom button of his coat unbuttoned—had come to summon them to break their fast.

They followed him forward to the dining car, and were seated at a table covered in cloth so white it almost dazzled in the light of lamps in fine brass fixtures. Servants, men in tailcoats and women in voluminous skirts, served them tea and coffee in fine china from silver pitchers,

iced water and even fresh-squeezed orange juice. As the
sun mounted higher and burned off all but bitter-end wisps
of fog lurking low in the hollows, they ate a sumptuous
breakfast. Brigid's usually healthy appetite had returned;
she ate well. Domi ate like a wolf pack. They were the only
diners, and the servants had clearly had been instructed to
deny them nothing. As long as they ate or drank, neither
plate, cup nor cut-crystal goblet was allowed to empty.

Yet despite the fact that they were isolated travelers
from a place infinitely far, and had known each other
years, some invisible barrier hung between them like a
membrane. So they dined alone together in silent splen-
dor. At the end, there was still food on Domi's plate—a
near miracle—when she finally pushed it away and
belched.

One of their near-silent guardians—Bright, this time—
appeared to guide them back to their compartment.

Later, perhaps three hours after departing from the
Lake Ontario siding, a change in the train's motion made
Brigid raise her head from the pillow she had propped on
the sill in their compartment. Outside, the clouds seemed
to open up ahead. Like a theatrical spot, a shaft of brilliant sunlight fell upon the towers of what appeared to be
a city all of white and gold.

Chapter 9

Grant came awake all at once.

For a moment he felt dislocation, as if he weren't fully conscious, but only knocking on its door. The impression was quickly crowded from his brain by the conviction that he was not alone.

He also realized he didn't have the dimmest notion of where he was. He was in a bed in a room half-darkened, he saw as he opened his eyes to slits. His mind and body were free of pain.

He smelled the scent of another person in the room. An unmistakably female presence. His ears heard motion behind him as he lay, he perceived, on his left side.

He spun and sat up quickly, a sheet whipping away from his bare chest and slipping half to the floor. A woman stood there, stark naked with dark hair cascading down over pale shoulders. She recoiled at the suddenness of his actions, but stood her ground. And smiled.

Though she did not speak, she didn't have to. The smile said all.

A small but insistent voice from the back of Grant's head said he should hold back, was promised to another. Before he could say or do anything, however, a terrible fatigue rose up like a miasma from the bed to envelop him. He wondered, briefly, just what was happening to him— or had happened. Then the dark cloud took him back down to the depths.

"EXCELLENT, EXCELLENT," said Zirak to himself. He was looking through a one-way synthetic window so cunningly contrived that inside the cell neither the subject nor the human female behavioral specialist could distinguish it from plain drab cell wall, painted texture and all.

The weak believe we must conquer humankind because of their weakness, the chief inspector thought. The strong know we must conquer because of their strength. "Are you so sure, Zirak?" demanded Phalanx Commander Akhdar. "Our more direct methods would have produced results by now. Sleep deprivation works wonders."

"Produced what results, Phalanx Commander?" Zirak asked. "The creature is neither scientist nor engineer, nor truly a technician. He's a warrior, as you are alleged to be. Would you learn of the tactics of his tribe—who don't exist in our world, and whom you will never face on the field of battle? Or have you learned a degree of humility, and suspect he might be able to teach you something?"

The edges of Akhdar's ruff rippled, and he blushed in bands of subtle color—mauve, gray, faint powder blue, fainter old rose—across his head and neck. "You're a civilian!" he barked. "What do you understand of such matters?"

"Nothing, Phalanx Commander," Zirak said in tones he knew the other would interpret as submissive, although the chief inspector's body attitude was neutral: near horizontal, eyes looking directly at the military Reptoid. "But I know two things. First that this man has many uses to us, including, yes, the intelligence he can provide. All of which will be most readily available to us if he voluntarily makes them so."

"Ridiculous to coddle such beasts—"

"And second," Zirak said in a tone of voice long perfected to override the witless interruptions of superiors without offending them, "that *captive* is claimed by the Chief Intelligence Directorate. Any dissatisfaction with that, or with the methods I choose to employ, you must respectfully take up at a pay grade far, far above my poor head indeed."

And he rolled his eyes meaningfully skyward, in a gesture universally understood among the members of the True Race trapped in exile here on this vile dirtball, even though the world's moon and its High Base hung well around the curve of the world, far from the daytime sky at this longitude.

"We have dosed him with subtle drugs, which weaken his discernation while leaving his intelligence and even his will itself fundamentally intact. And we provide pleasurable stimulus to counteract the unpleasant experiences your overzealous subordinates put him through, to win his favor back."

"Plain bribery!" Akhdar huffed.

Zirak performed a bow by tilting his body forward—the downward motion hiding the sardonic smile. "The phalanx commander is most perceptive," he said.

The general huffed and left. Zirak rose laughing silently at the uniformed back. Then he put the dolt from his mind, folded his arms behind the back of the somewhat shabby jacket he wore and turned again to study his latest acquisition with the intensity of the true enthusiast.

BEHIND HIGH WALLS of gleaming white stone, the Royal Hegemonic Palace in Gloriana rose like a fairyland castle. Brigid and Domi rode toward it through the capital's broad streets in a great white-and-gold carriage drawn by eight white horses with scarlet-dyed plumes nodding from their foreheads. A squadron of Hussars rode before and behind them in gleaming breastplates and helmets, with red, white and gold hegemonic pennons fluttering from their lances.

The city itself wasn't all of gold, as it first appeared to Brigid. The spires of certain tall or prominent buildings, like church steeples and a vast dome that Brigid gathered had some governmental function, were gilded. But many of the structures were built of white or tan brick and stone, much of it glittering with what she guessed was a high quartz or mica content, and the tiles on many steep-angled roofs were of a yellow-tan color Brigid was tempted to think of as topaz. The architecture was generally airy in effect, with even the most brutally plain walls, of warehouses and the like, supported by flying buttresses and pierced by many high windows with pointed Gothic-arched tops.

The streets around were thronged with people going about their business, mostly afoot, some in carriages or horse-drawn trollies. A few cars were visible, clearly powered by steam. The only mounted persons Brigid saw were obvious policemen, and cavalry like their own escorts.

The people in general looked prosperous in their quasi-Victorian clothing, the men all in hats and jackets, the women in long flowing skirts. They moved with a brisk ease, not, Brigid thought, as if they were subjects of a harsh police state. She saw no one shabby or visibly poor.

Overhead, airships drifted through the sky, sausage-shapes great and small. A few winged flyers were visible kiting against the clouds, whether gliders or the electric-powered ultralight airplanes Brigid couldn't tell. There also seemed to be relatively small dirigibles aloft with fat spindle gas bags; what depended from beneath them none came close enough for Brigid to tell, even with her glasses on. But they were numerous, and seemed to be becoming more so as the clouds yielded to blue sky and sun. She guessed they were one- or two-person craft.

The nearly translucent quartz walls surrounding the palace, which rose fifteen yards from the street, were interrupted by a gate of what looked like gray armor plates twice as wide as high, held together with rivets as large as dinner plates. Against the designed delicacy of the city and what was visible of the palace towers and spires beyond it looked almost shockingly brutal. Brigid could only presume this effect was calculated: a recall to reality on the very brink of a fantasy realm, that within the dainty velvet evening glove was a fist of iron.

The great grim plates slid sideways before the lead escorts with a vast groaning and creaking and blasts of steam from fixed engines behind the walls, to reveal black iron gates of looping, soaring, almost Art Nouveau tracery. These swung daintily inward to admit the glittering horsemen and the carriage behind into the palace grounds.

Even Domi was impressed. She came out of her sullen reserve to press her nose against the window and clap her hand in childish delight.

Brigid could see why: the place looked to her like pictures of Disneyland. Without the rides and the fuzzy character-costumes, of course, and not precisely, especially since she already had garnered enough scraps of this worldline's history to know Disneyland as such had never existed in this world. But, as with Cinderella's Castle in the long-lost theme park, the architects had blatantly been influenced by the works of castle-mad King Ludwig II of nineteenth-century Bavaria, a man so consumed by his hobby he had thrown over legendary beauty Lola Montez, inherited from his father along with the crown, to pursue it. He even secretly plotted to sell much of his own kingdom for funds to build more and greater castles in Africa, of all places, and was caught at it—whereupon he had drowned in a lake under what were termed "mysterious circumstances."

The palace was no single structure but a whole sprawling compound full of them, a city within a city. Although one great building, both wide and soaring, clearly dominated and was no doubt the Hegemonic Palace proper, there also stood a stone flotilla of ancillary buildings, barracks, storehouses and others whose function was not at all apparent, and an entire cathedral of some size, inter-

spersed among spacious gardens and pools and white ga-
zebos with gilded roofs. Brigid was reminded of Ver-
sailles—or the gigantic monument to socialist bad taste
and monarchic ambition built by Romanian tyrant Nico-
lae Ceauşecu in the late twentieth century.

"I'm pretty sure Gloriana is built where Toronto was
in our world," she murmured to Domi. "But this city had
to have been built from virtually the ground up. Toronto
never looked like this."

"Something knocked it all down," Domi said matter-
of-factly.

Their fantastic procession trotted grandly up to the central palace, which combined High Gothic features with
soaring mock-medieval towers and turrets. They halted
under a white porte cochere all the cavalry mounts coming to a stop at the same instant, as if their legs were wired
to a single circuit.

Bright and Cobden had seen the women into the carriage at a small tree-shaded station in a park a mile or so
from the palace. The locked doors were now opened by a
pair of white-liveried footmen whose powdered white
wigs contrasted with their dark, strong-featured faces:
both were clearly AmerIndians. Waiting behind them
stood a thin young man in black coat, buff trousers, white
blouse with cravat and dark-tinted half glasses. His skin
was pale and so glossy it seemed stretched too tightly
across his prominent forehead and supercilious features.
His hair was dark brown and curly. Behind him loomed
four strapping great-mustached guardsmen in white uniforms and gilt breastplates and helmets, so resplendent

that Brigid felt fortunate they stood in the shade of the porte cochere; in the sunlight they would have been blinding.

"Ladies, I am Sebastian Dalzell, chamberlain," the thin young man said, bowing perfunctorily as the Indian footmen handed Brigid and Domi out of the carriage. "I am to be your guide. Please follow me."

Brigid and Domi found themselves walking with surprising briskness down a wide marble corridor whose ceiling vaulted high above their heads. The decor was muted, the light, which seemed to fall from cunningly placed and concealed skylights as much as enter through high narrow windows, was just past dim and lent the place a cathedral aspect.

"The proportions are designed to intimidate," Brigid said in a low-voiced aside to Domi, "inside and out."

The albino woman grunted missively. "I'm hungry," she said loudly. The walls seemed to absorb rather than echo her words.

"I apologize for any and all inconvenience, ladies," Sebastian Dalzell said. "At the moment I fear we dare not tarry. We are running late, through no fault of your own, of course."

He pivoted smartly left down a lower-ceilinged, narrower, dimmer passageway lined with white marble busts set in niches on pedestals. Soft radiance fell from above like haloes at intervals of four or five yards. "After your audience, all your needs will be amply attended to, my word upon it."

Brigid glanced at Domi. Despite the outlander woman's

shorter legs she seemed to be having an easier time keeping up with the deceptively brisk pace set by Dalzell than Brigid, who was taller and longer legged than either.

He stopped at a door on the right. It was a solid-looking oak door with some subtle figuring on it, otherwise unremarkable. Two of the four palace guardsmen—they couldn't possibly be anything else in those comic-opera outfits—who had been clanking and jingling discreetly behind took up positions of rigid attention flanking the door. The other two assumed a sort of parade-rest posture behind the two women. Brigid noted a detail she had overlooked before: each wore a basket-hilted sword in a gold-fitted silver scabbard, straight-bladed and hung from a white baldric at the left hip, nearly vertical so as not to trip them when they walked. If they carried firearms at all they were well concealed.

"Ladies," Dalzell said, opening the door, "it is my inestimable honor to present you to Her Benevolent Hegemonic Majesty, Queen Fiona I, Protector of Humankind and Empress of North and South America!"

Chapter 10

To Brigid's surprise they were ushered not into a throne room, but what appeared to be a steam-age briefing chamber. It was long and narrow, with the usual decor: stained wood paneling, silver-figured wallpaper above, lush carpet of a deep grayish purple, brass gas lamps with mauve shades, dark yet somehow without seeming gloomy. Instead it implied comfort with great power. Two features dominated: a long table like a narrow ellipse, truncated at both ends, and the queen herself, lounging in a chair at the far end of it.

She was much younger than Brigid expected. She could be no older than her early twenties. She had dark wine-red hair, a red markedly different from Brigid's own, with a metallic, almost coppery sheen to it, wound in a braid tightly around her well-shaped head. Her features were classic and haughty, a trifle square, with a slender nose and eyes of a blue so deep as to approach violet. These gazed at the newcomers half-lidded as Her Majesty puffed on a long black cheroot.

Brigid could hardly smell the smoke. Mostly what she smelled was the scent of sprays of fresh lilac, presumably hothouse grown, in vases set on walnut pedestal tables at intervals along the walls to both sides of the table.

Fiona I wore tan jodhpurs, black calf-length riding boots, one crossed over her knee, and a loose blouse of what seemed bleached muslin with the sleeves unbuttoned and rolled up carelessly to her forearms. Her skin was very white, with the bluish undertint of a truly pale redhead. She appeared to be tall, at least as tall as Brigid, somewhat broad in the shoulders, of a general wiry athletic build.

"Your Majesty," Dalzell said, bowing almost perfunctorily, "may I present to you Dr. Brigid Baptiste and Miss Domi, travelers from far places."

"Perhaps," the young queen said, biting the word off. "Perhaps not."

She uncrossed her legs, swung around in her chair and leaned her elbows on the table. "Perhaps they come from a place as near as the surface of our own skin, which we cannot see. Right—" She snapped her fingers in the air "—here. Fascinating."

"Ladies," Dalzell said imperturbably, "you may now perform curtsies."

Brigid did, to the best of her ability, which was scanty. As she dipped down in what she hoped approximated proper respectful form, the corner of her vision snagged on Domi, who stood rod upright, glaring laser defiance at the queen. Brigid tugged at her sleeve. The albino woman, though much smaller, had muscles like wound wire; she resisted successfully. The net effect of Brigid's efforts was to pull herself almost off balance and transfer the locus of Domi's glare from Fiona to her.

Fiona sat back in her chair and looked lazily at them

again. "Young woman," she said around her cigar, "whether you bow or not, I'll still be queen."

"We'll see," Domi said.

Fiona laughed. "Spirit," she said. "It's actually easier to admire in one who isn't one's own subject. In guests—or even captives—defiance can possess a certain charm, whereas in subjects it's merely inconvenient."

Brigid tried to puzzle out whether there was something sinister to the young woman's words or not. She was already certain that, titles apart, it would be a dangerous mistake to underestimate the barely postadolescent Fiona.

"Where are you from?" asked the queen.

"You summed it up as well as anyone could, I believe," Brigid said. She paused a moment. "Your Majesty."

"You seem tentative, Dr. Baptiste. As if nonplussed to encounter me in such surroundings." She waved a languid hand at the flocked wallpaper and the portraits of glum men in uniform in ornate gilded frames. "As if you'd expected to find me in a throne room rather than a conference chamber. Well, I've a throne room, right enough—it'd hardly be suitable for the ruler of the world's greatest empire not to—but it's big, drafty, somewhat silly, and the acoustics are terrible. I prefer at least somewhat more intimate settings when there's something I actually want to learn. And yes, I am aware that juxtaposing silver and gold is in shocking bad taste. My great-grandfather's fault, actually, not mine. I'm quite powerless to do anything substantial—bad taste passed on for more than two generations becomes tradition, don't you know?"

So far Brigid understood the queen less the more she

was getting to know her. "I'll admit I wasn't expecting to encounter a queen in such a setting," she said. "But I'm more concerned about our status. Whether we are guests or prisoners."

"That's a metaphysical question, isn't it? For now it pleases me to treat you as honored guests, despite your small companion's continuing to glare at me as if hoping I'll melt. Then again you might well consider yourselves prisoners. You are not—for reasons of your own safety, as well as that of the hegemony—permitted to leave the palace grounds, or indeed the palace itself, without escort. I note your skepticism, Dr. Baptiste. You will have to accept my assurance that you are in peril. The world you have come into is in a state of flux, and much of the turbulence centers upon this my capital. And you two are valuable prizes that others will not be slow in attempting to snatch away from the hegemony."

She leaned forward. "But rather more to the point—you are prisoners in this world, are you not? Because unless I very much miss my guess, the marvelous device on which you were relying to take you home—"

As she spoke her right hand had dipped out of sight behind the table. Brigid scarcely noticed—until it came up holding the experimental interphaser she had carried in her back.

"—is quite inert in this world in which you find yourselves."

She turned the object over in her hands. "It does have a certain eldritch esthetic to it," she said. "If it weren't so unwieldy I might use it for a scepter. Who knows? I may anyway. An artifact of otherworldly science might be a most fitting emblem for the ruler of this entire world."

Domi snorted. "You dream big, you." She had reverted to the clipped speech of her Outlands girlhood, never a good sign for her self-control. "Big place, a world…."

Fiona laughed. She had a good laugh, uninhibited and full, yet musical. "It is, and I do," she said. "But once the Apocalyptic Engine is complete, that by itself should lay the world entire at my dainty feet, for none will then be able to resist my science." She said *dainty* with evident irony—since it was obvious from her boots that her feet were anything but.

Brigid felt her jaw drop, and even Domi recoiled. It was a moment, Brigid thought—like one in which one's kidnapper pulls off his mask to allow you to see his face—of revelation that had certain implications.

The young queen laughed again. "Don't be so alarmed," she said. "Yes, it is a state secret. And no, your lives aren't forfeit for hearing it. All the world knows of the Apocalyptic Engine and its equally enigmatic creator. As I believe you've been apprised, this world is full of spies. Like maggots in cheese."

Though her mouth smiled, her eyes dissected the two women in turn. It seemed to Brigid that the queen experimented with words as she spoke them, flicking them like a riding crop to see what response they might elicit—from wordplay and rhyme, to shrouded threat, to what from a monarch trod perilously near the vulgar. She was either a woman of quite remarkable intellect and insight or quite floridly mad.

Unless, of course, she was both.

Abruptly, the queen stood. Her carriage showed the grace of a gymnast, as well as the arrogance of a mighty monarch.

"I must say it has been a pleasure meeting you—both of you. My own private world is so circumscribed that it becomes stultifying. Sebastian will see you to your quarters, which I assure you you shall find more than comfortable—if I keep you in a cage, it is not merely gilded but plush and well-ventilated. You will, of course, be subjected to endless questions in upcoming days, which may become tedious. But I can promise you also that the last thing my people will want to know from you are details of your personal lives, so you need have no fears for privacy."

"But, Your Majesty," Brigid said, "surely you have questions—"

"Doctor, I lack scientific and technical expertise. I employ experts for that—the very best in the world, as it happens. The ones who shall ask you questions are ones who know the proper questions to ask. Whereas it isn't worth my while to know. I have little time for idle curiosity."

She smiled a curious half smile at Brigid and cocked her head to one side. "It killed the cat, you know?"

"Son," said the President of the Republic of Cíbola, "what the confounded, tin-plated, made-in-Malagasy hell are we gonna do with you?"

The office smelled of soap and violets, whiskey and cigars. A huge hand, crisscrossed by scars and liver-spotted with age, laid Kane's utterly inert and useless Sin Eater on the green baize blotter on his immense desk with gentle finality.

"Young Randy says you're a good man in a fight," the president said. "And of course you're a visitor from another world, and the yellow journals'll doubtless make a fuss about you. But in terms of news I can *use*—against the Silver Kingdom, the Domain of Kali, the Russkies, the Texians and, longer-term, the lizard boys and those damned Canadians—anything you might be able to tell us would be as fascinating and useless as this here piece of ironmongery."

"Let me guide an expedition into Canada to rescue my friends," Kane said without hesitation. "Your Excellency."

For a moment President Preston Archer stared at him. He was an enormous old man, with a great seamed square face that sagged only lightly around the edges. He had an eagle's beak of a nose with winter-blue eyes as keen and fierce as any bird of prey's looking out from beneath extravagant bushy brows. Like the hair that hung down in a magnificent fall past the collar of his lightweight ivory suit and the sweeping mustache that almost hid his mouth, those brows positively gleamed a silvery white. The ruffle-fronted white shirt he wore behind his jacket barely contained a massive belly, but he had chest and shoulders to match. The way he spoke and looked at Kane and held himself, even as he sat at nominal ease in an oak chair in his spacious but relatively Spartan office, said that even if the decades had taken toll on him, he was a force to be reckoned with. About as harmless as a Rockies avalanche or Great Plains twister, Kane judged.

Kane reflexively sized him up and reckoned he could take him. But his speed would likely be his sole advantage.

"'Excellency,'" the old man repeated. "*Excellency? What kind of hogwash these boys been feeding you, son?* Ain't nothing 'excellent' about a politician—and mind you I say that as a man who's been one, man and boy, for nigh onto sixty years!

"And as for your modest proposal, Dean Swift had nothing on you." Neither did Kane have any notion what he was talking about. "For that matter, maybe nobody has, for monumental brass, since old Erik the Red named a godforsaken glaciated rock 'Greenland' and sold plots of it to other Vikings."

He hammered a huge fist on the green blotter on the desk before him, causing a brass lamp with a green glass shade to leap into the air. "María Carolina! More elderberry wine, if you please. And see to our guest—voicing ambitions that vaulting has to have dried out the boy's throat."

A voluptuous Latina, with gray streaking the black hair piled atop her head and slanting, jade-green eyes, came into the room with a tray and a grand sweeping of the dark gray-green floor-length skirt she wore. Her blouse was mauve.

"María Elena?" Archer boomed. "What the Devil are you doing here?"

"María Carolina is busy discussing the budget with the senate," the woman said, pausing next to Kane's chair to pour dark purple fluid from a square cut-crystal decanter into his wineglass. Her eyes met his, lingered, and then she swept on to refill the president's cup—a silver mug built on a scale as heroic as him. "It's a slow day at foreign affairs, so I promised I'd spell her waiting hand and foot on you."

"Never should've made the woman secretary of finance," the president grumbled. "Skews a woman's sense of the priorities."

"You always fill cabinet positions with your ex-wives, dear," María Elena said imperturbably as she topped off Colonel Randall Rodríguez-Satterfield's glass.

"Well, third time's the charm," he said. He looked back at Kane. "Never had a peep from my critics—who are so abundant, bless 'em, they'll have to build 'em a whole new annex in Hell, come Judgment Day—about nepotism. I calculate being so blatant about it just takes all the challenge out of it, all the game."

Kane took a sip of his wine. Aside from knowing he didn't want to arm-wrestle the oldie, he didn't have any idea what to make out of the president of Cíbola.

The *new* president. After the collapse of the unlikely alliance with the hegemony, his predecessor—literally, in this case—had promptly been assassinated. In the ensuing snap election Archer had won in a landslide to a third term in the Big House. "We can be a pretty conservative people, some ways," Rodríguez-Satterfield had confided to Kane while trying to give him a rundown on Cíbolan history and politics concise enough it wouldn't make Kane's eyes cross. "But in this case I'm not sure if we keep electing him because you always know where you stand with him, or because you absolutely never know what he's going to say next."

"Now, Mr. Kane," Archer said, "you've got balls. Damn, did María Elena leave the room yet?"

"She did, Mr. President," said bespectacled Charles Glass, his aide, who sat beside his desk in an attitude suggesting an eager hunting dog. The resemblance was reinforced by the numerous hunting-scene prints that hung in frames about the dark-paneled walls—although these were outnumbered by battle scenes, both painting and sepia-tone photographs. These could have come from three centuries past in Kane's world—except the one nearest Kane had a little brass plaque beneath bearing the engraved copperplate inscription, The Retreat From Santa Fe, September 1, 2112.

"Thank God. Anyway, you got balls, and we Cíbolans admire balls. But to be real candid with you, sir, balls are really nothing more'n Rocky Mountain oysters yet to be harvested. If most of our enemies hadn't had more balls than brains, we'd've been plowed under ten times over."

"Major Kane is a most intelligent man, Preston," Rodríguez-Satterfield said.

Kane stared at him "Major?" he mouthed. Rodríguez-Satterfield winked.

"He's also extremely resourceful," the colonel continued. "Nor do I believe him to be a man who says things without reason, or speaks because he's much in love with the sound of his own voice. Though I have to admit I'm a little taken back by the breathtaking speed with which he cut to bone here."

"All right. Then, dammit, mister—Major. Suppose you tell me why in the name of a million tons of buffalo crap we should send an expedition skyhooting across three quarters of a continent to attack the highly fortified capital of the strongest nation in the Western Hemisphere, if not the whole blamed world!"

"First a question, if I may, Mr. President."

"'Preston,' if you please. That's who I am. President's just what they let an old fool play at being every few years, for entertainment's sake."

"Preston. What makes you so sure Baptiste and Domi—my friends—have been taken to Gloriana?"

Glass squirmed like a schoolboy needing to pee with his eagerness to answer that one. But Archer needed no prompting. "The limey," he said flatly. "Miles-Burnham's there. There's no place else they'd take them, because if there's a man on Earth who can find a way to make use of the advanced technological knowledge from your world on this strangely circumscribed globe of ours, it's him."

"Then so much the more reason to rescue them. Baptiste—Brigid Baptiste—was a senior archivist for the barony we both served before becoming fugitives a few years ago. That meant she had the job of reviewing records—historical, political, cultural and also technical—that survived from before our big nuke."

"So you caught a catastrophe that blighted your world, too, did you?"

"Yes, sir. About a century and a half later than you did, and man-made, not natural."

"I'm not sure you could call the Great Destructor *natural*, whatever the Hell it was. But go on."

"Now, Baptiste is not a whitecoat—not a scientist or engineer herself. But she was tasked with reviewing countless technical documents, including scientific papers and engineering blueprints. Some of which undoubtedly contained knowledge that is going to be transferable to this world. News you can use."

Kane leaned back and paused for effect. "Are you familiar, sir, with the term, 'eidetic memory'?"

President Archer leaned forward and placed his elbows on the desk before him. "Son," he said, "you interest me strangely."

Chapter 11

The shell's explosion produced an orange flash instantly obscured by a vast eruption of earth, sod and dense smoke. Through it rolled a land ironclad, seventeen yards long, with two-gun turrets fore and aft. From the top of the superstructure amidships, a Gatling gun smoked and rattled from behind a splinter shield.

"Ridiculous, isn't it?" Zirak, the being who styled himself Ishmael, murmured to Grant. They were standing atop an observation tower that overlooked the vast practice grounds. "A starfaring race, reduced to employing weapons and vehicles from centuries in its own glorious, if somewhat checkered, past." He expelled a breath and shook his head.

Grant wore a uniform of midnight-blue, with high stock collar and gold buttons. It was meant for an officer of the Reptoids' human auxiliary forces, although lacking rank or unit insignia. It seemed remarkably plain for this world, or at least the somewhat abbreviated and kaleidoscopic impressions Grant had received the past few days. Underneath he wore his shadow suit.

That still surprised him. That the Reptoids permitted him to keep such an artifact, which even his host-captor

Ishmael professed to represent technology far beyond their own capabilities, struck him as remarkable. Especially since the shadow armor, whose function was almost entirely passive and due to its composition, a weave of spider silk, Monocrys and Spectra fabrics, still worked, even when his subcutaneous biolink transponder and even his side arm didn't. Or he wouldn't be here.

Another big vehicle appeared through the smoke as other explosions boomed around it.

"Buried charges," Ishmael said, peeling paper wrapping off a toothpick and putting it in his mouth to chew. "Command-detonated to mimic heavy shellfire. Realistic training's one thing, but with live artillery accidents happen. War machines cost us heavily in scarce resources—and our race is the scarcest resource of all. Besides, with enemies on all sides, even though the damned alliance has broken of its own internal contradictions, authentic danger's none too hard to come by."

He shrugged, an oddly human gesture that happened to suit his differently designed shoulders. "Just leave St. Louis and drive."

Grant felt himself oddly flushed, as if he were submerged in slowly heating water. He was brooding again. He knew it; it was hard to control. The anger had always been there, he knew. But it was never far beneath the surface these days.

"Why did he say that?" he asked.

His voice sounded like a rusty steel grille being pulled from a storm drain. The lizard-man looked at him with a wrinkling of his brow. The Reptoids had fewer mimetic muscles than humans, but they were capable of a range of facial expressions, if comparatively subtle ones.

"Why did that bastard ask if I was their master or their slave?"

ZIRAK SCRATCHED his flat chin with a pair of taloned fingers to gain time. Several times the subject had recounted the story of his and his friends' arrival and reception at the hands of the Hegemonists. Initially he was kept unconscious and questioned under the influence of Reptoid drugs, then several times he was consciously debriefed by the chief egg inspector, who portrayed himself as his case officer. But strangely, this was the first time the subject had asked this question. It was a sign that his will was beginning to return—and that the most ticklish phase of Zirak's plan had begun.

Unlike many of his compatriots in the intelligence game, Zirak felt no attraction to lying for its own sake. A lie intrinsically complicated situations; it was hard to remember, and he knew from frequent observation, as well as bitter early experience, that the fact he personally was very good at lying was more a trap than a facilitation. He had therefore set himself to master the more abstruse art of carefully filtering the truth.

Therefore, as was his habit, he told truth: "You've heard a little about the great change that came over this world centuries before we arrived: the global devastation, enormous initial loss of life, which in turn was dwarfed by subsequent deaths to starvation, disease—and, of course, anarchy."

The big human nodded his long, powerful chin. "We had something a lot like that," he said in a voice so low Zirak's ears, evolved for a thinner atmosphere, had to strain to hear it. "Only it happened a century or so later. And wasn't a comet."

Zirak nodded. "Which I admit I find intriguing, my human friend. Although what hit this Earth doesn't seem to have been a comet. In any event, you may or may not realize that it struck during a North American conflict often called the War Between the States or the Civil War. Which was fought in part over the issue of slavery."

"I knew that."

A land ironclad stopped almost in front of their wooden tower. A heavy steel ramp winched groaningly down from the bow, with much puffing of smoke from the tandem stacks mounted behind the pilothouse. A squad of Reptoid infantry spilled out in their camouflage battledress and coal-scuttle ceramic-synthetic laminate helmets, bayonets gleaming on their bolt-action rifles. As the vast armored vehicles boomed out covering fire and the inevitable smoke pall began to settle over the scene, teams assembled portable Gatlings on heavy tripods and began to crank rounds down the practice range.

Zirak had to almost shout to make himself heard over the uproar. "When the aftershocks had finished circling the globe, the slaveholders of the Southern states discovered, like everybody else, that their firearms wouldn't work. The percussion caps they used to set off the powder charges contained tiny dabs of high explosive—and high explosives don't work here anymore." The last few words came out as though they tasted foul, although Zirak doubted the human could read their inflection; the True Race had had its own bitter experience of this world's Great Discontinuity, which they still tasted two decades later.

"So the guns the slave-owners relied upon in large part to subjugate their human property didn't fire. Only some old flintlocks, since black powder still works fine—as you can see for yourself right here. Not to mention hear and smell. And the slaves held a disproportionate number of those, among the light weapons that they were allowed to keep for hunting.

"They rose. The slaves were numerous, and most white men fit for military service were away fighting the Union. The rising spread carried by messengers and the movement of rebel bands. Communications were disrupted—long-range telegraphy was another casualty of the Great Destructor. Confederate soldiers could not be recalled to fight the slaves. Neither could Union troops be dispatched to put down the rising, as they no doubt would have been."

"So the slaves won?"

"Yes. I hope you won't take offense, but they didn't prove themselves greatly more enlightened in ruling than their masters."

"Doesn't surprise me. It's not my world, anyway."

"True enough. They exterminated the whites, by and large, throughout a large swatch of the southeastern sector of what had been the United States. The survivors were enslaved themselves. As word filtered out what had happened, African-descended folk began to emigrate to the newly liberated—or conquered—lands. Not always voluntarily—whites in the North were panicked by what had befallen their Southern cousins. There were massacres of blacks. Thousands more were simply driven from the homes and herded south like droves of cattle. And in time, as the rebel states began to coalesce into what would become today's Empire of New Africa, they themselves began military operations to forcibly 'repatriate' blacks from neighboring regions. Whether they wanted to go or not."

"So that blond son of a swampie whore's question—"

"Was deliberate provocation—in all the Americas, slavery only exists legally in the Empire of Brasil, the Dominion of Kali, where it's recently been introduced, and New Africa. And people of your skin color and general appearance are vanishingly rare outside of New Africa."

Grant shook his head. "Hell of a thing to say," he said. "Hell of a thing."

Out on the practice ground the Reptoid infantry skirmished forward as if they knew how, in short dashes, then diving to plowed earth to fire their rifles at distant earth berms. Sailplanes swooped soundlessly overhead, firing rockets like smoky comets. Lower down, an ultralight with a battery-powered electric pusher motor putted along seemingly not much faster than the troops who were advancing on foot, ripping away with its hand-cranked Gatling. Zirak took a risk and clapped his human companion on a powerful bicep, being careful to withhold his slightly retractable talons. The big human didn't flinch away or lash out in reflex anger.

"Come, my friend," the inspector said. "Let's go inside.

There's not much more than a fog bank to be seen here now, and I for one am working on a powerful appetite!"

KANE, DRESSED IN fine clothes that felt alien to his body, was trotting down the broad steps of the capitol with Colonel Randall Rodríguez-Satterfield and a group of his allies when a man broke from the crowd of spectators on the street below, strode up to Kane and slapped him across the face with a glove held in his right hand.

The blow caught Kane flatfooted. I'm getting complacent here, he thought, belatedly swinging up his own hands to defensive posture and jumping back. He repressed his reflex reaction, which was to jump on the slagjacker and pound him through the concrete steps to show him what it meant to lay hands on a Magistrate. He didn't know the lay of the land here—as this peculiar attack demonstrated vividly.

Rodríguez-Satterfield and his supporters didn't reach to restrain Kane, but moved swiftly, if subtly, to interpose themselves partially between Kane and his attacker—like the small, quick, clever dogs he'd seen them use to herd their great-horned cattle.

The man made no further move on Kane, which was the best move he could make. He was tall, almost an inch taller than Kane, with brown hair receding at the sides, cut medium short and slicked back, and razored sideburns spiking down scarred, tanned cheeks. His eyes were gray and his nose had been broken more than once or twice. He was slender as a rawhide lariat and dressed in an immaculate dove-gray tailcoat over white blouse and ivory trousers with slightly flared cuffs. The outfit differed little from what Kane had been stuffed into by Rodríguez-Satterfield family servants at the order of Randall's magisterial Aunt Cecilia, except Kane wore a dark blue jacket and blue-gray trousers with muted maroon stripes down the legs.

"You shall hear from my seconds, sir," the interloper said in a high, clear voice. "I suggest you appoint yours."

"I'm his second," Randall Rodríguez-Satterfield said, stepping up to Kane's right side.

"And I'll back him," said one of Rodríguez-Satterfield's friends who had accompanied Kane out of the capitol, stepping up on Kane's left.

"And I," said another.

"Go ahead and state your case, Silveiro," Rodríguez-Satterfield said. "Your seconds can call on me later to work out the gory details."

Neither of Rodríguez-Satterfield's associates looked particularly concerned by the incident, nor had either shown any sign of making a move toward the sizable handgun each wore beneath his long jacket. An unarmed man was the exception here in Cíbola, not least of all in the senate he'd just finished addressing, and a woman who was packing was considered unremarkable.

"My principals object to this man," the interloper said. He had some kind of an accent Kane couldn't identify. "His ludicrous and patently spurious claims offend them. They desire to foil his mad attempts to embroil the republic in desperately dangerous adventures far from her native interests. They therefore engaged me to chastise him."

And he turned and walked away.

"What the fuck, over?" Kane demanded.

"You've just been challenged to a duel, amigo," Rodríguez-Satterfield said.

"By a professional duelist," said the man on the other side of him. "João Silveiro, whose friends would call him Johnny. If he had friends."

Kane looked around. It was tubby, balding Ned Barker with his extravagant sideburns—Burnsides, they called them here—who had spoken.

"Who is also," said Francisco Burciaga, "a Brazilian assassin." Burciaga was so tiny he was almost a midget. He was so handsome, with his dark olive skin and raven's-wing hair and obsidian eyes, as to be almost pretty. Something Kane had not been at pains to point out to him. In the couple of days he'd spent here, largely at the vast Rodríguez-Satterfield estate northeast of Auraria, he'd gotten to know the type of men Colonel Randy ran with: richer than God and well-seasoned man-killers, if not full-on coldhearts.

For his part, no matter how much he missed its reassuring weight on his forearm, Kane was just as glad he wasn't carrying his now-inert Sin Eater. He gathered drawing down would have been a severe gaffe and possible sign of cowardice. He just hoped that, if things dropped in the pot, he'd remember to draw the burly double-action Taliaferro .50-caliber automatic revolver riding at his own hip, rather than just making a fist and expecting it magically to fill up with blazing full-auto handblaster.

"They're open about that sort of thing here?"

"It's a crime to assassinate somebody here," Rodríguez-Satterfield said, "not to be an assassin."

"A duel," Kane repeated. "You have got to be shitting me."

"Not at all," Barker said in a booming, affable voice. Like the president he had one of those big bellies that, if you took the possessor up on an invitation to punch him there, would hurt your hand. He had been a real swashbuckler in his time, a far-ranging trader who made and lost a dozen fortunes in some of this world's hairiest locations before settling down as an industrialist, manufacturing small arms and steam-engine parts in a huge factory complex forty miles south of Auraria. "It's one of our more distasteful folkways, dueling."

Burciaga flashed teeth in a quick white smile. "Not at all, my friend. It helps keep us a polite society. And culls the herd, so to speak."

"And that's as far as this line of palaver ought to go," Rodríguez-Satterfield said dryly, "unless we want another duel on our hands."

Both his companions laughed with an easy familiarity, suggesting this was not just a joke but an old one. Kane felt frank relief. He was no coward, but he was also not fool enough to want to get caught in a crossfire of friends falling out. Civil wars were always the worst.

Burciaga had a cattle ranch the size of a European count's fief—before Reptoid-backed barbarians overran the continent, anyway—out on the plains east of the capital, and was among the most highly regarded horse breeders of the upper Rio Grande. A position of high esteem in a world whose technology relied largely on literal horse-power.

He was also a successful militia cavalry officer who specialized in guerrilla tactics. He was also largely Apache—Chiricahua Apache, and what's more Mexican Chiricahua: the folk whose own name for themselves was *ndé'indaaí*, the enemy people. They ranged the southern reaches of Cobaltville, the barony Kane had served as a Mag and their reputation as fierce, implacable warriors was legendary.

"I've been here two days," Kane said. "How could I get somebody pissed enough at me to call me out?"

"What the man said, I reckon," Rodríguez-Satterfield drawled, producing a cheroot from an inside pocket of his black jacket. He proffered it to Kane, who declined the offer, then unwrapped it and lit it for himself. "The passionate appeal you just made to our august legislators to launch a fresh expedition eastward to spring your lady friends from Canadian durance vile."

"Word travels fast," Barker said, "what with telephone and telegraph. And speaking of which—" he nodded toward the foot of the wide stairs, where a mob or reporters stood waiting eagerly "—gird your loins. We're about to run the gauntlet of the gentlemen and ladies of the press. Which I fear will make your hair-raising escape from the Hedges seem like a walk in the park, Mr. Kane!"

Chapter 12

This part of the golden city, Gloriana, didn't look so golden. Brigid stared out the window as the carriage rolled through streets narrower and dingier than those that had first led her to Fiona's extravagant palace. The carriage was less grand and ornate—and the escort of horsemen in spiked helmets and glittering cuirasses, while smaller, seemed to have a less ceremonial intent.

Domi sat as far from Brigid as the carriage would permit. After the initial interview with Queen Fiona several days before, Domi accused Brigid of sucking up to the Canadians, and being overly impressed by their fancy manners and outfits and pretensions of royalty. Brigid claimed Domi was being immature and reactionary. The Canadians weren't perfect, but no one was, certainly not the refugees packed into Cerberus back home. Brigid felt Grant's absence keenly, too, but she understood it had come about through the actions of a renegade, a loose cannon. For their part the Canadians seemed to care deeply about social justice and order, and if they followed expansionist policies, it would have the effect of displacing social systems far worse.

"That what the barons said!" was Domi's shouted

reply. It was so manifestly unfair that Brigid, shocked and stung, had simply ended the conversation.

Those had been almost the last syllables the women had exchanged. Fortunately, Fiona had delivered on her promise of luxurious confinement: their quarters were a suite with two spacious bedrooms and even two bathrooms—so they had been able to share their imprisonment apart.

They were allowed to eat in their chambers for the most part, and when they were escorted from the suite by polite, soft-spoken men to be interviewed by other polite, soft-spoken men, it was most often singly.

Brigid had never thought of herself as a sociable person. An archivist's life was intrinsically solitary, and besides, denizens of an Enclave were not encouraged to form personal connections. Yet she felt her isolation keenly. There was no one here she felt a connection to, at least no one she knew, other than Domi.

If only it were Kane, she thought. And promptly stepped on the thought: it didn't lead anywhere she cared to go. Besides, in essentially Victorian Gloriana, she and a male co-captive would no doubt be kept scrupulously segregated except under closely chaperoned circumstances.

Still, Brigid acutely experienced something she had seldom experienced before. She realized with something of a shock, as she sat gazing out at shabby care-worn people walking bent over and hurriedly past, with occasional hooded looks cast at the carriage and its glittering, lethal escort, that for perhaps the first time in her life she was permitting herself to feel lonely.

She felt a pang at the unfairness of it all: for all its flaws life as an exile at Cerberus had brought her out of herself, forced her from her shell of apparent self-sufficiency. And now she was marooned, friendless in a realm more distant from her own than the Andromeda galaxy.

The carriage halted before a looming Gothic pile that, to judge by the lakefront behind, was a warehouse, or had begun existence as such. It was coated in streaked soot and grime. The rest of the block was similarly monolithic, smudged and run-down.

The cavalry lieutenant who led the escort opened the carriage's gatefold doors and personally handed the women out. A pair of troopers stood flanking a multiple-layered arched doorway with bolt-action carbines shouldered. Another pair stood to either side, facing warily outward down the sidewalk with longblasters at port arms. Brigid felt surprise: what on Earth could the queen intend in sending them to what very clearly was a rough part of town?

Still, part of her was amused: in her life as an exile she had had ample experience of the Tartarus Pits beneath various baronial monoliths. Which she had never laid eyes on as a lawful archivist and Enclave-dweller. And if these mirror-polished pony soldiers thought these streets were mean, she didn't know whether to pity or envy them.

"I'll leave a guard here at the door, ladies," the lieutenant, a middle-aged man with a face perpetually sunburned from campaigning, said to them with what seemed genuine concern. "They'll ring 'round for the carriage when your interview is concluded."

Brigid thanked him. Domi said nothing. She had gotten over the point of violent resistance, indeed of open display of any sort except the occasional sullen glance at her tormentors.

Inside they found a great echoing cathedral space, filled with café-au-lait light, drifting dust motes, and...mechanism. They stepped inside, necks craned upward, looking in wonder and puzzlement. Great gears turned lazily in complicated trains, some seeming barely supported; ratchets caught and released, cams turned, great pistons thrust and returned, driving flat ringlike brass dials as wide as houses; a complex dance of steel and turned brass.

"Ladies, welcome!" a clear tenor voice cried. Striding across the floor toward them came a figure not much larger than Domi, dressed in tan breeches, a white blouse with sleeves rolled up and a green waistcoat. His youthful-seeming face was clean shaved beneath a great mass of unruly auburn hair. He had half glasses pulled down to the tip of his long nose and a black smudge on his cheek. He wiped his hands on a rag. "Please forgive my manners for not meeting you at the door! I am Dr. Nigel Miles-Burnham."

"Good morning, Doctor. My name is Brigid Baptiste. This is Domi." The albino woman had produced a yellow apple from within the red-and-yellow dress their servants had stuffed her into that morning and bit into it, gazing around with ruby eyes huge.

"Welcome to my workshop," the scientist said. "Rather a shocking breach that you must introduce yourselves. I suppose the army dropped you off at the door and bade you shift for yourselves. They're rather fearful of what I'm about here. I do believe they more than halfway suspect me of witchcraft. I apologize, Dr. Baptiste, Miss Domi, and I assure you I am entirely charmed to meet you both."

Brigid raised an eyebrow.

"Ah, please forgive me again," he said. He stood before them, hands behind his back, bobbing up and down on the balls of his feet. "Of course I've been told to expect you. After all, it was I who predicted your arrival."

He seemed to teeter on the brink of uncertainty how to proceed. Brigid offered her hand. Miles-Burnham hesitated a moment longer, then grasped her hand fervently in both of his and shook it. His hands, slender but disproportionately long for his height, were surprisingly strong. The hands of a craftsman, it seemed, not a cloistered scientist.

"That's right," she said, smiling to put him at ease, as it suddenly felt important for her to do. After all, she told herself, if we have any faint hope of returning home, he's it. "Your instruments detected our coming."

He smiled. He seemed rather relieved than offended that Domi hadn't offered her hand. "Well, not quite, Doctor. You'll think me mad, and I beg of you not to tell our mutual hosts. But the plain fact is, I foresaw your arrival in a vision."

GLEAMING DULLY in the afternoon light that spilled into the whitewashed chamber from tall clerestory windows, the curved blade descended toward Kane's forehead. He strove to bring his own saber up to parry the cut, but the cavalry-style weapon, heavy to begin with, felt as if it weighed twenty-five pounds. Fatigued with terrible rapidity from the unaccustomed exertion, the very muscles of Kane's forearm felt turned to lead.

It was hopeless. The sword flashed down between Kane's eyes. It stopped with the curved blade's tip an inch from the skin of his forehead.

It hung there a moment, motionless, then whipped away. "Very well, Mr. Kane," the sword master said in a crisp accent that sounded like an amalgam of German and French, as he stepped back. "You are a man of exceptional physique, conditioning and skill. Your reflexes are superb. Your eye is keen as a prairie falcon's. You learn as if absorbing through the skin. I salute you."

His mouth set into a razor slash in his pale face, where it seemed hardly more than just another scar. He was a head shorter than Kane, his close-cropped hair salt and pepper. His eyes were dark and intense under eyebrows like lines drawn in charcoal. He had been introduced as a Walloon, whatever that was, and had been one of Europe's leading sword masters before the continent fell into barbarism, an event that had taken place less than five years before.

"But you got me dead to rights," Kane said, gratefully lowering his sword. The cool Front Range air of the practice room was like fresh spring water. He drank it greedily down.

The small, square head nodded micrometrically. "In ten years, I could make you a swordsman."

"I got two days."

The sword master shrugged. The gesture was purely

Gallic. "Then you can learn to make a brave show," he said, "and not disgrace yourself in dying."

"TELL ME AGAIN," Kane said, sipping blackberry wine, "how it works out I have to fight with swords?"

Colonel Randall Rodríguez-Satterfield laughed. He and Kane sat in deep leather chairs in a sitting room of the sprawling hacienda. Huge oil paintings in gilded frames covered the walls. Navajo rugs in stark geometric patterns covered the maroon tile floor and the white *bancos* standing out like benches from the walls. The furniture was wood, heavy, stark and dark, with frequent piercings, usually in the form of Maltese-looking crosses.

"A peculiarity of the system the way it's evolved here on the Front Range. I suspect our distinguished forebears wanted to distinguish themselves from effete Easterners and their European-imitating ways. The challenger, as the injured party, gets to specify weapons."

"What keeps guys from just going around challenging people they know aren't as good as they are with their weapons of choice, and just hacking them down?"

"Damned little," Rodríguez-Satterfield said. "That's a problem inherent in dueling anyway, if you think about it. We're a commercial society at heart, so our mode of dealing with it is to allow the hiring of substitutes. We admire a fighting man, but understand there're plenty good men who aren't good at it."

"And me without the jack," Kane said. "If only I'd remembered to bring my vast fortune across."

Rodríguez-Satterfield laughed. Kane had told him

something of his world and even his own past in it. He liked these people. They had treated him well. He could have lied his ass off. But what was the point? It was a lot more work than telling the truth, and he might sacrifice some of the good will he'd built up if one of these shrewd raider-and-trader types caught him out in an inconsistency. And he didn't want to risk losing any shot at he had of talking them into helping him try to rescue Brigid and Domi.

He'd given them all the technical information he was able to. He had managed to hold back the secret of his shadow suit; they'd never searched him or his effects. There was no pressing reason for it. It wasn't as if Cíbola was going to mount an invasion of Cerberus anytime soon; hell, from his tales of Program of Unification and the society that raised him, whose regimentation horrified his hosts a lot more than the fact it was secretly stage-managed by a race of hybrids, they were if anything sympathetic to the freedom fight being mounted by Lakesh and his cronies. But Kane just liked to keep an ace in the hole.

For his part he was glad to do anything he could to help the Cíbolans over the Canadians. The equation was simple in his mind: the Cíbolans treated him decently and better than decently. The Canadians had gunned down his best friend and kidnapped him and his female friends. He owed the bastards hurt for that. And the Cíbolans, freshly stung by the collapse of their alliance with the hegemony, were by and large eager to lay hurt upon the Canadians.

"You might," Randall said, as a tiny dark Indian looking woman in a dark dress, high-collared and sweeping in the skirts, refilled their goblets from a cut-glass decanter of the Rodríguez-Satterfield home vintage, "consider declining the bout."

He held up a hand the color and consistency of a hide lariat wound on hard wood. "I know it goes against your instincts as a warrior. But what's the point to coming all this way and throwing your life away, hey? I assure you, I and my family would think no less of you—and you have a home here as long as you desire."

"What's the downside?"

Rodríguez-Satterfield raised an eyebrow, then laughed. "Another otherworldly idiom. If only the doubters could hear you speak, they'd doubt no longer. Presuming, of course, that their doubts aren't just assumed for political purposes."

He shook his head. "The problem is it would discredit you in the eyes of the public. You'd doom your own cause."

Kane set the glass down on a small round table beside his chair and leaned forward. "I don't understand what's got people in such an uproar. They don't want to believe me, fine. They don't want to pay for or go along on an expedition back east, fine. Why hire a fancy-pants South American coldheart to chill me?"

"We're beset by hostile neighbors, as our esteemed president told you. Lot of people reckon we don't need to go looking for enemies."

"What about your fight with the Reptoids?"

"That was the reason I and my family opposed the whole thing."

"You were against it? But you were right there in the thick of it. Obviously, or I wouldn't be here."

Rodríguez-Satterfield shrugged and grinned in a cavalier way. "It was an adventure, and we're essentially juveniles who have a hard time resisting a rousing adventure. Maybe that's characteristic of most of our cultures in the world today, frankly. I'm an officer of the militia, as you know, and my comrades rely on me. I could go on the expedition without approving of it. So I did. I was far from the only one."

Kane sat back. He was dressed in dark trousers of some sturdy material that nonetheless felt soft to the touch, and a loose white shirt or blouse with the sleeves rolled up. Though the sun was rising toward noon and outside the late-summer day was more than warm, inside it was cool and smelled vaguely moist.

"Now we've incurred additional enmity from the invaders and the Canadians, as well," Rodríguez-Satterfield said, "without making the Silver Kingdom or the devotees of Kali love us the more. We've spent much treasure. And blood, which, commercial as we are, is still more precious to us. So it's no wonder that some people might be seriously worried your wild and emotional—but nonetheless quite compelling—appeals for still more foreign adventuring might work. After all, the promise of new military and fabrication technology, blended with the prospect of rescuing maidens fair—"

He threw back his head and laughed. "How could any good Cíbolan resist?"

The corner's of Kane's mouth stretched in a lupine grin. "Somebody is."

"Apparently so. And nothing says your secret enemy

has to be Cíbolan at all. This is a cosmopolitan city despite its remoteness from the sea—the biggest between lizard-held St. Louis and the Pacific. We have visitors and emigrants from many nations, including Texas, the Silver Kingdom, and even Kali's domain and the hegemony. Any one of them might well be alarmed at the prospect of this expedition of yours actually succeeding."

"You let enemies live openly right here?"

"We value freedom above all, my friend. And we know that if we trade it for what we imagine to be increased security, what we wind up is unsafe slaves. Besides, what's a few open enemies? The real danger's the ones you don't know about, yes?"

"So I can kiss goodbye either to my prospect of rescuing Baptiste and Domi, or my life. Either way it looks as if they're screwed."

"They are if you continue to think in such a way, young man!"

Kane's head snapped around. A small birdlike woman dressed in a long black skirt and a stiff white blouse with high lace collar had come into the room. The skirt brushed the floor so that she seemed eerily to be gliding across the dark red tiles without moving her feet. Randall Rodríguez-Satterfield had jumped to his feet. Kane joined him, as much from the personal force emanating from the small, trim figure as from a desire to pretend to manners he didn't have by imitating his host's example in this courtesy-ridden society.

"Dama Cecilia," he said in his rude Spanish accent.

"Mr. Kane." Her English, like her nephew's, was precise; he suspected they kept a touch of Spanish accent as a means of distinction, since most of the really important people in the republic, at least of the ones he'd met, had some degree of Spanish blood and were at some pains to show it off. He also suspected their Spanish would be fully flawless, but he'd never know.

"What do you mean, Aunt Cecily?" Randall asked.

"What I mean is that should your young friend maintain a negative frame of mind, he's beaten before he ever engages this hired killer."

Kane felt his cheeks grow warm. He had, near as he could parse it, just been called a bitch by a little old lady he could press over his head one-handed.

She was also the absolute autocrat of the house of Rodríguez-Satterfield—which meant, in real terms, far more powerful than President Preston Archer, at least in his official role. If Kane said or did anything she took exception to, he'd be lucky if all he got was tossed on his ear. Not that the prospect scared him—but if that happened, his chances of getting these people to help him rescue Baptiste and Domi got kicked to the curb with him.

"Sorry, ma'am," he said, his voice rough with the unfamiliar effort of containing his emotion—and the unfamiliar mix of them. "But are you saying that if I just *think* I'm a better swordsman than this Brazilian, I'll win?"

"Not at all. My nephew tells me you're a fighter by profession, Mr. Kane. Is that correct?"

"Close enough."

She came close and gazed into his face. It was quite a squint from that range; she was no taller than Domi, if as tall. Her coal-black eyes were disconcertingly direct and intense as a laser.

"You move and hold yourself like a man who can take care of himself," she said. "Got the worst of it a few times, though, by the looks of you."

"You should see the other guys, ma'am."

She uttered a caw of laughter. "Now that's the spirit! The sort of spirit a woman likes to see in a man, even if she's ancient and decrepit as I am."

Over her head Kane caught sight of her nephew rolling his eyes behind her back.

"Now, then, do I understand that you've been in a considerable number of battles, Mr. Kane? And that you've won them all?"

"All the ones I had to."

She smiled. "Good. Then you can win this fight. By changing the way you think about it. Nothing could be simpler."

"Now you've got my interest up, Aunt Cecily," Rodríguez-Satterfield said. "How does a man win a sword fight by thinking about it?"

"By forgetting the sword," she said, "and remembering that, once the handkerchief is dropped, it's just a fight."

And she smiled sweetly into their looks of amazement, like a grandmother who'd just handed out Christmas toys.

Chapter 13

"It's like being inside a giant grandfather clock," Brigid said.

Miles Burnham beamed wider. "Rather."

For the first time in a week of visitations the scientist squired Brigid on a tour of the elaborate mechanism that dominated the great space of his warehouse-laboratory. Like mice they had scampered up what seemed endless rickety metal stairs and uncertain ladders. Brigid never felt a stir of trepidation. Miles-Burnham exuded such joyous vitality that it was impossible to feel danger in his presence.

Or at least, from such mundane perils as dizzying heights and precarious perches.

Now they strolled along a catwalk with great gear trains meshing and clacking right above their heads and a sort of pendulum swooping in space nearby. Escapements caught and let go. Rather than the metallic cacophony Brigid would have expected, the air vibrated with something akin to music, complex cricket rhythms overlaying the basso beat of the massive steam engines concealed in an outbuilding that drove the huge works.

"Each train of gears, each sequence of mechanism," the small but remarkably handsome scientist said with more glowing joy than pride, "represents some abstruse function of the many mansions of the multiverse, at least as I perceive them."

He flashed a smile at Brigid. She felt a certain tremor in the depths of her stomach. She kept her face in its usual neutral expression, as befit a senior archivist.

"The shafts are lathed and the gears are cut in a dedicated shop on an outbuilding behind this one," the scientist said, continuing down a metal-lattice catwalk at least two stories above the concrete floor. "I do no small amount of the work myself, being if I may flatter myself a mechanic of no mean ability."

Brigid had spent the past several days here. In a massive outpouring she had not only shared a great data-dump of technical information with the scientist, but had told him some of her own story. He had listened to all with the eager interest and wonder of an inquisitive child. The technical information his mind seemed to suck in like a sponge, even when it concerned areas of which he had small knowledge or prior experience. Yet the personal details of her life interested him no less. He seemed as fascinated at learning the facets of her life, her personality—her soul—as the myriad marvels of a science which the ability to perform high-energy experiments had driven light years beyond his own in ways.

They had come to a halt on a platform high up near the vaulted ceiling of the vast warehouse. He waved a happy hand at the plenum of mechanism surrounding them. "You might consider this mechanism a metallic metaphor or allegory for the functioning of the multiverse."

"Apparently the concept of multiple realties is not un-familiar here."

Miles-Burnham laughed. "We have been operating under severe limitations, like a man attempting to scale a peak with his foot imprisoned in a bucket of concrete. Yet the Great Change itself forced us—once we were able to think again in such terms—to confront certain cosmological truths.

"We understood there remained a realm of high-energy physics from which we were barred. Sadly, nothing till now has given us an explanation as to exactly what has happened to us, much less how. High explosives do not function here. Electrical generation is a paltry thing—we can store up substantial charges in the batteries we have developed, but cannot transmit power over any distance. We can communicate rapidly over distances by telegraph using simple binary codes, but only by means of a complex and fragile network of amplifying stations along the line. Radioactive decay has long been observed in our laboratories, yet we find ourselves unable to harness it as you have in your world."

She brushed a strand of hair back from her forehead, where it had been stuck by the sweat of exertion in climbing to this height. She had scarcely been aware of the effort. "Maybe that's a good thing," she said with a halting smile. "We almost destroyed our world by harnessing those particular forces."

"Ah, but, as you say, you had help." Then he stopped, set his small jaw, cocked his head to one side. She had recognized the gesture as a sign he was cogitating.

"Ah, but possibly you are right. After all, we've accomplished prodigies of destruction with the limited means at our disposal. Who knows what high-energy frightfulness we might have unleashed, left to our own devices? And yet I cannot find it in me to say that it is good to have any form of knowledge-seeking prohibited—for I cannot believe that God would create anything which He did not intend for humankind to know."

He leaned his elbows on the tarnished brass safety rail. "Yet it is undeniably true that God had seen fit to test us—and tantalize us. We still have lightning, as you have seen. The Aurora is visible in high latitudes, both north and south, indeed more powerfully than ever before the change, if surviving accounts are to be believed. High-energy reactions *do* still take place within the Chrissinger Radius, in which the Great Discontinuity holds sway. But God in His wisdom has seen fit to deny them to us. And even to our nonhuman rivals for supremacy upon this planet now. I wonder at His sense of humor, sometimes."

She smiled at his mysticism. Away down below she noticed Domi, sitting at a table with Norman, Miles-Burnham's butler, leaning forward in earnest discussion. The butler was a very tall man with gray hair and sweeping side whiskers framing a narrow, bald skull and gaunt face, dominated by a beak of a nose and a single vivid blue eye. The other eye was covered by a black patch. He always held himself ramrod straight, which suggested military training more than butler school, at least to Brigid. He was infallibly and unflappably polite, and obviously devoted to the scientist whom he served.

She frowned, hoping Domi wasn't leading the old man on.

"Did God tell you about our coming?" Brigid asked Miles-Burnham lightly. Instantly she regretted it, it rang as patronizing in her ears—the last thing she felt, or intended, for she was in awe of this man's intellect, and felt a dwarf beside him. She simply felt a desire to be friendly with him, even playful.

Yet if the great man took offense he showed no sign. "In my experience God is not quite so forthcoming upon matters concerning this sphere," he said, "although perhaps if I asked Him, He would tell me. But that seems quite like cheating—when my special blessing is to so enjoy finding these things out on my own. No, it was simply a vision I had during one of my journeys upon the lightning path. I told my hosts my instruments had detected your party's imminent arrival, in order that I might be taken seriously. Our modern age gives great lip service to religion, but mostly to its forms, as you may have observed in the palace. And scarcely any heed to matters spiritual."

"Indeed," Brigid said a bit faintly. While Lakesh was certainly prone to discuss outlandish cosmic theories, and sometimes even more outlandish realities, and while Brigid herself had experienced many things that fell well outside the maps of conventional rationality since she had escaped from Cobaltville, she was unaccustomed to a man so devoted to hard science speaking unabashedly in terms of spirituality.

"Perhaps you would consent to join me in one of my sojourns," he said.

"I'd be delighted," Brigid said. She didn't really mean it. She feared this man for whom she felt such profound respect and…well, the affection due a friendly individual who was also a towering genius.

A tinkling sounded far below. "Ah, the bell," he said. "That must be Chrissie, back from holiday on Prince Edward Island. I'd challenge you to race me down the stairs, but I'd hate to be responsible for either of us taking a tumble and breaking our necks!"

"IT'S A POLICE STATE."

Domi's flat statement kicked Brigid from her sepia-toned reverie like a physical blow. The ride home to the palace through Gloriana's evening streets was already less comfortable than usual. Dusk had the effect of blurring the unpleasant harshness of the lakeside-dock district where Miles-Burnham's warehouse stood, and as lights came on with evening the central part of Gloriana appeared more golden and glorious than even in full sunlight, and the palace a true fairy castle. But Domi had radiated sullen eagerness like heat from a pot-bellied stove since their carriage had pulled away.

And Brigid was out of sorts. Chrissie turned out to be one Miss Christina Battersea, a soft-voiced, pleasant young woman, in appearance even younger than Queen Fiona and in manner vastly so. Not that she acted immature, Brigid had to admit; rather the queen had, even in their brief encounter with her, displayed the personality of a case-hardened middle-aged cynic, instead of one more commonly found in a woman in her early twenties.

Chrissie was somewhat shorter than Brigid, and despite the flowery flounciness of her pale blue-and-white dress, obviously more slimly built. Black curls spilled down either side of her finely sculpted face, and she had clear blue eyes and a fine straight nose.

It was taking a massive effort of Brigid's potent will not to hate her. Her easy, if relentlessly courteous, confidence made Brigid feel gauche, as her size and porcelain-doll features made the older woman feel unwieldy and older. Her easy intimacy with Miles-Burnham had given Brigid a spike of something she wasn't quite willing to call jealousy on top of her resentment at the intrusion of this overly cheerful personage.

"What did you say?"

"It's a police state. This place you're getting so fused-out about. This ville. This whole country."

"If that's so, wouldn't they bug this carriage?"

"Norman says no. Not their style. Also not easy. They got no microelectronics, remember?"

"Norman?" Brigid's furrowed brow shifted from a frown of annoyance to one of puzzlement. The statement made no sense to her. Norman was a mere servant. Why would he discuss matters so clearly above his competence? "How would he know?"

"Because he was one."

"One what?"

"Secret policeman. Spy. Whatever. He was an RHMP agent. Did lots of spy stuff, sabotage, everything. Then he started to get old, and got hurt. So they pulled him out of the field, and retrained him, and set him on somebody who scared them. World's greatest scientist. In the Kingdom of Britannia. Your new lover boy, Sir Nigel."

"He is *not* my lover boy."

Domi shrugged. "You never listen to your woman side," she said matter-of-factly, "so no wonder you're the last to know. You're in love with him. He must be good at that, getting people to love him. Norman spilled the beans to him inside six months. Long before they had to skip from England."

"That's the most ridiculous story I've ever heard."

Domi grinned at her in the plush off-white gloom of the carriage cabin. "More ridiculous than us even being here, with all these blimps and guys on horseback with metal hats and pointy sticks? More ridiculous than me dressed like this?"

It didn't precisely answer Brigid's objection. Then again, the objection hadn't been strictly rational. Brigid subsided.

"Norman told his bosses he quit. Told 'em to back off Sir Nige. Made it stick, too—he has some kinda hold on them. Something on somebody important, I betcha. He hasn't told me yet. Might not—he's a pretty tough and smart old dude."

"A manservant?"

"I told you, he wasn't always that! Anyway, do you think Sir Nigel'd let anybody stupid stay near him? You always underestimate servants anyway. Just like most of these people. Another reason why you like them."

Brigid felt her cheeks growing hot. "Even if what you claim Norman said to you is true, it doesn't make sense for Sir Nigel to come here if the hegemony was spying on him."

"You told me they told you everybody spies on everybody." Domi laughed, deriving apparent sadistic satisfaction from the effect she was having on Brigid's composure. "But Britannia and Canada were all tied together, as well as rivals—cousins, like. And Nigel and his friend the Queen of Britannia needed a place to go when the barbarians came and rousted them out."

"The Queen of Britannia?"

Domi nodded. "She was Nigel's protector and patron, sorta. She's Queen Fiona's cousin. So they had a lot of adventures, and wound up here. Made the papers all over the world."

"Indeed." That much would be easy to check. If she chose to bother. She wondered how the British queen, whom she couldn't help picturing as the old and stumpy Victoria, felt about being beholden to a slip of a girl like Fiona.

"Also I think it was like a kind of payoff for the Canadian sec men backing off Nigel. When the barbarians grabbed Britannia, the whitecoat set up shop here serving Fiona. He's not too happy about it, though, I can tell you."

Brigid shook her head. "Surely he would have mentioned something—"

"Why? Why he should trust you? You were sent to him by Fiona and her spy-masters. He's supposed to be picking your brain for intel they can use, remember? Why would he not figure you'd snitch on him?" She produced a peach from somewhere in her pale green dress and began to munch it.

"Why for that matter would Norman trust you?"

Domi grinned again. "Got my ways. Doubt it?"

Brigid frowned. I want to believe he spun Domi a tale to impress her. It was certainly natural for a man to want to impress the diminutive albino woman. Yet for all her lack of faith in Domi's mental rigor, she knew that Domi was in some ways the most streetwise of the Cerberus operators. It was certainly no easier to pull wool over her blood-colored eyes than Grant's brown or Kane's wolf-gray ones. Whereas I'm clearly the innocent....

She took a deep breath. "Still. There's an underside to every society, every culture. Even Cerberus. Haven't you done some things you regretted, Domi?"

Domi gave her a quick angry looked, morphing—so Brigid thought, anyway—into grudging respect. "A few. Not so many as you mebbe think. Or, hell, mebbe more."

Brigid nodded. "We don't get perfection from ourselves. Why expect it from a whole population—even a whole government? Clearly Her Majesty's government has the most benevolent intentions, and manages—at least a good part of the time—to act upon it."

Domi shook her head in vigorous negation. "You're blind," she said, "cause you don't want to see. You should listen to Norman."

"What does he say about Dr. Miles-Burnham?"

Domi looked at her with her head cocked to the side like a curious pup. "He talks of him like a god," she said hesitantly. "He worships him."

Brigid nodded. "Haven't you ever heard the expression, 'No man is a hero to his own valet.' "

"No. What's 'valet'?"

"Let it pass. Norman, who knows him best, says Miles-Burnham is a good man and a great one. Yet Miles-Burnham serves the hegemony."

It was Domi's turn to nod enthusiastically. "He's all bookworm-naive just like you! Easy to fool by people who dress nice, say please and thank you, know what adverbs are, that kind thing."

Cheeks flushed Brigid turned her face to the window of the carriage, and looked without particularly seeing as the streets and structures of Gloriana grew golden again and they returned, at last, to the palace.

Chapter 14

Brigid came awake all at once, aware someone was in the bedroom with her.

"Shh," a voice said softly in her ear. "Take it easy. Don't holler or raise any fuss."

"Domi? What are you—?"

"Escaping—no." A hand clamped on Brigid's upper shoulder as she lay on her side. "Don't say anything. I'm giving you the chance to come along."

"How can you possibly escape from the palace?"

"Made contacts with the servants while you were rubbing elbows with the fancy-pants. Not everybody feels about their masters like Norman does."

Brigid tried to roll onto her back. Domi's hand resisted a moment, then let go. Brigid sat up. Domi stood by the bed, dressed in dark, oversize man's clothes.

"You fool. What good do you think this will do you? Don't you see our only chance to get home is through these people?"

"Lakesh won't leave us here," Domi said. Her head was down and her underlip jutted mulishly. She and Lakesh had been lovers for a while. Although Domi was as much and often irritated with the Cerberus director as any of them, she still felt a strong attachment toward him, and her customary strong sense of loyalty.

"Domi, don't you know? It won't do any good. The interphaser can't work here. Just as our communicators and our firearms don't work. Lakesh *can't* bring us back. There's no device he could send across to us that would work given the limitations on higher-energy operations."

Domi's face worked soundlessly for a moment. Brigid felt a stab of irritation at her stupidity for not grasping the fact: hadn't the evidence been enough? Hadn't they been told often enough what the altered rules of physics were here?

Be fair, she told herself. She was too angry to listen, in a state of defiant denial.

"So running away won't help you, Domi," Brigid went on gently. "Whatever chance we may have, it's here, with these people. Uncomfortable as I know some of their ways make you feel."

"Yeah, uncomfortable." Domi shook her head slightly and uttered an ironic laugh. "You're comfortable here, aren't you? With all their rules and order and running people's lives—for their own good, of course. You're still a baron's bitch at heart!"

Brigid's slap rocked her head around. Brigid instantly regretted striking her. Nor was it because she knew Domi was dangerously volatile, with a wild animal's inclination to lash out if physically attacked.

That's not who I am. What's wrong with me?

Domi raised her head and grinned at her. Brigid winced at the stark way her red palm imprint stood out against Domi's milky skin.

"That one cut to bone, huh? I shoulda known all the time. It's not 'cause the barons're evil you turned against them, but just because they turned on you. Here all this time you've just been looking for the right master to put the collar on."

Brigid found herself swelling with an emotion she was little familiar with: true anger. Many of the things she had witnessed and experienced in the past few years had sickened or appalled her; many were the times she'd been terrified. But seldom angry. Anger was not an emotion she was used to permitting herself to feel; it was unbecoming to an archivist, whose life was all cool dispassionate detachment.

She turned and started to swing her legs from beneath the gold satin coverlet to stand up. "This is absurd. You don't know what you're saying or doing. I'm going to call the guard. They'll sort this out. You won't be punished— you never gave your parole—but I'm afraid we'll be seeing further restrictions."

"That's all you think of me," Domi said softly. "I'm some kind of exotic animal. Can't really think, not responsible for my actions. Enough of you. I'll give you a chance for freedom. You pick your nice plush-padded cage. Okay, then. I let you. Don't try to stop me, though."

"Domi, listen to yourself!"

"I hear myself real good. You listen to me, for once. You get back in bed now and be quiet—one way or other. When they find me gone, you don't know nothing—you woke up, I'm gone. You don't make no trouble for the servant 'cause the servants can make trouble back, promise you. Anyway, if you tell your new masters I talked to you, they'll think you helped me run."

She grinned again. "They suspect that anyway—sec men always do, just like back home. But they still want what you got, shouldn't cause you much grief—for a while. When they done with you, though…"

Domi turned and slipped away, leaving Brigid alone with her tumult of thoughts.

"I THOUGHT THIS was supposed to be a private massacre," Kane said.

The sun had yet to put in an appearance. A band of pallid light was slowly expanding out over the plains, pushing the great black jeweled dome of night up and over their heads and down behind the Rocky Mountains. Kane stood with Rodríguez-Satterfield and his other seconds in the twilight on short, slightly dew-slicked grass, late-summer brown, in a shallow valley by a small stream. A single gnarled cottonwood tree stood on its bank near where Kane's party stood, the only tree in sight. Kane was wrapped in a frock coat; it was surprisingly cold, given how scorching the days still were.

To one side of the dueling ground the land heaved away in a series of ridges and valleys still shadowed by the sun; to the other it rose in a single slow sheetlike slope to a crest somewhat over a hundred yards away. It was there Kane looked when he spoke: it was beginning to be lined with carriages, black cutouts against a scarcely lightened sky.

"The vultures gather, my friend," Francisco Burciaga

said. "A public affair of honor, so-called, always attracts a certain sort of spectator."

"I didn't realize it was public," Kane said. He accepted a hit of coffee from some kind of bulky insulated flask offered by one of the Rodríguez-Satterfield *vaqueros*. The hot, bitter liquid warmed him. He had declined coffee laced with brandy—he didn't want alcohol taking the edge off him. The Cíbolan coffee was, as usual, touched up with an unsweetened cocoa.

"Presumably Silveiro's principals want to insure your death or humiliation are as widely witnessed as possible," the diminutive man said, "so as to discredit your presentations before the senate most completely."

He nodded with his chin toward where several groups, carefully kept a certain distance by mounted Rodríguez-Satterfield *vaqueros*, were setting up bulky box cameras on tripods. "They didn't neglect to inform the so-called gentlemen of the press, either, you see."

"I think to see our friend Henry's hand in that," Randall Rodríguez-Satterfield said. Henry Purcell was another of the colonel's close friends and allies. A tall, lean, big-jointed man, with heavy, handsome features, Purcell was the only person Kane had seen since Grant's death who appeared to have any African blood. His skin was a deep golden-russet, his large deep-set eyes mahogany, his hair, receding and cropped unfashionably short—although that didn't stop him sporting Burnsides himself—was bronze with a tendency to tightly curl. He was a newspaper editor and columnist, and unlike the colonel himself or his other friends Kane knew of, seemed to possess nei-

ther military experience nor great means. He was however
well-known in the republic and beyond for the audacity
of his views and the vivid yet tightly reasoned way in
which he presented them. "He's looking to dramatize the
heroism of Mr. Kane, in bravely facing up to a skilled professional killer. It might do some good, at that, selling people on our little scheme, my friend."

"If I survive."

"There's that, of course."

A black steam carriage appeared on the long slope
above. Its windows were curtained in heavy dark fabric.
It seemed to Kane more the size of a small omnibus than
even a largish personal vehicle. It even had six big wheels.
Doors in the rear opened, and out came the tall spare
figure of Silveiro the duelist, in immaculate white. Three
men in dark coats and top hats emerged after him: his seconds. Kane had seen them before, when they met with
Rodríguez-Satterfield, Burciaga and Barker to arrange the
terms of the duel. They were undistinguished enough.
Two of them looked like generic coldhearts to Kane, the
third like a lawyer, pale and stocky. Despite the Cíbolan
mania for privacy, Purcell had managed to learn that they
were hirelings themselves, a couple of minor bravos who
made most of their visible income as what amounted to
bouncers and, for a fact, a lawyer.

As if from the mists rolling along the stream the duel
master and his retinue appeared. The master, the event's
head referee, looked more like a preacher than anything
else: an enormously tall, inflexible, cadaverous specimen
in a stand-up collar and frayed black frock coat. Or an un-

dertaker, perhaps. They marched with a ceremonious air to the particular spot appointed for the duel to take place, a discreetly staked patch of level grass beside the stream near the lone tree.

The opposing party took up positions about twenty yards away. The tall and saturnine Silveiro did not engage in a staredown with his opponent, nor strut around and bluster like a professional athlete from a twentieth century sports vid in Kane's world. He flicked Kane a single incurious glance, and then ignored him.

Kane didn't have much stomach for strutting around and cracking wise himself. He shed the long black coat keeping him warm against the chill-edged morning breeze. Beneath it he wore loose trousers and a sleeveless blouse, both black.

Beneath that, he wasn't wearing his shadow armor. It would've been too obvious. There were other reasons, too, but Kane didn't care to look at them too closely. He didn't want to think of himself either as having a death wish or getting soft enough to give a stoneheart an even break.

The chief official and assistants took up position midway between the enemy groups. Rodríguez-Satterfield and Burciaga went forward to speak to him, as did Silveiro's two seconds. Barker stayed back as if to reassure Kane with his presence. He didn't pepper Kane with encouraging patter, but stood in silence, frowning slightly, hands in his pockets. Kane was glad.

He missed his Cerberus friends.

The crowd up on the ridge had swelled to what seemed

like several hundred. Overhead the sky had begun to color. Some pink horsetails of cloud hung off to one side. The air smelled of moist earth and brush. A pair of assistant officials like tanned, almost sexless, monkeys briskly and impersonally frisked Kane to make sure he bore no concealed weapons, nor wore any armor other than the approved ten-yard swatch of silk wound around his gut beneath his shirt. He endured their impersonal attention stoically. Glancing toward his opponent, he saw Silveiro doing likewise.

Why shouldn't he? It's just another day in the office to him.

The seconds marched back to their contestants, each carrying a long polished-walnut case. Rodríguez-Satterfield opened his before Kane to reveal a saber with a long, gently curved blade and wire-wound hilt with a dull-finished steel basket. A plain, high-quality wep; Silveiro was being presented with its identical twin. Kane hefted it and looked across at his opponent.

"Let's do this thing," he said.

He and Silveiro were brought to stand facing each other three yards apart while the chief referee, in a high-pitched drone, recited some ritual offers to both to kiss and make up. Silveiro refused with a tense head shake; his long, scarred face was slightly flushed, as if he were beginning to feel a certain excited anticipation. Kane, whose guts churned, simply shook his head, as well.

The referee ordered them onto guard. Kane raised his sword, held it steady. Silveiro did likewise, without any kind of fancy flourish or salute. The official stuck his black-sleeved arm in between them, counted three, then called, "Begin."

Cautiously Kane sidled forward as the saber master had taught him, blade questing forward as if it were an extension of his arm. He'd actually fought with swords before, if not particularly well. It still didn't feel like an extension of his arm.

That would be his Sin Eater, lying inert in a carved oak chest in his spacious bedroom at the Rodríguez-Satterfield digs, having been disassembled, measured, photographed and studied at length by envious experts, who, obviously, would never be able to duplicate it or get it to function.

The blades kissed at what Kane thought of as the sweet spot, a handspan behind the tips. At the tiny singing sound and vibration down his arm, Kane felt his heartbeat spike.

A smile spread across Silveiro's sallow, scarred face like an old wound reopening. With a flick of spring-steel wrist he beat Kane's blade aside as if the arm holding it were overboiled spaghetti. He lunged forward, cocking his saber over his left shoulder for the stroke that would split Kane's skull like an overripe melon.

Chapter 15

"We first landed on this planet in the year 2175, local," Ishmael said, walking slowly across the field from the small, grounded airship beside the big human with his tail up and head down and hands clasped behind his back.

He wore what looked like an Earth-style tan trenchcoat retailored to his differently proportioned torso. Their boots squelched in muddy furrows, driving already trampled and withered shoots of some indigenous crop deeper into the ground. Behind them the all-human dirigible crew struggled to dog the unwieldy craft to the ground against the rising predawn breeze.

"Although 'landing' is not exactly the right word. Because our advance craft were following a trajectory calculated to effect direct grounding without entering orbit first, they had no warning and no chance when suddenly, their control systems failed. We built them sturdy—most of the craft, our investigations established later, were reasonably intact when they impacted at near cometary velocity in some fields on the east side of the river. Of course, the less speculation about the fate of the crews and assault units during the extraordinary furnace-like heat of decontrolled entry, the better."

Grant grunted. Zirak glanced up at his companion. A human lackey danced alongside holding an umbrella over his head. The big black man walked with his head tipped forward, leaning slightly forward, so that without hurrying he still seemed to move with relentless force. He didn't seem to care whether the rain fell on him or not, and his face streamed like a polished mahogany idol's.

"Two years later all was in readiness for a second attempt. Our grand fleet built a base on the Moon, where the technology that had brought us across the stars still functioned. We sent down a force in glider-type assault landers, with special control systems that worked by purely mechanical means, not the high-energy microelectronics that failed so spectacularly the first time."

He sighed. "They encountered the same problem as you, my friend—the primers in their projectile weapons, made of tiny mounts of high explosives, wouldn't go off. Of course their energy weapons went dead, too. They were quickly defeated by the humans. To be fair, the humans didn't kill indiscriminately. They took a lot captive, and treated them humanely—while draining them of every bit of information they could.

"It was five years before we began to mount the final attack wave, which won us footholds on this world twenty years ago. We developed a technology similar to that used by the natives for their firearms—our caps are small glass lenses with two compartments containing chemicals, inert when kept separate, which instantly burn at high temperature on contact with one another. Not as efficient as high-explosive primers and, as you no doubt imagine, horribly dangerous at first, until the technology matured. Of course our weapons must be black-powder based. One of our greatest delays was arranging to mine or synthesize the necessary compounds without a living planet to derive them from. Think charcoal. On the Moon. And of course conventional automatic weapons are quickly rendered unusable by the vast quantities of fouling the propellant produces. We had to derive our own version of the multi barreled system known as Gatling on this planet...."

Zirak was rattling. He wasn't entirely in his comfort zone here. His subject's affect stayed flat as a deader's EKG. He wondered if the drugs Grant was dosed with were having too strong an effect. They were a temporary expedient, after all, meant to suppress his critical faculties and cloud his memories long enough to help the skillful Zirak interrogate him.

The smell hit them first.

A few lights burned in the village, bluish, battery run, emplaced by the infantry company that had secured the place. Zirak absently returned the salute from a squad commander whose zeal caused him to forget that you didn't salute civilians.

The first body was that of a small girl. It sprawled in the mud where a raider's lance thrust had caught it in the back. The skin of bare arms and legs was ashy with death, although the corpse as of yet showed no signs of bloat. Zirak felt a momentary disappointment she wasn't clutching a doll, and none lay just beyond reach of stiff outstretched chubby fingers. It would have been far more dramatic.

The big human's face showed little reaction. But the light reflecting from the balls of his eyes changed, one to signify their turning to look again as they narrowed ever so slightly. Zirak's knowledge of human body language was very good, and he missed very little.

They moved on. The fires had gone out, leaving the simple clapboard shacks as sad slumps of charred ruin. Here the stink of ashes was even stronger than that of death. But there was death here, in plenty. Bodies were strewn in the muddy streets, half out of charred doorways.

"Why'd you bring me here?" Grant asked.

His heavy handsome face showed no sign of reaction to the stench of week-old death. Zirak was skilled enough at reading human facial expressions to be sure of it—not that most of his compatriots, themselves Earth hatched and reared among the tailless, could not have recognized *that* look when they saw it. Of course it helped that, in the humid heat of late summer and nearness to the Mississippi Valley, most of the decomposition had already occurred, and the smell had begun to diminish.

"To show me man's inhumanity to man?" Grant asked. "Been there, done that."

"Something more specific," Zirak said. "These humans lived at peace among us. These villagers were under our protection. They were killed for collaborating with us."

"Who killed them? Those redcoat bastards who took my friends? Or one of their allies?"

"Not exactly either, much as I'd like to blame them. This was done by irregulars—bandits."

They had stopped in the middle of the devastated village. The bodies lay heaped together here, in a sort of little square or plaza. Despite the fact that most structures had burned to black frame skeletons, the place was undeniably primitive. From hours of interviews Zirak had the impression it was still nice by Outlands standards in the reality his guest had left. But here the rain was powerless to dilute the reek of dead humans. It was like a physical assault.

"Lot of bandits," Grant said. He had wandered outside the umbrella's rain shadow. He swiveled his streaming head slowly from side to side. "To chill this many."

"The world is a disorderly place, my friend. Chaos breeds disregard for law—and thus, for human life. Some hate us. Yet they take it out on their own kind.

"You have told me you were raised and trained to serve the dominant North American government on your world."

The big man's eyes snapped to Zirak at the apparent non sequitur. A moment later he turned his still impassive face to bear on him like a searchlight.

"You once believed in the ideals of the system you served," Zirak plowed on, "even though the system had become corrupted, had betrayed those ideals, even as it eventually betrayed you."

Grant stared at him and still said nothing.

"What you see here is what Program of Unification was meant to prevent in your own world. It was flawed and grew corrupted. But its ostensible aims—the ones you were trained to uphold—were laudable."

He looked up at the man's face. "You can serve those ideals here. Now. You can help us bring order and decency to this troubled world. We're not perfect, but surely you agree—he gestured about him at the corpses putrefying in the gentle rain—we're better than this."

Grant grunted again. "Thought you wanted to pick my brains for whitecoat stuff."

Zirak shrugged, smiled. "Ah, my friend, but you are not a whitecoat, to use your colorful idiom. Which I find quite delightful. In any event, you are, for instance, a veritable font of information on the flying, combat tactics and maintenance of rotary-wing attack craft. You have told us wonderful tales of your Manta Trans-Atmospheric Vehicles. Which we likewise have, and cannot use. Of course, our brethren on our lunar base might be able to profit from your data, but we cannot."

"Use big mirrors to communicate, do you?"

Zirak blinked three times rapidly at the human. Beware of underestimating this one, he told himself briskly. He is far more than the blunt instrument he appears to be. To his knowledge no one had ever mentioned how the planet-bound Reptoids communicated with their great fleet in space.

"You are very clever, Grant," he said. "Our lunar base generally uses lasers to communicate with us—more directional." And no security breach to concede: it wasn't as if the confounded tailless nation-states didn't know it already. And while Reptoid codes and ciphers managed to stay a consistent step ahead of this planet's frighteningly resourceful and dogged cryptographers, it scarcely mattered for more than Race pride: the humans found out most of what passed between the permanently separated forces through their spies, omnipresent as ants....

"Your splendid armor, most of whose properties are structural and hence unimpeded by this world's peculiarities, provides us a rich field of study. It represents a number of significant advances over our own art." And, oh, would those chauvinistic drones in the Talon bepiss themselves if they knew I said that! He made a note to include it in his report of this encounter. As if in passing.

"I'm surprised you let me keep it."

Zirak shrugged. "It is a token of our esteem and good faith." And besides, even you must sleep sometimes, my friend. Of course the technicians wanted to cut the shadow suit up into little pieces the better to analyze its structure and operation. Let them whine like terrestrial dogs, Zirak had long since mastered the arts of bureaucratic intrigue. At which the techs were notably deficient...

Indeed, he thought, by far the greatest portion of my efforts to advance the Race are spent in *circumventing* the Race.

"And also," Grant said with one of those smiles Zirak had long since learned not to mistake for expressions of friendship or pleasure, "you want something out of me."

Zirak nodded. "We do."

"What?"

"Your help. You are in your own lexicon an expert commando." It was another alternate-world import Zirak savored: *commando* to this world's humans meant a small, independently operating military force. "We need your services. You can help train us—our own elite warriors, I believe, have much to learn from you. And you could work wonders with our human auxiliaries."

"You want me as an instructor?"

"In part. We would also like to employ you on certain crucial missions. Nothing prejudicial to the interests of your fellow humans—because we intend none such. But if you would gain a measure of revenge against those who insulted you in the most demeaning terms and shot you down like a dog and kidnapped your friends into captivity—can offer you that."

A corner of the man's wide mouth lifted slightly, slowly. Not even Zirak could decipher the expression shift.

"How about a chance to spring my friends?" the huge human said.

Zirak nodded slowly, pretending to ponder. For once his subject's unlooked-for quickness of wit—so belying his brutal appearance—was helpful rather than the reverse. Zirak had been struggling with how best to broach this very subject.

"It might be," he said, "just possibly, that you could prove instrumental in rescuing them."

Grant nodded. "I'm in."

Zirak blinked again. "Like that?"

"Like that."

Walking back to the airship, enjoying the return of clean wet smells of rain-drenched soil and greens, Zirak pondered what he had learned. Of human behavior—or at least the mental landscape of this remarkable specimen trudging at his side.

Zirak was pleased with the hand circumstance had dealt him—for once. Events at the ville once called Nickleberry had unfolded as he had described them. It had not proved necessary to stage an atrocity. Although that was well within the Race's purview—and Zirak's, although he would have regretted the necessity. But it was part of his compact with himself that he should never let the affection—actually the love and even esteem—he felt for his pets divert him from zealous performance of his duty.

He had thought it was an especially sweet favor from Fate that the occupants of Nickleberry, east of the great Mississippi, had one and all descended from refugees from the periodic and brutal political upheavals in the Kingdom of New Africa, which had long become more a patchwork of feudal fiefs than a kingdom in any real sense. The legendary freedom fighter for whom the ville was named had led them here and won acceptance from the government of the then-Great River Republic a century before the first, abortive Reptoid landings. His descendants—as most of the villagers were indeed rumored to be—had in turn acquiesced to Reptoid rule. Their relations with their overwhelmingly white neighbors had been far from placid, and they suffered frequent depredations from New African river pirates who still regarded them as traitors.

Zirak was immoderately proud of his awareness of such distinctions as racial subgrouping within humankind, unlike a majority of his races. Those distinctions mattered a great deal to the human natives.

Yet it seemed to make no impression whatever on Grant that the massacre victims were, like him, black.

Which only showed, Zirak thought, how much remained to be learned about these fascinating beasts.

And knowing the human couldn't read his own body language, he allowed himself the tail-swinging swagger of one who had not only won total success in his current project, but had also guaranteed himself years more pursuit of his beloved hobby.

Chapter 16

Gleaming dully in the pale light of dawn the saber hacked downward for Kane's face.

As soon as his own blade was knocked aside he launched himself forward without even trying to whirl the weapon back around into position. He tucked his chin to his clavicle and raised his right arm bent forward.

Whatever move Silveiro had been expecting from his opponent—probably to stand there like a sheep caught in headlights as his saber split his skull—it came from the lexicon of classic swordplay. This move didn't.

The professional duelist's basket hilt slammed down with painful force on the juncture of Kane's neck and shoulder. Kane's forearm bar caught Silveiro in the armpit and blasted him backwards off balance and flailing.

Kane was after him, hacking downward with the saber held in both his hands. Back on more familiar terrain, the swordsman caught himself, deflecting the stroke to his own left.

Before he could riposte, Kane had seemingly blundered into him again, slamming him with his left shoulder. His weight pinned Silveiro's sword arm between their bodies. He brought up his right hand and punched Silveiro in the face with his own steel basket.

The duelist staggered back, blinking, with blood streaming from his broken nose. This time Kane gave him no chance to find his way back to the familiar continuum of sword fighting. Lunging forward, he grabbed the Brazilian's sword-hand wrist with his left hand to control the wep. Still half-blind with the pain and shock of his broken nose, the duelist instinctively seized Kane's right wrist.

Kane slammed his forehead down onto the bridge of Silveiro's nose, knocking it askew and snapping his head back. Then he brought his right knee up hard between his opponent's legs. The air exploded out of Silveiro's lungs in a gagging burst.

Kane let him fold. He released Silveiro's sword arm to drop an arm onto the back of the swordsman's neck and guide his face into a rapidly rising knee.

Silveiro went to all fours. His head was down and streaming blood onto the ground. Kane took a step back and gave him a good running kick to the ribs, knocking him onto his back. He heel-stomped him in the solar plexus, completely winding him. Then he walked over and stepped deliberately on the wrist of Silveiro's sword hand. He ground with his heel until the fingers released the hilt. Then he kicked the saber away.

"Want any more?" Kane asked conversationally. "Plenty more where that came from, I'm barely just warmed up."

Silveiro lifted up his head. His face was a mask as bloody as a man flayed. He raised a feeble left hand and shook his head.

"No," he croaked. "Please, no more."

"In my world," Kane said, "Brazilians know a thing or two about street fighting."

He thrust his own saber tip first into the turf. He turned to the referee. "What now?"

"Well, that last shot to the stomach was not, strictly speaking, considered fair."

"If you wanna prop him up on his feet I'll be happy to throw him another beating."

"No, no. He has conceded. And I don't think it was solely due to the questionable blow." He turned to face the crowd, which Kane realized was applauding wildly. He had heard nothing during the brief, brisk encounter but the sound of his own breathing.

"Mr. João Silveiro of Belem in the Empire of Brasil has surrendered. Mr. Kane, a visitor from parts unknown, has won the duel. His honor stands vindicated."

Kane reached his left hand down to Silveiro. The Brazilian stared up at him blankly. Then he clasped his subjugator forearm to forearm. Kane hauled him to his feet as if he were a child.

"Thank you," Silveiro said through pulped lips.

Kane shrugged and started to walk away, toward Rodríguez-Satterfield and his friends, who surged forward in a jubilant knot. The duelist's seconds made no move to help him.

A gasp from the crowd drew his attention up the ridge. The side of the long black steam car in which Silveiro and his seconds had arrived had fallen away. In the wag's bed a pillar-mounted Gatling gun began to roar and flame.

Silveiro danced like a puppet on a string as a stream of .45-caliber slugs sleeted through him. He fell down dead before he hit the ground. The bullet stream began to walk toward Kane, who had thrown himself down at the first yellow flick of muzzle-flash.

Fascinated, he watched little geysers of dirt and grass erupting, closer and closer to his eyes.

"I SAY WE PRESSURE HER," said the man whose big crimson face clashed horribly with the scarlet of his tunic. "Lean on her some, don't you know?"

A ripple of agreement came from the half-dozen other men, some also in uniform, some in civilian garb, gathered around the briefing table. The single woman in the room, who wore a gray dress that for all its severe simplicity clung perhaps a bit too tightly to her supple form for decorum, and whose hair shone a dark metallic red in the light of the gas lamps, sat back in her chair with chin down and eyes brooding and unfocused.

"Stands to reason," said a weedy, tweedy man with a receding chin and protruding eyes in a tenor voice. His manner suggested eagerness to mount what seemed the cresting consensus wave. "Our window of opportunity, so to speak, won't stay open forever. Our enemies will most assuredly make some move soon. They're already fearful of the Apocalyptic Engine."

The air was stuffy and overly warm, crowded with the smells of soap, sweat, wool slightly damp from the humid day, pomade and the residue of cigar smoke. The sovereign permitted none but herself to smoke in here, a thing almost as scandalous as the garment she wore. Queen Fiona's intense conservatism was mostly confined to the arena of politics, and mostly to others.

"Preposterous," said the man lounging at apparent ease at the table's end most distant from Fiona. He wore a scarlet tunic and had a shock of straw-colored hair, a blond mustache, slanted long pale green eyes like a lynx. The others reacted as if an electric shock had been passed up from their overstuffed chairs into their overstuffed bottoms. The high-ranking leaders, both civilian and military of the queen's secret council, were not accustomed to being contradicted, especially so bluntly—and by one so junior. It was the act of a man who would seem to care little for his life, let alone career.

"Has none of you learned anything in years of playing the game?" Lieutenant Colonel Rafael Mackenzie asked, voice still as languid as his posture. "You can't pressure a boffin like that. They're stubborn as mules and delicate as egg porcelain at once. If you push or pull them they won't budge. If you break them they stay broke—and are no bloody use to anybody."

The use of the final adjective, with obscene connotations, caused another shock to ripple through the generally well-padded features of his hearers. Yet the Devil Mackenzie had no fear for his career while Fiona sat on the throne, and others were well advised to look to their own purses, wives and even lives when he was in the vicinity.

"Lieutenant Colonel, you forget yourself—" the officer with a face like a crimson balloon began.

"On the contrary, General. I *remember*. We have successfully followed a hands-off policy with Miles-Burnham. He's building the Apocalypse Engine for us, or had you forgotten? Had we given into your initial impulses to pull his fingernails out for him not long after he arrived in our midst, he might not be proving quite so dexterous in Her Majesty's service, eh?"

The important men in the room, middle-aged or older one and all, exchanged angry glances. "Damned impertinence—" began another man in civilian garb, who had a damp receding hairline and hanging jowls like a hound's.

Mackenzie grinned. "What I get paid for, Colonel."

"Dammit, the man's too circumspect! And for all that he's a guest upon Your Majesty's hospitality, and hails from the mother country. His goals and ideals are hardly the same as ours."

The youngest person in the room cleared her throat. Instantly the others grew still. Even Mackenzie subsided, although he regarded his sovereign with amusement in his pale green eyes.

"Time presses, Rafael," Queen Fiona said. "It presses us hard. Because of the damned leaky *sieve* which is all we or anybody else can apparently contrive by way of security, everyone in the world knows we have the wretched woman, and they know she's a treasure house of otherworldly technological lore. It's but a matter of time before foreign agents start swarming around her like flies to a jam jar."

She sat quite upright now. Her eyes blazed as she swept them around the table. The council tried to sit at attention, almost quivering to her scrutiny.

The Devil Mackenzie seemed to sprawl even more bonelessly in his chair, like a great cat relaxing in the sun. "Let me remind Your Majesty, she is unburdening herself to our esteemed guest, the professor, and quite nicely, too. The man seems to have quite the way with women." Something about that seemed to amuse him greatly.

"But he's hardly a professional military man!" the general burst out.

"He in no way understands the demands of industrial production," said the stout, balding civilian.

"He is not trained in interrogation," said the tweedy man, his mustache twitching like rabbit whiskers.

"Do you, gentlemen, feel yourselves intellectually superior to the greatest scientist of the age?" the queen asked in a voice like silk rustling. Or a snake in fallen leaves. They subsided instantly.

"So long as our goose continues to lay golden eggs," the monarch continued, "you shall not be allowed to dissect her. Surely you don't believe our good lieutenant colonel advises restraint out of squeamishness?"

The others exchanged glances. More than one face had grown a shade paler, or even two. They had heard the stories of Mackenzie's exploits. Some, indeed, had read the dossiers…

"No more do I. For now we will continue to do what is bringing us results."

She turned her fierce gaze on Mackenzie, who showed no reaction. "Yet my patience is not infinite. Understand me, gentlemen—one way or another, this Baptiste woman will *not* be allowed to fall into other hands!"

"I GOTTA ADMIT," Kane said, accepting an iced mint julep from one of his host's innumerable granddaughters, distinguishable by their piercing blue eyes, "that for the first time I actually appreciate the value of an armed populace."

The Gatling concealed in the black steam carriage had fired plenty, but not long. As soon as it opened up, everybody among the onlookers, including women and even a few older children, had suddenly produced handguns and started returning fire. Kane had a particularly vivid image of an elderly lady in a sunbonnet happily blasting away with a revolver seemingly as big as her own head held in her bony fists.

The coroner, according to a recent rumor, had dug two pounds of lead out of the actual gunner. He had died almost instantly—the last shots creeping their way toward the bridge of Kane's nose had been fired by his dead hand and inertia on the crank. His assistant gunner hadn't been so lucky, to judge by the horrific shrieking that immediately followed the explosion of the carriage's steam boiler. But the audience obligingly kept firing right along, even into the sudden steam cloud that obscured the vehicle, and put him rapidly out of his misery, as well. The driver had had the sense to jump clear in time and was claiming ignorance.

"It is the cornerstone of our liberty, Mr. Kane," said the slender editor, Henry Purcell, who stood with Kane, Randall Rodríguez-Satterfield, Barker and Burciaga beneath the shade of a giant Russian olive tree in a tan suit and top hat.

"You think? I'd figure a newspaper type like you would say that was freedom of the press." Not that that was a concept Kane had either great allegiance to or familiarity with. He had been raised to regard such freedoms as dangerous irresponsibility. While he had been forcefully awakened to the truth that just about everything he'd ever been told growing up was a lie—about human history, the nature of the baronies, even who and what he was—it didn't mean he'd quite sorted out where he stood on all such matters yet.

"Indeed I do," Purcell said, smiling and nodding. "The right to be armed is in truth the first freedom. None of the rest are worth a hang without the means to protect them, wouldn't you say, Mr. Kane?"

Kane scratched the back of his head. "My experience," he said, "nobody actually *has* anything they're not equipped to kill to hang on to. But then, I come from a pretty rough playground."

"I find the existence of a world in which that rule does not apply far harder to conceive of than that of the Earth you describe, Mr. Kane."

Much of the population of Auraria was crowded onto the lawn of Preton Archer's hacienda. The president of the Republic of Cíbola had no official residence, no less an authority than President Archer himself had explained to Kane the republic didn't want to privilege politicians any further than they had to. But Archer was clearly a man of means, to judge by the size of the white house atop the lawn-covered hill on whose slopes the party was taking place.

Conspicuously absent were the gentlemen and ladies of the press, who had followed Kane here, dogging the Rodríguez-Satterfield steam car with rental steam carriages of their own, hanging out the window and shouting questions. Archer's own gauchos, led by several young men with lean brown faces and startlingly pale blue eyes, had herded them on horseback—cutting them out from the crowd like cattle from the herd where needful—to a pavilion beneath a giant spreading cottonwood at some remove from the big house, where a collation had been laid out especially for them. As far as Kane could see at this remove, they were being treated as grandly as the president's other guests. But if they tried to stray to the main event they were intercepted by horsemen and chased back none too gently.

Kane sipped his drink, feeling the pleasant burn of strong alcohol on his tongue and throat. He pointed to the members of the press. "How about that? You call that freedom of the press?"

"Property rights trump it," Purcell said. "They're free to write what they like. Pres is free to keep them off his lawn. Would you rather they be let loose on the man of the hour again, Mr. Kane?"

Kane shuddered and let that answer for him. At Rodríguez-Satterfield's counsel he'd allowed several questioning sessions with the local mass media, including one in the immediate aftermath of the duel.

"I don't notice any of the presidential offspring turning up on horseback to run you out, Henry," he said.

The editor laughed. "I'm an invited guest," he said,

"and I mind my manners in person—if not always in print. We value manners highly, Mr. Kane. A trait, by the way, of our world in general, not just the republic."

"And how do people on your world regard good manners, Mr. Kane?" a voice asked from behind.

He turned. The voice had not been familiar, but the accent was. Very.

A man had approached holding a glass of blood-colored wine, product of a vineyard Archer owned down the Rio Grande Valley about where Albuquerque used to be in Kane's continuum. He stood slim and as effortlessly erect as a steel blade to his full height, a head less than Kane's. He had dark blond hair slicked back, matching small precise mustache and beard. He wore a sky-blue tunic decorated with a discreet splash of medals, white trousers with red stripes down the side. A monocle was screwed into his left eye. His eyes were dark and slightly Asian looking.

"We can take 'em or leave 'em," Kane said. "Generally we leave 'em."

"Mr. Kane," Purcell said, "permit me to present Colonel Vasily Arkadyevich, Count Arkov. He's the Russian imperial consul to Auraria."

Kane shook the offered hand. It was slim and painfully well-manicured, but it also felt as if it had wound wire over steel armature beneath the skin. Kane was just as glad he didn't try any hand-crushing games with the man, despite his size and foppish demeanor.

"Pleasure, Colonel," he said. "Or do I call you Count?"

Arkov grinned. "You can call me anything you like," he said, "except late for dinner, as they say around here."

"I thought Russia was at war with the republic, Colonel."

Arkov shrugged. "No formally declared hostilities exist. The incidental unpleasantries that arise—these are the very reasons the czar sees fit to maintain me in moderately luxuriously style, a stranger in this most strange land."

"Not that it matters much," Purcell said. "We've got official delegations from everywhere, including places we are actively fighting, like the Silver Kingdom. You'll no doubt be meeting some of them—they're all invited, too. We'd even have Kali-ite representatives if they'd send any."

"Why the sudden interest?" Kane hadn't met a bunch of foreign types before on his public appearances.

"Most immediately, today's duel," Arkov said.

"Why should it make any difference to you or your czar that I beat up some Brazilian chiller?"

"Aside from the fact the outcome was unexpected— you are to be commended for your unorthodox tactics, as well as your prowess in applying them—what I find significant were the lengths to which parties unknown, but possessed of substantial means, were willing to go to silence you. Or failing that, to silence the man they hired to dispatch you. It has tended to erase the last doubts people might be harboring as to the authenticity of you and your claims."

A hand like a bear paw descended on Kane's right shoulder from behind. A wave of whiskey breath enveloped his head.

"Sorry for pussy-footin' up behind you, son," boomed the voice of the republic's septuagenarian president. "Thanks for not laying some of that whoop-ass on me. My poor old bones'd never take it."

Smiling hugely beneath his white mustache, he said something in Russian that ended with "Vasily Arkadyevich." The consul smiled and bowed.

"I yield to your hostly prerogatives, Your Excellency," he said. "Mr. Kane, it has been a pleasure to meet the famous man from another world. I hope we might extend our acquaintance at some time in the near future." He turned and marched away.

"Nice boy, that Vasily Arkadyevich," Archer said with one arm draped around Kane's shoulders. Kane normally didn't welcome physical intimacy from anyone, much less another man. But something about Archer's force-of-nature personality made it easier to take. He was still glad when the arm dropped away after a moment.

"Slip a stiletto in your kidneys in a heartbeat if he thought it'd help his czar," Archer said. "But beyond that, a stand-up guy."

"I notice," Kane said, "he never denied he was the one who sicced Silveiro on me."

Archer guffawed. "Boy's catching right on!" he said. "Henry, he's getting the hang of this world of ours. He just might make it."

"I get the impression," Purcell said, "that if anything, the intrigues of our world are mild compared to his."

"Better mannered, anyway," Kane said.

"I don't think Arkov had anything to do with it," Archer

said. "Mind you, not that he'd have batted an eye shaking your hand and congratulating you like he did if he had."

"What about the Texians?" Purcell nodded toward a somewhat boisterous party of men about fifteen yards away, who were making gallantries toward several striking young women in flounced skirts.

"Naw. Not their style. I'm thinkin' it was the Silver King's bunch. But it could've been the Danes, the Minnetonkans, Canadians even."

"Perhaps a bit of overkill for the Canadians," Purcell said.

"Not all of 'em are the Devil Mackenzie, Hank. And the hit had a certain style, you got to admit. So maybe I shouldn't be too quick to exclude the possibility it was him. Though I still doubt it."

The lining of Kane's throat had grown cold at the mention of the Canadian operative's name. "Why don't you think it was Mackenzie?"

Archer looked at him for a moment. "That's right. You met him face up. Randy told me he was the one who had your friend killed."

"Yeah."

"I'm sorry. As to why it wasn't him making a play for you—somebody made a good-faith effort to kill you today. Maybe two."

"Yeah."

"You're still alive, I notice."

Kane looked at him a hooded moment. "I'm not that easy to chill."

"I appreciate that, son. You surely proved it this morning. But just remember, Mackenzie's not a man who feels real constrained to play fair."

Kane's mouth smiled. "Neither am I."

Archer laughed again. "I believe it. Henry, we got us a real wildcat by the tail here, don't we? Glad he's on our side."

"Am I?" Kane asked.

For a moment Archer looked at him, close and sober. "Of course not," he said. "You're on your own side. And your friends from back home. It's only natural. But let's just say I hope we can stay allies."

Something about the way he said it made Kane's eyes narrow and his gut constrict. Archer nodded ever so slightly.

"Colonel Randy called," the president said. "The senate's voted on the proposal that the republic officially undertake to rescue your friends from the hegemony."

He laid a hand gently on Kane's shoulder again. "Sorry, son. They turned it down cold. Memory of the last debacle's just too darned fresh."

Chapter 17

Brigid's breath condensed on the glass of the carriage window as she watched the evening streets of Gloriana roll by. She almost expected frost to form. It was unlikely; the window was double glazed for insulation, and the doors sealed with synthetic gaskets. It was quite warm inside the luxurious interior.

Outside it was cold. The people hurried against wind, clutching threadbare garments close about them, holding their rounded little hats to their heads. Although it was but early September, winter came early at these latitudes, her hosts had told her. Earlier than it once had; though long ago, the records showed it. It seemed to be another by-product of the Great Change, although the tremendous nuclear winter caused by the Destructor's passage should have ended within a few years, as skydark in Brigid's home line.

Brigid was growing frustrated. Mornings, in the weeks since arriving in Gloriana, she had passed by reading mostly newspapers and history books, and in mild exercise on the extensive palace grounds. Evenings she dined alone or with quietly convivial groups of male and female courtiers evidently selected to put her at her ease and engage her in conversation she would not find boring: the art, culture, history and current events of this world.

In fact she found it fascinating and did enjoy it; she also took for granted her clever companions all reported her every word promptly to hegemonic intelligence. She knew far more than she liked about the ways and wiles of internal security. Domi's accusations, she still believed, had sprung from paranoia fueled by her near pathological hatred of authority. But Brigid took for granted her charming hosts were spying on her. From their perspective it was a matter of survival.

Out on the street a pair of men with close-cropped hair and beards and black-and-white-striped prisoner's attire scrubbed at a stone wall under the supervision of a stone-faced police officer in blue uniform and helmet with a strap beneath his lower lip. They were apparently trying to efface a stylized but rather surprisingly detailed graffito of a white rose.

Brigid pressed her nose to the glass. She had begun to notice symbols chalked on walls in white, but never before had been close enough to see clearly what they were.

An intercom connected the interior of the carriage with the driver's box up front and on top. Brigid had never used it. She wondered now, with a vague pang of guilt, if perhaps she did identify too strongly with the rulers here and took their servants and other commoners for granted.

She pressed the button. "Yes, marm," a voice said promptly from the golden grid.

She leaned her face toward the pickup. She knew such devices were neither powerful nor sensitive. "That symbol those men are cleaning off that wall," she said. "Can you tell me what it's all about, please?"

A pause, as static crackled. Miles-Burnham had assured her they were caused in this world by micropotentialities, differences in the probability stream resolving themselves. It struck her with sudden chill that perhaps the topic was impolitic, even forbidden. Surely they'll realize I've nothing to do with their internal politics, that I couldn't know!

She wondered at her own burst of trepidation: after all, hadn't she decided to aid these people because of their civilization and thoroughly institutionalized compassion? What then had she to fear?

"Bad business, marm," the driver's voice came back at least, still deferential but gruffer than before. "Anarchy, it is. Bad business indeed."

LIKE TOY FIGURES on a glittering music box the dancers whirled on the palace's hangar-sized dance floor. Though she had little appreciation for music, the scholar in Brigid thrilled as she viewed the spectacle from a railed terrace overlooking the floor. They waltzed to melodies never composed on her own world—unless hummed once by an anonymous prodigy and forgotten, squatting by a campfire in the Outlands somewhere.

She wondered what it would be like to be out there, dancing, whirled by a man's strong arms. In general the prospect left her cold; even the measured evolutions of the waltz seemed to her wildly Dionysian, bloodless as she knew that made her seem. And anyway she didn't know how to dance. She would only make a spectacle of herself. People would laugh at her gracelessness, her gaucherie. Just the thought made her long to flee to the refuge of musty library stacks…or a laboratory. Someplace she might feel at home again.

Unless…unless the arms of a special man were whirling her. She thought briefly of Kane. It brought only a pang of loss, a memory of pain. He was gone. He was thousands of miles away across a hostile continent. He might as well be back in their home casement. As resourceful and resolute as he was, he would never reach her here. Not alive.

A generically handsome staff subaltern hovered by her elbow, which was covered in the emerald velvet of her evening glove. Her hosts—to call them anything else risked giving into the paranoia that had driven Domi out into the gutter—had seemingly thrown a succession of them at her in the weeks she had spent shuttling between the palace and the warehouse district. While her photographic memory naturally filed away every detail of facial characteristics, carriage and mannerisms, her conscious mind scarcely bothered trying to tell them apart.

"Excuse me, Lieutenant Olsen," she said to the current make and model, "will Dr. Miles-Burnham be here tonight?"

He blinked at her, nonplussed. "The scientist chap? Why, yes, uh, Doctor. Rather a surprise you'd ask. Frankly, I'd think you'd have had enough, being bottled up in a musty old lab with him all day every day answering questions."

She smiled absently at the lieutenant. "That makes me all the more eager to encounter him in a purely social context."

BRIGID WAS ALREADY seated at the long table, with its dazzlingly white cloth of Irish linen, when the scientist was cried in by the heralds stationed at the door. He wasn't being fashionably late. Ironically for a man who thought so deeply and to such profound effect about the quiddities of time, he was scarcely ever aware of what time it nominally was. She looked up quickly from her still empty porcelain plate, at which she had been gazing unfocusedly while ignoring the chatter of a duchess on one hand and the drone of a major general of artillery on the other.

Miles-Burnham wasn't alone. He had Chrissie on his arm, regal and slender in an ice-blue gown, with her dark hair piled atop her head, but for one tress hanging like a dark vine over one bare shoulder. Her slim, graceful beauty made Brigid feel quite bovine in her strapless green velvet evening gown, with her own firefall hair twisted up behind her neck and caught by a great golden broach with emeralds lent her for the occasion, despite the fact that masculine eyes strayed so often to Brigid and lingered so long even she was aware of the fact.

She became aware of Chrissie being announced, according to the local tradition of saving the best for last: "—Majesty, Christina II Regina, Queen of Britannia in exile!"

Belatedly Brigid realized the small diamond tiara Chrissie wore wasn't for show. Throughout the brilliantly lit hall the glittering throng stood to applaud for the fugitive monarch and the global celebrity who had aided her escape from the Reptoid-allied barbarians who overran her island kingdom, Europe's last bastion of civilization south of Scandinavia. Feeling clumsy and reluctant, Brigid joined them. Her own applause was faint.

She felt several kinds of used. Irrational, she knew. Yet she couldn't help it. But after all, Chrissie Battersea had never claimed *not* to be Fiona's cousin, the Britannian queen.

Squiring his monarch to their seats to either side of the empty chair waiting at the head of the long table, Miles-Burnham caught Brigid's eye. He gave her a big, slightly embarrassed smile. It righted her tumbled gyros. Somewhat.

Trumpets blew. Queen Fiona made certain her entrance was no anticlimax. Nor was it: scandalized, half-hushed comment rippled round the room. The neckline of the skintight black spaghetti-strap gown encasing her taut-muscled body plunged clear to her sternum. Every other female bosom in the room, including Brigid's, was discreetly covered to at least the collarbone. Striding with imperial hauteur, Fiona went to her chair, was seated by a white-jacketed servant, and the meal began.

"SO YOU ARE THE WOMAN from another world."

Chewing a piece of asparagus, Brigid nodded. She had a feeling her manners weren't quite up to imperial standards in this manners-obsessed world. She was content she knew enough to chew with her mouth closed. She had limited patience for such trivia no matter how enticing she found them when observed from an outsider's vantage. It was convenient that her status as famous cosmic oddity granted her a certain leeway.

The man seated across from her seemed no less a striking nonesuch in these surroundings than her. He was a tall, powerfully built man who looked to be in his middle twenties. He wore a tunic of white as dazzling as the tablecloth, with gold epaulettes and trim, and a discreet patch of medals on his left breast. A ring of gold braid encircled the top of his head of crisp, black, short hair. It was almost redundant: even Brigid, who put no great store by her ability to read people, would have taken him for royalty by his bearing, the arrogant power he projected, though he was effortlessly polite and his speech mild. His announcement, shortly before the Queen's, had caused something of a stir, as well: apparently he had arrived unexpectedly that evening by ship down the St. Lawrence.

He was a black man, the first she had seen in the hegemony, the first she had seen since Grant's murder. Like Grant's, his skin was not particularly dark. He had a great bulging forehead, its force only emphasized by the fact his hairline had already begun to recede.

"I am, Prince John," she said, clearing her mouth. "It seems everybody's well aware of the fact."

"Perhaps more than you know, Dr. Baptiste," he said. His eyes were a pale brown with a hint of some other color—gray…or yellow?—that lent them an almost spectral quality. The unusual color, added to the intensity of his gaze, was quite unnerving. "For you are said to be assisting Dr. Nigel in the creation of his fabulous Apocalyptic Engine."

"With all respect, Your Highness, I don't really know what you're talking about," she said, dabbing her lips with a napkin embossed with a monogram consisting of a giant crown and FIR—for Fiona I Regina—in gold.

The prince smiled. The expression didn't reach his eyes. His teeth were strong and white. Brigid wondered if his subjects back in their kraals had teeth so fine. She doubted it. He had undoubtedly grown up in privileged and luxurious surroundings, whether abroad or in his native Kingdom of kwaZulu.

"You don't?" the prince asked. "Your reputation makes you a woman of formidable intellect—as one might presume, from someone who was chosen to cross the time streams. Are you really so ingenuous?"

"What do you mean?" she asked.

The prince had laid down his eating utensils and fastened all his attention on her like a lion its dinner. Thinking about it, she decided he would not lack for credibility among the kraals and warriors of his homeland, either— that he would, with a change of wardrobe, fit in perfectly.

"It is known throughout the world that Dr. Nigel is developing a device to twist the fabric of reality itself," he said, his voice low and resonant, almost hypnotic. So much so that she brought herself up sharply. "As did the Great Destructor itself, so long ago. When he has completed this great work, then the hegemony shall possess unanswerable power over this world, despite the best the Reptoids can do in their laboratories hidden away upon the far side of the Moon. You convey to him your vast store of knowledge of the science of your own strange world. Do you truly not believe such information does not advance this undertaking?"

The muted clatter of eating and service and murmur of speech around them seemed to have faded. Her vision had contracted until she saw only the prince's handsome face and compelling eyes, as at the other end of a tunnel. She wondered why her subconscious reacted so strongly, here in the midst of the very stronghold of the mightiest power on Earth.

"Prince John, I am myself an archivist by training and inclination. It may be that by the standards of someone as worldly and trained in the nuances of diplomacy as Your Highness, I am ingenuous indeed. All I know is that, out of gratitude for the hospitality shown me by the hegemony, and of esteem for Dr. Miles-Burnham's brilliance and the…the greatness of his soul, I have freely shared with him all the knowledge I possess. As for this Apocalyptic Engine, all I know is what I have heard whispered a hundred times, which is little more than the name itself. I have not seen any such thing, nor has the doctor spoken of it to me."

Her cheeks were burning by the time she finished, and her breath was fast and high in her throat.

"As perceptive as you clearly are, Dr. Baptiste," the prince said, "are you sure you would know such an engine if you laid eyes upon it?"

Before she could frame an answer he went on, "And you are most generous in your gratitude to the hegemony—or am I incorrect in my understanding that its troops shot down one of your companions in cold blood the very day your party emerged into this world? A black man, to be specific?"

She turned her eyes toward her plate, on which the splendid meal she had been served mostly sat in the piles she'd pushed it into with her silver fork to make it seem as if she were eating.

"Really, Prince John," her escort said, "is it really quite the thing to badger the doctor so?"

He transferred his gaze to the young subaltern. It was like twin particle-beam weapons shifting aim. For her part Brigid could have kissed the boy.

"The terrier confronts the lion," the prince said. "You are to be commended for your spirit, boy. If I have offended the lady, I ask her forgiveness as a stranger in this land. We speak bluntly in my land, which we call Heaven."

The word for Heaven was Zulu, her inner pedant reminded her. Heaven was an empire that comprised the greater part of the African continent south of the Equator. It was less wealthy and technologically advanced than the hegemony, or so the Canadian texts had it. Even they conceded its status as a military superpower.

"Your apology is accepted, Prince. We are both strangers here, after all, and I'm none too sure of my own manners."

"It would appear you have little to fear on that score, Doctor." Prince John smiled again and nodded. "Nor are you the first to name Dr. Nigel a mahatma—his magnanimity has long been as far fabled as his intellect. I do beg leave to wonder whether his grasp of the spheres and the ether exceeds his knowledge of his fellow humans and their petty politics."

"It might be so, Your Highness. I possess but little understanding of such matters myself."

"Perhaps you might consider coming to visit us in kwaZulu," the prince said. "It would be fatuous to speak of broadening your horizons, but at the least we can afford you a different perspective on this curious, tormented world of ours."

"I am flattered, Your Highness. But really, the matter is out of my hands."

He smiled with apparent blandness. "We must all bow our heads to Fate, Doctor."

"May I have this dance, Dr. Baptiste?"

She stood on a terrace overlooking the dance floor, once again a brilliant whirl of Gloriana's elite. Mainly she was watching Miles-Burnham, sitting to one side of the floor engaged in animated conversation with Christina and her cousin.

Although she was aware of the pressure of many eyes, Brigid never expected to be asked to dance. She wasn't the sort of person who got asked to dance. She turned, about to offer something by way of polite refusal, and found herself staring into almost self-luminous sea-green eyes. The last eyes on the continent, except perhaps Kane's wolf-gray ones, she would have expected.

Without conscious volition she found herself among

the dancers, turning with the best of them in a nonwiden-
ing gyre, dancing as if she knew how behind the master-
ful lead of Rafael Mackenzie.

"Perhaps you should let yourself get out of the laboratory more often, Dr. Baptiste," he said in her ear.

"I really don't belong here," she said faintly. She felt
instant shame. She had faced down deadly danger not just
to her body but to her soul. Yet this entire evening she'd
been behaving, and worse, thinking of herself, as if she
were some bashful helpless adolescent.

"That's the spirit," he said uncannily. She realized he
had read the change in her eyes, the tension of the body
he held in his arms. He's good at what he does, she
thought. Underestimate him at your peril.

"What are you doing here?" she asked in a voice that
sounded more like her own to her than it had all evening.

"Keeping watchful eye on you," he said. He looked
very dashing in his scarlet tunic, pink pants, high black
boots polished to an obsidian finish. His straw-colored
hair was somewhat wild, as if neither it nor he could be
fully constrained, even in settings such as these. He was
a most handsome man, she had to admit.

He nodded past her bare left shoulder with his chin.
"Notice those worthy Oriental gentlemen standing by the
column."

Fluted columns with flowery Corinthian capitals
sprouted here and there around the great festival hall,
probably more for effect than to hold up the ceiling. A pair
of men stood beside the one indicated by Mackenzie, turbaned and bearded, wearing medal-splashed khaki tunics

with red sashes over blue trousers. Each carried an enormous saber in a gold-chased scabbard.

"Are those—?"

"Representatives of the Satguru of the Dominion of Kali," Mackenzie said. "Here to get a closer look at you. Just like your friend from dinner."

About a third of the way around the ballroom stood Prince John. He was flanked by two tall and heroically muscled warriors in traditional garb: leopard skins, assegai, pure-white bull-hide shields as tall as they were.

"They seem to be playing to racial stereotypes," Brigid said.

"Precisely," Mackenzie said with a grin. "They play upon our fears, and at the same time seek to disarm us with the reassurance that they're beneath us after all. Also they bolster their self-regard, show their defiance, by claiming the very primitive traits we whites disdain 'em for are really their greatest strengths."

She looked at him in surprise. He laughed aloud. "Did you think I was just some brute torturer? Her Majesty can pick those off any shrub she passes, in Gloriana alone— and not alone the meaner sections."

Brigid frowned. She didn't like the ramifications of what he said. He's a renegade, she told herself; with a shock like a blow to the belly she remembered he had killed her friend.

"In the end they're just foolish apes, these wogs," he said. He put his mouth near her ear and added in a whisper, "Just like the rest of us."

From across the ballroom came a muffled bang. Then

screams. Brigid turned to see white smoke whirling up from beneath the bandstand as dancers scattered like panicked birds.

Chapter 18

The sentry's neck broke with a sound like a green tree limb snapping. Grant eased the convulsing body down out of the shine of camp lights into a puddle of dark and water.

For a few breaths he crouched behind the bulk of a land ironclad, streaming rain. He wore only his shadow suit, a web-gear harness, a bulky rucksack. He needed no more; it felt good to be stripped for action again.

He carried two handblasters. One, tucked in a shoulder holster beneath his left arm and covered with a flap against the mud, was of a design radically new to this world, an actual autopistol firing from a box magazine. It used a new propellant developed, like the wep itself, in the Reptoids' lunar labs. It mimicked gunpowder by burning rapidly and producing enormous quantities of gas in a hell of a hurry, pushing the projectile before it, but created less fouling than did black powder. It was a top secret item; Ishmael had stressed it was not to fall into enemy—he scrupulously avoided saying *human*—hands.

The other handgun, riding in a hip holster tied down to his thigh, was to Grant's mind a far more curious design.

The hegemonic armored battalion was laagered close behind lines of infantry dug into trenches shivering in night, rain and icy mud. Despite the collapse of the anti-Reptoid alliance this was very much an active battle zone. The periodic sky flashes and thuds that made the wet earth vibrate beneath Grant's soles came more frequently from mortars and rifled guns than lightning and thunder.

The land ironclads crouched like dormant dragons, awaiting the call to attack or defend against a penetration of the line by their armored cousins from the other side. Grant could smell hot metal and coal smoke to all sides, heard a banshee keening somewhere off to his left as excess steam was vented to the night sky. The crawlers' boilers were kept heated so that they could run up a full head of steam at short notice.

Despite the camp's proximity to the front, the camp lay mostly quiet in the vile weather. A few sentries walked among the squat shapes and the neat rows of low tents in which the crews slept, bolt-action rifles slung to their shoulders. A huge water tank dominated the scene, a wooden box ten yards long and half that high and wide, lined, according to Grant's Reptoid controllers, with a great bladder of flexible polymer, supported on a stout wooden frame and rising up fifteen yards against low clouds lit by the sullen glow of fires and swept by spotlight beams.

Grant dragged the dead sentry around the stern of a land crawler. The vehicle was perhaps ten yards long, with a modest two turrets fore and aft, and an armored smoke-stack between. It was driven by great cleated tracks running on a line of wheels, much like tanks in Grant's own world. He tucked the corpse out of sight beneath the tank's belly between the tracks.

Bending at the waist, more from the need for stealth than the weight of his rucksack, Grant moved out for his main objectives. He kept to the shadows, which were in abundant supply. With practiced grace he placed his feet so as not to splash in the puddles of water. Such noise as he made, the rain covered.

A giant shadow rose before him like a mountain range. It was the centerpiece of the camp, and likewise the armored battalion: a land monitor, a monstrous crawler of three segments coupled together like train cars, each with its own set of tracks and engine to drive them. It bristled with stacks and turrets and guns; to Grant it looked like a sizable sea-going warship that had been sawed into segments and stuck back together far inland. It carried by itself more firepower than a full platoon of the lesser tanks.

He wondered how the monster moved in weather such as this without miring itself to the upper deck in mud. As he got closer he realized each of the tracks was over two yards wide, wider than he himself was tall. It was a truly monstrous machine, huger than he first realized.

He shed his ruck. Without hesitation he dropped to his belly in the mud; squeamishness was one of many common human traits ground out of him as a Mag Division cadet before his voice changed. He crawled under the land monitor's rear segment, dragging the pack by a strap. He didn't actually need to go all the way down. He could have duck-walked easily in the space between lower armor and ground. But he preferred crawling, even if it more resembled mud swimming, since it was less likely to cramp his thighs.

During the premission briefing Ishmael had rolled his eyes at Grant when a uniformed military intelligence officer, another lizard man, insisted on pointing out in great, pedantic and altogether unnecessary detail on a chart just precisely where each and every boiler was placed: dead amidships, bottom of the hull. The place logic dictated they *had* to be, for maximal protection and also efficiency in driving the treads.

Like all armored fighting vehicles Grant knew of, the land monitor had to economize on weight where it could; as it was, it massed over two hundred tons. Thus it had relatively thin belly armor. Enemies seldom got direct shots at the underside of a tank—especially one this gigantic. It flowed over obstacles, when it could surmount them at all, like a monstrous if sectionally deprived centipede, so that after the first segment had briefly exposed its belly climbing, its full armor then shielded the middle segment, which shielded the end segment in turn.

Grant reached the first segment's center and dug a parcel out of his pack. With no high explosives, there were no shaped charges on this world. But apparently good old thermite—iron oxide and aluminum powder—functioned just fine. Grant unwrapped what felt like a stiff plastic covering from a doughy mass of adhesive goo impregnated with the stuff and slapped it against the rust-streaked metal plate above. Then he placed a second charge, in a sort of stout iron pot, on the ground directly beneath. To each he affixed an initiator. Then he pulled the tab in each, which began the chemical timing sequence.

He now had ten minutes. But the fireworks were due to begin before then.

He crawled on, moving and acting with purpose but without haste, repeated the actions on the next two segments. Ishmael had gone way out on a limb for this one, entrusting him not just with a mission vital to an upcoming offensive designed to crack open the hegemony's defenses but with top-secret tech that, the Reptoid assured him, the humans could not duplicate and were in fact unaware of.

Mission, technology and Ishmael's thick and somewhat grubby neck were all safe as far as Grant was concerned. He had been confused the first few days, after awakening from what he thought was his own death. But the fog had passed. The things Ishmael had shown and told him had helped him get his mind right. He knew now what he had to do, and being Grant, he would do it, no matter what the cost.

As for the mission…it wasn't Grant's nature to fail.

He emerged from beneath the bow of the mighty land monitor, stood up, shrugged his ruck over his broad back. The mud was already beginning to peel off his shadow suit of its own weight. Time now to go gently and exfiltrate this place, make his way overland toward the rendezvous where Ishmael and a few trusted human auxiliaries—not traitors, but born and raised under Reptoid rule, which seemed as legitimate to them as human governments seemed to those born into them—waited with horses for a dash back to Reptoid lines. By that time, if all went well, the Canadians would have a great many more pressing matters on their minds than pursuing them, if they were even on their trail....

But all never goes well, even in undertakings far less chaotic and perilous than war and snoop-and-poop commando sorties. Grant heard the creak of a rain-rusted metallic hinge almost directly over his head and cursed himself for forgetting that.

A technician in a leather helmet with loose chin straps poked his grimy head out of a hatch. He stared down at Grant with open-mouthed astonishment.

Before anything could come out of that open mouth, Grant spun and brought up the handgun from his hip. It was a magazine air pistol, capable of firing five shots semiauto from a canister of compressed gas clamped beneath the barrel. It was as heavy and almost as bulky as Grant's Sin Eater, but offered no great punch.

It was, however, almost completely silent. With no more noise than a quick plosive breath it spit a bullet that struck the tech between his wide staring blue eyes. His body spasmed once and then sank down noiselessly out of sight.

But Grant's luck tonight, like hourglass sand, once it had run out, was gone. Behind him he heard the throaty bark of a German shepherd—much used by human armies because they could sniff out Reptoids at some distance—and a sentry's challenge: "Who goes there?"

BRIGID CAME AWAKE all at once. Her nude body was completely encased in chill sweat.

She had slept uneasily, dreaming of Domi. The albino

woman was grinning at her with malicious triumph. She had played one of her mad pranks, and Brigid had no doubt it was directed straight at her.

The "explosive device" placed under the bandstand had turned out to be a stink bomb. Mackenzie had hurled Brigid to the dance floor and flung himself atop her, then leaped up and raced to the bandstand, where the orchestra was trying to flee and falling into a panicky thrashing knot over its own instruments. Cries of "Gas, gas!" rang out, adding to the terror.

But Brigid had quickly recognized the rotten-cabbage reek of methyl mercaptan. In the twentieth century the substance had been added to natural gas so that leaks could be detected by smell. She knew at once what the device was.

A stink bomb.

She also, in an intuitive flash, knew instantly who was behind it even before Rafael Mackenzie stood up from behind the bandstand holding—somewhat scorched and tattered—a single white rose.

Several of the dancers still hugging the hardwood around her gasped, "The white rose of anarchy!" Brigid realized the significance of the symbol she'd seen scrawled on the wall, and why the authorities were so eager to efface it.

Domi had been a busy little outlander in the weeks since escaping the palace in the dead of night.

Brigid realized what had awakened her from her uneasy dream. A soft scuffle of movement, a curious smell.

She was no longer alone in the room.

And the sound was no inquisitive rat: the smell, not unpleasant, was that of a slightly sweaty masculine human body.

Brigid had no weapons. Her one option was a loud scream. She filled her lungs to deliver one. Before she could, a heavy callused hand closed over her mouth.

She bit.

Her assailant was definitely hard-core. He grunted but didn't let go. She sank her teeth deeper, worrying the hand like a terrier with a rat.

An open-handed buffet slammed the side of her head. Sparks arced behind her eyes. She let go the hand as her head was knocked straight back down to the pillow.

She heard a harsh hissed word of command. Then she heard a hiss of a different kind, a gasp, a wetly sucking noise.

Blinking, she sat up. A burly black man wearing a loin-cloth dropped to his knees beside the bed. As he did, the long tapering blade of a stabbing spear, gleaming in the low gaslight, retracted into his chest.

Brigid opened her mouth to scream. Something whipped past her eyes, down. Then a cloth was tightened hard and fast over her mouth from behind, garrote fashion. In a flash she felt it tied off behind her neck.

The big warrior who had speared the man who seized and then slapped Brigid stepped back to stand beside an even taller man. Like the others he wore only a loincloth. Brigid recognized him at once despite the radical change in profile from when she'd seen him last.

"I gave instructions you were not to be harmed, Dr.

Baptiste," Prince John of kwaZulu said low in his gigantic chest, in a lion-hunting cough of a voice. "I mean to see my orders carried out. Bring her, Usibebu."

Brigid felt the bed bounce beneath her as someone sprang past; she had never felt him come onto the bed in the first place. It was another Zulu warrior, smaller, darker, and lither than the four or five others in her field of vision. She realized he had gagged her with a pillowcase. He seized her by the biceps, then, with a quick eye roll toward his ruler, bowed and gestured her forward with mock courtesy.

The men were all armed with short-hafted spears, which the prince had identified at dinner as *ilkwa*, and flimsy-looking clubs, seemingly mere hardwood sticks with big bulbous ends. Brigid wasn't deceived: she recognized knobkerries, which could crush a man's skull at a stroke. The scene resembled some kind of Victorian caricature, or perhaps racist nightmare: near naked primitives in a white woman's plush boudoir. But there was nothing comical about these men. They were plainly what back home would have been called coldhearts.

The door was flung open. Prince John strode forth in the lead. Usibebu bundled his captive out right behind. Brigid's door gave onto a gallery overlooking one of the numerous foyers and halls of the great palace. The procession marched to a nearby stair that wound down to the ground floor.

John reached the head of the stairs, pivoted—and stopped.

Brigid peered over the rail. Her heart jumped into her throat.

Rafael Mackenzie stood halfway up the stairs with a saber in his hand, pointed at the prince's bare chest three yards away. Behind him stood four palace guardsmen in gold-and-white uniforms. They clutched bayonet-tipped rifles in white-knuckled hands.

"Leaving us so soon, Highness?" the operator said with a smile. "Really, you should try to be less predictable. The game's no fun if it's too easy."

"You think it easy to thwart me, Devil?" The prince gestured.

Brigid winced as the tip of a stabbing spear painfully thrust up under the angle of her jaw.

Chapter 19

The sentry held a carbine in one hand and the quivering-taut leash of the guard dog in the other. Grant snapped two shots toward the pale, straining face. The compressed-air wep made two soft spitting sounds and the man fell.

The dog, freed, snarled and charged. Voices shouted from several directions. Grant sensed other forms moving through the drizzle around him. Like more conventional silenced weapons back home, the air pistol was a tool for the murder of the unexpecting, not self-defense. Not trusting its stopping power, he holstered it, drew his autopistol, fired twice.

The special propellant produced giant orange-flame blooms, as well as cracking reports. The dog uttered a yip of pain, fell face-first into the mud almost at the big man's feet, kicked briefly, stilled.

Men materialized from the gloom behind rifles tipped with glinting bayonets. At least four, then half a dozen. "You, there! Put up your hands."

There were too many, from too many sides. Grant knew from painful recent experience, not his first, that his shadow suit would probably prevent the high-caliber but relatively low-velocity bullets from killing him. He also knew enough hits would incapacitate him. In disgust he stuffed the experimental handblaster back into its holster and folded his hands behind his head.

If I'm awake and not too busted up, he told himself, I might yet get a play.

The soldiers stopped in a circle around him. The ridiculous gaudy finery of their uniforms was concealed by streaming rain capes that hung around them like wilted flowers. Grant towered over them like a black colossus. They stared at him with pale faces until an officer strode up and took charge in a brusque voice.

At his command, a trooper peeled Grant's pack off his back. Grant had to lower his arms briefly to let him do so; unfortunately he got no chance to move. Instead he had to raise his hands again while the Canadian, grunting in surprise at the unexpected weight, let the sack swing in a barely controlled drop into the standing water and mud several yards away.

The officer paced before Grant with hands behind his back, perusing his captive. He was a head shorter than Grant, even with a polished metal helmet beaded with water.

"What have we here, hmm? A black man? Who are you, fellow? Aren't we a little far from New Africa?"

From the corner of his eye Grant saw the trooper plucking at the strings and straps that secured the rucksack's outer flaps. "My name is Grant. I'm a Magistrate from Cobaltville. Baron's business. Official."

The officer frowned. "What on Earth are you on about?" He shook his head. "Makes no difference. The interroga-

tors will winkle the truth out quick enough. Norton, Fur-
long!"

A pair of soldiers slung their rifles and moved in on the
big man from either side.

The man kneeling over Grant's grounded pack got an
outer flap to open. The small explosive device within went
off with a head-splitting crack and a dome of glaring yellow light.

The booby trap wasn't designed to set off the remaining explosive contents of the ruck. Nor did it. It did just
what it was intended to: provide a diversion in case its carrier was captured and his captors got grabby and inquisitive.

The trooper sprawled backward hands gone, uniform
front shredded and smoldering, too stunned to scream
from the black gape where his mouth had been.

All heads snapped toward him—except Grant's. The
soldier on his right was frozen with hand outstretched to
grab or frisk him. Grant seized the wrist and spun from
the waist, driving with his legs. Caught midstride and off
balance, the soldier was easily yanked into a stumbling
run, across Grant's front to slam into his comrade closing
from the left.

Grant used the man's momentum to propel himself forward. As the troopers collided and fell in a tangle of limbs
like players from an ancient slapstick vid, Grant drove in
on the officer. The man clawed at his side arm's holster
flap. Grant's right fist arced in a brutal backfist, powered
from the waist and supercharged by the great muscles of
thighs and back.

The officer's head snapped around, his eyes rolled up in his lolling head and he dropped to his knees.

As he pitched bonelessly into the mud, Grant darted past. A rifle barked from his left. It was answered by a thump and groan from his right as the big slug went home in another trooper. The men closing in were caught in the crossfire.

A soldier barred his way, thrusting with bayonet-tipped rifle. Grant swerved left, swung his right hand down and across, slapped the rifle beside the sight, pushing barrel and blade to his right. He felt the bayonet's tip gouge his right side as he kept charging, protected from the razor-honed steel by his shadow suit. Grant drove a forward elbow slam into the soldier's face, snapping back his head. Seizing his shoulder and taking him down with his left hand, he snatched the rifle from his unresisting grasp with the right.

Another trooper charged from the left. Grabbing the rifle by the muzzle, Grant swung it two-handed like a baseball bat. Gripped that unorthodox way, it outreached the soldier's own bayoneted weapon. The butt slammed against his ear below his helmet. He fell with limbs wildly asprawl.

A hundred yards away, at the center of the bivouac, men shouted hoarsely as a long tent took sudden flame. An alarm began to wind. The handful of troopers still confronting Grant found their eyes drawn that way.

Grant ran up on another, who blocked his escape route to the wire. The man thrust for him with his bayonet. Holding his stolen rifle in a more conventional way—and unwilling to risk losing the wep by getting its bayonet stuck through a Canadian trooper's body—Grant parried the blow with the full-stocked barrel and then butt-stroked the soldier full in the face. The man fell thrashing and mewling in the muck.

The conflagration near the water tower was attracting a lot of attention. The burning tent belonged to an officer. Yellow flames darted high up against the night sky despite the persistent rain: the waterproofing chemicals the Canadians used on their tent-canvas burned quite spectacularly at a certain temperature. It was higher than the flame of a spilled kerosene lantern—but not higher than the temperature achieved by the Reptoid-made incendiary pencils Grant had thoughtfully placed among the tents beforehand.

But several of the soldiers who had surrounded Grant still had their feet—and were reclaiming their presence of mind. Shots boomed behind him. Bullets ricocheted off the dark, angular shapes of land ironclads ahead of him as he ran for their shelter.

He threw himself into a forward roll. It ended on his back with his feet pointed the way he had been running and his head toward his pursuers. Rolling onto his stomach to a prone shooting position, he shouldered the rifle, elbows propped in muck to hold the rifle. Aiming at the center of a dark shape he thumbed off the safety and pressed the trigger.

The rifle kicked his shoulder and erupted a big red fire flash. The shape fell down.

A second shape to its right emitted its own yellow fireball. A bullet splashed water over the left side of Grant's face. Working the action by pure reflex, Grant switched aim, caught a quick picture through the sights and fired again. That soldier dropped, as well.

Leaving the rifle Grant sprang up with an explosive push of his forearms. Before his surviving captors, if any, had rallied enough to shoot at him again, he had darted between a pair of comparatively light crawlers, each with but a single turret and little larger than a civilian steam coach.

The charges he had placed on the legs of the scaffolding that upheld the giant water tank blew. The legs buckled, toppling the massive wood framework tank forward. It crushed five of the dozens of soldiers gathered to fight the burning tent, or just stand and spectate.

Then thousands of gallons of water inundated the rest.

Grant was bellying through the water-filled channel he had dug under the wire perimeter when the charges he had laid beneath his second main target, the great segmented land-monitor, went off like a young volcano.

"GO AHEAD AND SHOOT THEN," Prince John thundered, "and be damned!"

"Can't, Highness," Mackenzie said, still grinning his mad, bad, Errol Flynn grin. "Loaded firearms are not allowed in the palace proper except by special orders. Relic of Queen Fi's grandsire, Leonard IV. Bit of an eccentric, the old chap, but you know how traditions are."

The prince brandished his spear and his hardwood club. His arms looked carved from mahogany trunks. "You want her, come take her!"

The grin widened. "Why, Highness, I believe that I shall."

He advanced. His men followed him up behind their bayonets.

Brigid's two captors dragged her back by the arms. The one on her left kept his spear pressed painfully up under her jaw. The kidnappers could have turned and carried her off the other way. But that would have meant going deeper into the palace, away from escape. And anyway, she suspected that ran counter to Prince John's temperament.

Mackenzie sidestepped up the stairs toward the towering, glowering prince with his blade extended. The long tapered-triangle blade of John's stabbing-spear darted toward his face. Steel rang as Mackenzie parried with an inward wrist turn. The sound turned into a sibilant scrape as Prince John turned his own wrist in and over, seeking to bind the Canadian's blade. Driving it downward, he launched a whistling overhand smash with his knobkerrie.

Laughing, Mackenzie danced back down the stairs. His blade sang free of the spear. The club's head whipped harmlessly past his face.

He hurled himself into a clashing, slashing whirlwind attack, driving steadily upward. Even with two weapons and consummate skill the burly Zulu warrior-noble was hard pressed to keep the broadsword out of his flesh. He gave ground, step by furious step, until Mackenzie mounted the landing to fight on level ground.

Prince John roared wordlessly. He swung a backhand

blow of the club clutched in his left hand at Mackenzie's momentarily open face. The only way the scarlet-tunicked Canadian could keep from having his skull or cheekbone stove in was to slip the blow, ducking back and turning away. With a triumphant cry in his own language, Prince John closed in, thrusting his *ilkwa* for Mackenzie's vulnerable left armpit.

But Mackenzie was still in motion. He continued his evasion into a spin. Brigid knew that turning your back on an opponent in a fight was usually death; she'd seen men die of it. But Mackenzie's skill was superb and his speed supreme. Quicker than Brigid thought possible he whirled clear around and swung his sword in a brutal cut that caught the spear just behind the head.

Had the metal of the head not extended in a socket several inches down he would have hacked through the hardwood shaft. As it was he threw his whole weight against blade and spear shaft, pressing left hand to right wrist for additional force. He slammed the larger man back into the wall with his own weapons crossed over his huge, bare sweat-streaming chest and trapped by the broadsword.

"Go!" Mackenzie shouted to his men. They crowded past to engage the prince's retainers.

The fight had distracted Brigid's captors. She felt their bodyweight shifting forward in subconscious expression of their desire to help their leader. Their fingers no longer felt like iron clamps on her bare flesh.

She sagged to her right. Her weight was not inconsiderable. When it all become sudden deadweight, the clutching dark hands slipped. She fell against the hip of the man on her right.

Before the warriors could react by seizing her anew she drove her right elbow into the loincloth of the man on that side. He doubled with a gagging cough.

Usibebu, the smallest, lithest of the warriors, held her left hand. He snatched her arm again, grinning.

Brigid snatched the other man's spear from his slackened hand and, catching the shaft with both hands, drove it into Usibebu's lean belly with all her strength and mass behind it.

A Zulu retainer went down with a bayonet through his heart. A redcoat soldier's skull was dished in by a horizontal knobkerrie blow that came in beneath the side of his gilded helmet. Bellowing, Prince John pushed himself off from the wall, flinging the lighter Mackenzie away. The Canadian hit the balustrade at the small of his back, teetered as if about to go over backward and fall to the marble floor seven yards below.

Jaw set, brows furrowed, sweat starting on her face and streaming down her ribs, Brigid trudged forward, pushing the screaming Usibebu back. She felt the stretch of skin, and then felt and heard the rip as the spear tip came out his back. A second later it grated against the smooth polished stone of the wall.

Shouting triumphantly, Prince John swung his knobkerrie in a screaming overhead arc. Mackenzie turned right way from it. The head crashed down and rebounded from the marble rail. Then Mackenzie's blade arced up and down to sever the slender shaft a handspan behind the head.

Propelled by a strength belying the apparent slimness of his wrist, the blade turned and came up between the men's bodies. Its tip pressed the dark skin above Prince John's sternum so that it turned white.

"Checkmate, Your Highness," Mackenzie said with a smile. "I believe you know the derivation of the word?"

Prince John of kwaZulu glared at his. The white of his eyes had gone red as blood. But he threw down the spear to clatter on the carpeted floor. At a bark of command in his own language the weapons of the others clattered to the floor.

"You have killed no king today, Mackenzie the Devil," John said, drawing himself rigidly upright. "I claim diplomatic immunity."

All this exchange was spoken loudly to be hard above the screaming from Usibebu, who was still pinned against the wall by Brigid. She ignored his howls and furious flailing and indeed everything around her. She was totally focused on pushing forward, forward, with the blood-slippery spear. Her fists and forearms were red with blood; it had begun to drip onto her breasts and trickle down the dome of her bare belly.

"I believe you can let that one go now, Dr. Baptiste," Mackenzie called without turning his head. "If you wish, I'm sure Her Majesty will see fit to present him to you as a trophy—pinned like a butterfly to a board!"

Brigid let go. With a scraping of spear tip on stone, Usibebu slid down the wall. Once the terrible exertion relaxed it seemed that all the energy drained from her. She swayed, abruptly lightheaded, and almost toppled sideways before recovering her balance.

Chapter 20

Colonel Randall Rodríguez-Satterfield slapped Kane on his shoulder. "See what you have set in motion, my friend?"

He had to shout to make himself heard above the cold wind of the dirigible's passage. The two men stood at the forward rail of the twenty-gun Aero-Dreadnought *Liberty's Lady*—a reference to a concept personified, not a statue that, in this world, had never stood in the New York harbor. The sun had already ducked behind the Rockies to portside; the sky was streaked rose and shades of blue and an amber light still filled the cloud realm, making the clouds seem solid and softening the harsh outlines of the great airships spread to either side of them.

Kane nodded somberly. His lean frame was wrapped in a black greatcoat with wolfskin collar. "Have a hard time believing it myself."

Paradoxically, the defeat of the motion that the Republic of Cíbola should lend official aid to Kane's scheme to rescue his friends from the heart of Canadian strength had brought him directly here, in the midst of a fleet embarked to do just that. The Cíbolans were averse to unnecessary military adventuring, especially in the wake of the failed alliance with the Canadians against the Reptoids. The expense in treasure and lives was simply too great.

To be undertaken by the republic itself. The Cíbolans, it seemed, were a people who believed in government doing as little as necessary. But they were more than willing to do it for themselves. Even when it came to foreign military adventures.

"I still don't quite understand how this all works," Kane said. The same legislators who had voted against the republic participating in the mad scheme had thronged forward looking to participate privately themselves, as investors, directly or both. Several of them captained ships of the flotilla. President Preston Archer had been the first to ask to buy in, although the insistence of his current and former wives had kept him home.

"We can be pretty hard for outsiders to reckon," Rodríguez-Satterfield said. "Which doesn't mean to imply we always understand ourselves, mind. Just put it down to natural cussedness."

"I still don't understand how private citizens could come up with a war fleet."

The other laughed. "It's not as if these Aero-Dreadnoughts are yachts, each owned by a sole proprietor. Although two are. The rest are either owned by subscription, or by great houses."

"Such as Rodríguez-Satterfield."

The colonel grinned. The ember tip of his cheroot glowed like a red eye as he drew on it. "You know it. This ship is ours."

"How can you afford it? It's hard to see how even a big

family or a bunch of investors could swing something this expensive. Much less an individual."

On anything deeper than a purely intellectual level Kane had only a rudimentary understanding of price. Economics in the baronies amounted to force, fear and guilt, like all the rest of life; a Mag's needs were provided for, as they were defined, by the Division. If for some reason a Magistrate needed something a civilian had, he took it. He didn't ask. If there was a price involved, it was what the Mag exacted from the civilian's hide if the lousy slagjacker tried to hold out on him.

But even before leaving Cobaltville, along with most of what he thought he knew about his world and even himself, Kane understood that war was a pretty wasteful, resource-intensive undertaking. Although the Mags seldom engaged in anything near a fair fight, they expended lavish amounts of ammo in combat. Wear and tear on their vehicles was pretty severe even without battle, given the harsh conditions of the environment in the barony of Cobaltville. Nothing Kane had seen since fleeing the ville had lowered his assessment of the resources it took to go to war.

"Remember, we have no regular military," Rodríguez-Satterfield said. "Our forces are essentially all militias. What the government of the republic can do is vote to mobilize the militias and place them under government command. As was done for the anti-Reptoid alliance with the Canadians."

"And as the senate refused to do this time."

"Right. The great houses need warships to protect their

interests, against pirates, privateers and enemy incursions. They're pricey but we build and maintain them anyway."

"But everybody doesn't pay," Kane said. "And you still protect them."

Rodríguez-Satterfield shrugged. "Either way, we must protect ourselves and our interests. What would you have us do, defend only our own spreads and let raiders plunder our less wealthy neighbors at will? That won't fly. Besides, we're talking about our employees, our customers, our neighbors. There's noblesse oblige involved. And yeah, more than a little family pride and plain old ostentation."

"How about the single-owner ships? Are they owned by the richest guys?"

"Not at all. I mentioned privateers. You know what they are?"

"Not exactly."

"They get letters of marque from their government to prey on enemy shipping. That makes them pirates with licenses."

"So these private owners—"

"*Arabella*'s a prize," Rodríguez-Satterfield said, pointing to a vessel flying to starboard. Then he pointed to port. "*La Llorona* was a subscription warship. Her captain was lucky or good, and was able to buy out the other owners from his shares. Neither owner is cash rich—the things're expensive to maintain, as you'd reckon, and George is paying off his loan. But they've got valuable assets, and if they can operate successfully for a few years, they'll be wealthy indeed."

Kane rubbed his chin. "But the other ship owners—if this isn't an official Republic of Cíbola operation…"

"You got it," Rodríguez-Satterfield said. "We're all privateers. If we can win access to the knowledge stored in your lady friend's head, the potential return is unbelievable. And even if we can't make it pay—well, if her knowledge enables Miles-Burnham to complete his Apocalyptic Engine for the Canadians, neither our weapons nor our wealth will be worth buffalo flop anyway. All the costs of this expedition and more are worth it, if all we do is prevent that happening."

Kane looked away to starboard, into the great bowl of night that was the Plains. The wind buffeted him and howled in the rigging, booming off the swollen sides of the vast gas bag overhead. His friend Colonel Randy wasn't saying something, but Kane heard it loudly anyway.

These Cíbolans loved life. But they weren't afraid to risk it. Kane got the distinct impression most of them would rather go out in a blaze of glory than live badly— or worse, dully.

While they had shown themselves anything but bloodthirsty, they were not a whit more squeamish. If they saw a need that blood be spilled, they were ruthlessly direct in spilling it.

Their overriding priority was denying the knowledge cached beneath Brigid's flame-colored hair to the minions of the feared and hated Queen Fiona. That was as key to the expedition's widespread popular support as the daring rescue of a beauteous damsel in distress, which had fired the Cíbolan imagination.

If Brigid couldn't be rescued, they would do what they had to do.

That's ace with me, thought Kane. You got your games. And I got mine.

WITH A FLASH of yellow-white light that spilled in through the skylights, the gas lights sputtered and died out.

They had been working late. Brigid's handlers back at the palace had been pressuring her in their ever-so-polite ways. Her explanation—that she couldn't tell Miles-Burnham what he needed to know unless she herself knew what was needed—had fallen on ears of stone.

She understood. The vultures were circling—over her. Outside the high white-gleaming palace walls events rushed to a head, and even if no one could say yet exactly what it was, it seemed scarcely conceivable it would be good.

A flat slam of sound, like a giant slapping a tabletop, rattled the warehouse windows and vibrated up through the concrete floor. Overhead the great clock movements continued to click, catch and swoop half-seen—dark forms, half of mechanism and half of myth. For some reason they chilled Brigid's spine.

Norman, Miles-Burnham's tall, cadaverous man's man with the black eye patch, stepped forth from an alcove. Already Brigid's eyes were adjusting; the darkness wasn't total. At least some lights still glowed in the city, reflecting back into the warehouse off the low cloud cover that had been spitting sleet all the dreary day.

"The anarchists will have blown up the Cavendish Street gasometer," he announced.

Miles-Burnham half turned from the table where he sat in his shirtsleeves, listening intently to Brigid. She was telling him of how she began to glimpse the true outlines of the history of her own world, when her superiors within the Archives Division set her to reviewing certain sequences of anomalous events in its twentieth century. So importunate had her hosts become that Brigid was uneasy spending so much time talking about her mere past. But when she faltered, Miles-Burnham, in his eager and affectionate way, urged her, please, to continue—one never knew what details would prove vital to his current enterprise.

"Why the anarchists, and not the mob?" Miles-Burnham asked.

Norman set a candle in a silver holder on the table between the two. It stood against one wall of the crowded workshop floor. The candle's orange glow sent strange shadows capering across the scientist's boyishly handsome face.

"The mob would scarcely have so much focus," the butler said. "They are aroused and bent on venting their outrage. Shouting in the streets comes a lot quicker to the mob's mind than such decisive action as blowing up a power station. And where would the mob lay hands on the needed casks of black powder?"

Miles-Burnham nodded. "You're right, of course, Norman. As always." He turned to smile ruefully at Brigid. "I am lost in the world of politics and strategy, as I am in everyday life. Only the esoteric, I fear, seems truly real to me."

"It's what you have me for, sir," Norman said matter-of-factly. "Speaking of which, if I might broach a concern—"

"What is it?"

"It may be merely coincidence. But the gasometer that has been knocked from service serves this location. That you are assisting Dr. Nigel in his research is known to the entire world. No doubt the anarchists know it, as well."

Brigid felt a constriction like a chill hand clutching the base of her throat. Despite being raised in an atmosphere of extreme paranoia, Brigid had grown complacent here. Prince John and his warriors had been declared persona non grata and now waited on the warship that had brought them, rolling to anchor in Lake Ontario, awaiting the conclusion of tortuous negotiations and bureaucratic permissions required for their departure. Even their attempt to kidnap her seemed but an aberration, an exotic adventure, almost...if men hadn't died. All that despite the fact that by the standards Brigid was accustomed to, security was laughable on this world.

The anarchists would perceive themselves as having as great a stake in denying the hegemony the unanswerable power of the Apocalyptic Engine as Canada's rivals in the game of global domination. They might well seek to destroy the engine, or the laboratory in which it was putatively being built. Or...worse.

"Are you saying they might threaten us, man?" Miles-Burnham seemed genuinely shocked.

Norman nodded. "It is highly possible, sir."

Miles-Burnham was shaking his head. "I don't understand these matters at all, I fear."

"It's rather simple, sir," Norman said, "begging your pardon. The anarchists may believe you are in process of putting into the queen's hands a weapon of unanswerable power."

Miles-Burnham stared at his man with wide eyes reflecting the candle glow. "Do they honestly believe that?"

Norman nodded. "As does Her Majesty's government, sir."

Laughing, the great scientist shook his shaggy head. "Wherever did they acquire such a foolish idea?"

Norman's eye flicked to Brigid, who sat leaning forward. She realized her own expression must be thunderstruck.

"I suspect they have talked themselves into it," the butler said. "If I may offer a word of advice—it might be prejudicial to the interests of Dr. Baptiste to disabuse them of the notion."

"Huh? Ah, quite, quite. You are ever the man of the world, Norman; I am in your hands in these affairs."

He stood up, wiping his hands on some cotton waste from a bin. "Very well. You clearly cannot stay here any longer tonight, Brigid, delightful as I find your company. There are soldiers guarding the place—they'll escort you back to the palace and keep you safe from anarchists and those poor unfortunates protesting the latest tax increases."

SHE HEARD THEM before she saw them. Their voice of their rage was like distant surf.

The coach's route back to the palace took it past several public squares. The one square closest to the waterfront, was dominated by a central equestrian statue, its bronze green and pigeon streaked, of a stout muttonchopped general in a cocked hat scowling and brandishing a saber. She thought of him as General Unpleasantness; he didn't appear to be someone she should regret never having met.

A throng of people surged around the statue's base and filled the square like an angry sea. Many were the ragged people she was used to seeing on the streets of this district, walking with quick steps and lowered heads. Others looked more prosperous, their clothes finer, cleaner and better filled out.

Between them and the broad avenue along which the carriage rolled, with its plumed and cuirassed cavalry escorts riding before and behind, stood a line of redcoat infantry with pith helmets and fixed bayonets.

A young man with disarrayed hair mounted the statue's pedestal. Clinging to the horse's raised bronze foreleg he began to exhort the crowd, punching the air with his fist. Between distance, the crowd roar and the double-paned window Brigid couldn't make out his words. But she heard the cry of the mob itself increase in pitch and volume.

It was a district of tall, somewhat narrow brownstone and yellow-brick buildings, most of them three or four stories with steep-pitched roofs broken by multiple gables, and elaborate but sturdy-looking black ironwork guarding doorways and small courtyards. It looked overall shabby-genteel, as if to sum up the stations and nature of the mob itself.

Snow began to fall, sparse, but in big fat flakes, slowly drifting in the still evening air. As the coach neared the midpoint of the square Brigid saw the line of soldiers shoulder their rifles. As she pressed palms in horror against the chilled pane, flames stabbed from the muzzles, pale in the garish gas light. Puffs of smoke like dirty cotton balls appeared between the red line of soldiers and the civilian protestors.

The reports sounded like a platoon of distant woodpeckers rapping hardwood. Screams filtered through the window, ghostly. As the soldiers racked their actions Brigid saw people staggering, people helping each other to stand, people falling, people lying—some moving, some not. Then a second ripple of fire flashes and distant-sounding knocks, and the scene was momentarily obscured by the gun smoke as by a fog bank.

But not before Brigid saw the youthful orator torn from his perch as by invisible claws.

She pounded on the button of the low-powered electric speaker that connected her to the driver in his covered cab up front. "Please!" she shouted. "We have to do something!"

"Begging your pardon, marm," the reply came back, "but why? They're only getting what's coming to them, as they don't want to pay their share."

Pay their share. Norman had told her in a quiet aside, as he held the door for her into the surprising chill of the night, that the new tax raises—to pay for the hegemony's

boundless ambitions and the ceaseless wars it spawned—
would close down hundreds of businesses in the glittering capital city alone, throw thousands out of work and
drive them from their homes. The hegemony had a com-
prehensive social-welfare program, one of the things that
attracted Brigid to it. Yet it seemed willing to condemn
tens of thousands to hunger and exposure in order to provide benefits for others, as selected by some cold and
cruel calculus none had revealed to her.

What she witnessed now was murder wholesale.
Through a momentary rent in the curtain of gun smoke she
saw a woman holding a child limp in her arms. Smoke obscured them as a fresh volley clattered.

From a street on the side her coach was approaching
charged a squadron of cavalry. She recognized the silver
breastplates and pink pants of the Cherrypicker Hussars.
They drove into the crowd swinging straight-bladed
broadswords. Some used the flats. Others didn't, and
Brigid saw sprays of blood arcing in the air as the cavalry
troopers raised their swords to strike and strike again.

"Stop! Please stop!" she cried to the unseen driver.

"Can't, marm," came back the polite disembodied
voice. "Orders. And anyway, there's nothing to see here,
nothing at all...."

Chapter 21

"Please, Nest-Master," Chief Egg Inspector Zirak said. He held himself in a position of ritual abasement, facing the viceroy of St. Louis with arms folded across his chest, his snout almost touching the floor, his stubby tail high. "The threat exists. It must be taken seriously. And other powers are already on the move."

He was crossing a bridge and well he knew it. To use the imperative case with one so many ranks senior was asking for instant reduction to the lowest caste of all—organic fertilizer. Yet his status within the intelligence directorate offered no little protection: the Race were a pragmatic people, and it had long since been figured out in a collective sort of way that intel officers more subservient than objective tended to lead their masters blithely into fire-sack ambushes. Also, Zirak had an impressive string of successes to his personal credit.

He also knew full well that a major error here would zero out the ledger and then some: the compost heap for him.

"Really, Zirak," Nest-Master Szu said, elevating a stubby right forearm to allow its human tailor access to its pit with a cloth measure, blue chalk and a mouthful of pins. "Surely you exaggerate the seriousness of the threat. They are, after all, tailless. And while this strange human female comes, like our own prisoner, from a world unaffected by the Great Discontinuity, such secrets as she might impart will by the same token apply only to her own realm. Our own scientists on the Moon can only provide us advances in locally applicable technology with the most agonizing slowness. The tailless are inferior to true Folk. How can this tailless one tell the hegemonists anything which can truly harm us?"

Imbecile, Zirak thought.

"Please, Excellency," the human tailor lisped through its mouthful of pins, "shift your weight back."

Szu did so, pivoting his body at his hips to raise his own upper torso almost vertical. A silk jacket of a royal blue that was almost self-luminous encased his pudgy body. Big gold buttons marched in two rows down the front, and great golden epaulettes clung to the shoulders with gold braid loops swooping down from them like gilded alien octopoids. Over the back of a human-style antique chair— from the Danish-held region of France, early twenty-first century—a pair of gold breeches hung, neatly folded. They would reach down to the backwards pointing "knees" of the viceroy's powerful hindlimbs, which were actually the heels of his long digitigrade feet.

"Please remember, sir," Zirak said, "that she has the help of the greatest human scientist, Dr. Nigel Miles-Burnham."

"Yes, yes," Szu said, fluttering his fingers. He was clearly more interested in the fitting than in the trifles his subordinate was troubling him with. "Still, the sum of our achievements is far greater than theirs—that's why we're fit to rule."

"So much the more reason, Nest-Master," Zirak said, "to take the steps necessary to secure this woman's knowledge for our own scientists to study. At one remove, granted—but think of what they could achieve!"

The tailors stood back momentarily. The wispy mustached one in charge kissed his fingertips. Nest-Master Szu struck a pose, while an assistant tailor adjusted a cheval glass to the proper angle.

"Suitable, suitable," the viceroy murmured.

"Nest-Master!" Zirak said, scarcely able to contain himself. Aside from the opportunity to advance the glory of the Race, he had ulterior motives. Along with possessing an eidetic memory, his client Grant said, Brigid Baptiste was a woman of striking beauty for a human, possessed of creamy skin, large round breasts, trim stomach, full hips, topped by hair like flame and emerald-green eyes. Himself a remarkable specimen of his kind, Grant had conveyed these details to his friendly interrogator in an almost analytical manner: he had never felt terrific attraction to his longtime comrade Baptiste, he claimed.

But Zirak was adept at manipulating humans' motivations and feelings so that their actions conformed to the Race's interests. Once Brigid had been secured to the People where she belonged and returned to propinquity with Grant—vigorous, strong, harshly handsome, consummately male and her sole point of contact with her own world—Zirak was sure matters would take care of themselves.

He felt perspiration start on his forehead. He might have felt abashed that he was more excited at the prospect of being able to observe two splendid specimens of this curious species at their even more curious mating than by the welfare of the Race. But to show off such a pair engaging in copulation for the delectation of select, discreet audiences would enhance his prestige as mightily as the intelligence coup the coupling represented. And shame was as little a component of the Reptoid makeup as xenophilic voyeurism was a giant part.

"Your hat, Excellency," said the odious wispy tailor, holding up an extraordinary triangular confection of blue silk, gold trim and white plume. The already plump Nest-Master swelled visibly. He nodded—another gesture borrowed from these strangely compelling inferiors—and with the air of conferring monarchy the tailor placed the ludicrous hat on his broad-skulled head.

I'm losing him, Zirak thought, in a fever now of frustration and anxiety.

"It suits you marvelously, Nest-Master," he said. In the hierarchy of the Race, a little groveling was never out of place. In fact Zirak thought his lord and master looked a complete buffoon, as if the tailless apes had dressed one of their homely little pug dogs in a similarly Napoleonic suit-of-pretense. "I hope that events away north in Gloriana won't spoil your opportunity to debut your sartorial magnificence to our grateful subjects, Most Resplendent Male."

Szu's eyes narrowed to slits and flicked toward him, glittering from behind lowered lids. "What? What do you mean? Dammit, Zirak, don't mumble! Out with it."

"The Apocalyptic Engine," Zirak almost mumbled.

"What? What?"

"The Apocalyptic Engine," Zirak said loudly and crisply, making the most of a chance to repeat the phrase for the benefit of Szu's subconscious—never deeply buried, in his estimation, since it had so little stacked atop of it. Zirak had a little experience in dealing with the psychology of his own race as well as the tailless. "The diabolical device being created by none other than Dr Nigel Miles-Burnham. If this extradimensional refugee woman provides him the key to its completion, our dreams of raising this world from its muck of ignorance and barbarism will crash in the mud themselves."

"But how? She's tailless, too. How could she possibly provide him the means of advancement so far beyond what our own fleet scientists can achieve?"

"Her people have achieved interdimensional travel," Zirak said. "Our Race has yet to master faster-than-light flight."

"Do you—do you think that's possible, Zirak?" he all but whispered.

Zirak nodded sagely.

"And this human captive of yours, this Grunt." Zirak forbore to correct him; he knew when to hold his tongue, as well as when to let it run. "You are certain he will cooperate? He is, after all, one of...*them*...himself."

"A most astute observation, Nest-Master." Of the blisteringly obvious. "But it was the Canadians, after all, who shot him down like a dog after insulting him. We have shown him how his own fellows on this planet, this very continent, treat humans of his degree of pigmentation as animals. And, finally, he is of lusty nature even for a human—and the captive woman is described as most toothsome, prime flesh indeed, Most Excellent One."

It was one of Zirak's points of pride in his expertise—his mastery of a multiplex and risky art—that he seldom if ever had to resort to telling an outright lie.

"Ah, yes, yes. These humans are lusty fellows, aren't they? Incredible they can rut at any time of year, I am still amazed by such a fluke of biology." He was space-born himself, of eggs stashed in cryo-storage when the fleet departed the true nest and thawed and quickened during the many-year-long braking on approach to this star system. "We can count on him, then?"

He scowled. "Your head on it, Zirak."

Zirak merely bowed. The genuflection had the effect of hiding his smile. *Once again my master chooses to belabor the obvious.*

AFTER the chief egg inspector had departed—frightful fellow, really, with a truly shocking fashion sense, yet wasn't it always thus with Intel wonks?—Szu remained mired in thoughtful reverie, an environment neither familiar nor congenial to him.

He didn't understand what the confounded ape Miles-Burnham was driving at with his Apocalyptic Engine. That was no dishonor; he was no scientist himself, and besides, neither human boffins nor the fleet's lab drones on the Moon's bare backside had the slightest conception, either, although they tended to try to bury the fact in avalanches of syllables. But all the experts agreed that if Miles-Burnham thought himself onto something, then—tailless or not—he was.

And everyone agreed on one more thing: if he attained his Apocalyptic Engine it would be a very bad thing for anyone who *wasn't* Her Benevolent Majesty, Fiona I, Queen of Canada.

In this dark mood he allowed his tailors to divest him of his new uniform, which had temporarily lost its zest for him, and ignored them as they bowed and scraped backward from his chambers.

Is it true? he wondered, scowling without seeing toward a portrait of Kantar V, who had reigned over the Home System when the fleet set forth decades before. It was one of the few artifacts rescued from the disastrous second wave of invasion and as a plain photographic print, one of the few of actual use on this wretched mud ball. Can the tailless apekin *really* threaten us?

He already knew the answer. His own scientists had been pestering him incessantly since the extradimensional visitors had arrived. Squeaks had even been heard from the high station, where the Race's technology still functioned in full glory, relayed tortuously by coded flashes of light down from the night sky...when the cursed climate allowed it, and didn't block the signal with clouds.

He had never known any other climate, of course. Not planetside. There were times he longed for the gangways and compartments of a ship of space, even the stale recycled air, which after all he had grown up breathing. An environment, above all, under control.

Whereas everything about this world defied control. Even the fabric of reality itself.

Slowly, reluctantly, he set aside his hat, divested himself of his splendid blue coat and hung it over his trousers. He was sticking his own head out by authorizing his spy's mad expedition: such a raid would require risking a substantial portion of his Folk, machines and resources despite the fact the Race's foothold in the central Mississippi was sorely pressed on all sides by barbarians and bandits. Even success would be costly.

He did understand that success could also bring great rewards. Perhaps the ultimate reward: final victory over the recalcitrant denizens of Terra. The prospect filled him with warmth like the white sun of a home world he had never seen save in holograms. He would be a hero, could breed without restriction, spread his seed wide.

But the impertinent Zirak had also convinced the nestmaster of the catastrophic consequences of failure. To think these strange creatures might threaten the very fleet! It would certainly look bad on his quarterly efficiency report.

Slowly he began stripping off the white silken shirt. He hissed an obscenity as a side seam tore. He would put his master tailor in the torture chair for the shoddiness of his work, and let him experience the wonders that could be wrought even with trickle currents.

And he would send a coded light-flash message to the

fleet to begin preparing the Wormwood Option. In itself that would entail loss of face for him.

But the decision renewed the warm feeling spoiled momentarily by the tearing of his fine shirt. Now, even should Zirak's raid with his huge half-alien black-skinned human fail, the Canadians would still never use any Apocalyptic Engine to ruin the glorious plans of the Race.

Because the engine, its creator and the human female from a strange and terrifying world where the tailless commanded wonders unknown even to the Folk would themselves be destroyed in the blink of a nictating membrane.

Chapter 22

The first Kane and his companions knew of approaching danger was when a storage tank on the western edge of the compound exploded in a red ball of flame.

The Cíbolan fleet, now joined with a pair of Kiowa- and Comanche-crewed freebooters from the Kai-Gwe Republic, had put in at a fueling station on the Red River, not far from St. Boniface, capital of the Republic of Assiniboina. It had been in gouged in red earth out of deep woods, with pines and firs towering all around the great field. That was something of a shock to Kane: in his world, leaving aside the fact all this was in the midst of the Winnipeg hellzone, this was prairie, flat and grassy where anything grew at all.

The field resembled a farm for giant mutant mushrooms. Half a dozen football shapes squatted swaying at pylons dotted around the field, refueling and topping off their tanks with water.

"Lakota!" somebody shouted, as another explosion gouged a crater in the middle of the vast tending area.

Kane was heading to the commissary to meet Rodríguez-Satterfield. He'd been out for a run inside the perimeter of the landing around. He had wanted to stretch

his legs in the woods outside but had been vigorously ve-
toed by the short, dumpy, damply mustached Métis station master and his looming Woods Cree sec boss, a
great-chested man with an eagle-beak nose to match the
sideways feather at his nape, and a pair of glossy black
pigtails hanging down his wedge-shaped back. His build
and manner put Kane achingly in mind of his lost friend
Grant, and in general appearance and demeanor he would
have fit right in with Sky Dog's crew back home.

Given the proclivities of Sky Dog's self-proclaimed
but largely ersatz Lakota, Kane was real glad he hadn't
been out walking the woods when the genuine article
came to call. A green shape came rocking and lumbering
out of the underbrush at the eastern end of camp: a small
tank, with a stack smoking away behind its single turret.

Pale orange flame flashed from the stubby barrel. Kane
saw the side of a great gas bag flex as the shell went home.
If it exploded he couldn't tell.

The great airships were frighteningly vulnerable down
here almost on the ground like this. But probably less
than the Plains raiders thought. They were inflated with
helium, not flammable hydrogen, and the giant envelope
contained a number of discrete bladders, called *ballonets*,
that even sported some kind of self-sealing system. Bursting one or several would not fatally compromise an Aero-
Dreadnought's ability to maneuver, or even—more
crucially in the here and now—to rise.

And the warships of the air were built to withstand their
own kind, who carried weapons far larger than the puny
twenty-ton land crawlers now creeping from the woods like

a pack of steam-powered beetles. As the crew of the tank found when one of the airship's four-inch broadside rifles spoke in return. The shot smashed the turret root and exploded both shell storage and the boiler. Kane saw the turret rise a yard into the air on a gusher of orange fire. Then the tank was completely obscured by a swirl of steam and smoke.

Back on Kane's Earth, the risk for AFV crews was being cremated alive within an armor-plated oven. In this world the risk was more being parboiled.

He didn't get long to ponder the agonies of the tank crew, if any had survived the shell strike and explosions. Rodríguez-Satterfield came racing by and clutched his arm.

"Better seats upstairs," he said, rolling his eyes skyward. Gatlings had begun their droning songs, from the tanks steaming out of the woods and from the airship gondolas. "And if you want to get a few licks in at the savages, the high ground's the place to do it from."

Kane followed him. He hadn't sorted out racial relations on this world, or even this continent. He knew too well blacks were despised most places—they were accepted, if not commonplace, in Cíbola—and he had heard a couple big Cree stonehearts referring to the Lakota as *les sauvages* within half an hour of landfall this morning. For what all that was worth.

Four airships rose rapidly into the high white sky. Black smoke boiled from amidships of one. Two more tanks were smoking and steaming wrecks on the ground.

A spine-scraping cry made Kane spin. A horseman

bore down on him, black hair flying, dark face contorted under paint. A hatchet with feathers bunch-tied beneath the head was upraised to split his skull.

He thrust out his right arm, hand curved to receive his Sin Eater....

"Damn," he said.

Two shots cracked from behind his head, so close he felt hot particles sting his right ear. The Lakota went over his pony's white rump, which was marked with red hand-prints in paint.

"I've heard tell," said Randall Rodríguez-Satterfield, his drawl barely audible above the ringing in Kane's ear, "that in combat, what a man most trains to do, he does. Don't you think you better fill your hand while you got some breathing space, amigo?"

"That's two I owe you right there," Kane said, reaching out the .50-caliber Blessing revolvers he wore under the frock coat he'd donned against the northern autumn chill, each beneath an armpit.

"*De nada*," Rodríguez-Satterfield said, coolly breaking his own piece open for a quick reload. The Cíbolans, anyway, used moon clips, a sort of spring-steel star that held six cartridges in position to be stuffed quickly into a revolver cylinder. The partial empty he dropped into a palm, thence into a pocket of his wolfskin coat. "Nothing's too great for a friend of the house. Not to mention the fact that if you go down, most of the point of this fool's errand goes with you. Now we'd best move with a purpose, or our ship will leave without us."

They raced toward *Liberty's Lady*. Painted horsemen in

dark blue coats and loincloths whirled about them, shrieking, brandishing lances, firing handguns, carbines and even
sawed-off shotguns. The Woods Cree security contingent,
who didn't wear uniforms but dressed in a combination of
native and European-style garb, had come running out to
fight with them, which they did with a kind of mad gaiety.
Kane saw one warrior wearing a loincloth and a blue-and-
white flannel shirt come flying off the railing of a bunk-
house porch to tackle a passing Lakota lancer clean off his
pony.

A knot of horsemen spotted the two dashing toward the
Aero-Dreadnought, now the only one still tethered to the
Earth. They swooped down toward them. They didn't
shoot. Either they had exhausted their magazines for the
moment or desired to count coup by striking their quarry
down with handheld weapons.

A warrior closed from Kane's left, swinging a saber
around his head. Kane turned as he ran and blasted him
with both his handblasters. The way the balance shifted
when the heavy barrel and cylinder assemblies, recoil-
driven, reciprocated to recock the pieces after each shot
still felt weird in Kane's hands. But hours spent practic-
ing on the Rodríguez-Satterfield spread came in handy.
The warrior's head snapped around as a heavy high-caliber, low-velocity bullet caught him above his left eyebrow and snapped his head around as crimson sprayed
from the back of his head.

A horse reared right before Kane. He blasted shots into
its belly from both revolvers. The horse screamed shrilly
and fell away to Kane's left with blood pennons streaming.

"Kane! Behind you!" Rodríguez-Satterfield shouted.

Kane dived forward, across the stricken horse, which had rolled almost onto its back and was falling back onto its side, still thrashing and tearing the air with its hooves. At the same time he thrust his two handblasters down along his body and fired at the rider closing rapidly with him from behind, spear raised to spit him. A hoof caught Kane a stunning blow on his left hip. A big soft slug took the charging Lakota in the right shoulder, causing his body to twist that way. A second bullet struck him in the bare left armpit. He was toppling from his mount as Kane cleared the horse he'd shot.

He remembered to tuck his shoulder and roll. After a short, bumpy ride he wound up on his back on the dew-slick grass.

He was staring up into the rage-contorted features of the man he'd unhorsed. The Lakota raised a hatchet to split Kane's skull. Kane aimed his handguns back at the flat, muscle-ridged belly and pulled both triggers.

The doomful sounds of both hammers clicking on spent primers was almost as loud as gunshots would have been.

Screaming triumph, the warrior swung down his hatchet. As Kane desperately tried to roll clear, thunder crashed from somewhere beyond his boots, which were pointed back the way he'd come from. The warrior jerked as a bullet hit him in the belly with an audible thump. He folded at the waist. Another shot slammed home between his right shoulder and his corded neck, boring transversely through lungs and viscera. A third knocked a chunk out of his skull, with heavy black hair still sticking to it. He fell in a sodden mound.

"We carry two guns because that's the quickest reload," Randall Rodríguez-Satterfield said, holstering the revolver he'd just fired and drawing its mate as if to drive his point home. "Ammunition must be plenty cheap in your world."

"It's these damn Bronze Age blasters," Kane said as Rodríguez-Satterfield stretched down a hand and helped him to his feet. "Don't feel I can get a decent amount of firepower shooting just one at a time."

"Your people must've mastered the art of missing fast enough to catch up," Rodríguez-Satterfield said. "Let's cut stick—"

His last words were drowned in the iron-edged thunder of a full broadside of the *Lady*'s eight starboard side guns. Explosions ripped the field hard by the forest. A storage building was shattered in a whirlwind of planks. A booming secondary explosion accompanied by a billow of dirty white, lit from below by a series of orange flashes, showed where another Lakota whippet tank had been destroyed.

Kane holstered his blasters and grabbed up a Canadian Foley carbine dropped by one of the Plains raider riders. Its wooden furniture, pale-stained maple buttstock and forestock that went clear down flush with the muzzle, was decorated with patterns of brass tacks driven into it. He cranked the action to make sure the piece would fire at need. A tarnished brass cartridge spun away into the grass, but he saw a second slide into the chamber.

The two men took off at a run for the airship. It hung over them like a levitating mountain. Either recognizing the long, lean wolf of a man in the black coat that slapped the thighs of his black trousers as their prey, or merely with their chase-reflex stimulated by their flight, Lakota peeled away from whirling dogfights with mounted or foot-borne Cree and came streaming between burning buildings from all over the field in pursuit, yipping like coyotes.

Rodríguez-Satterfield cracked shots as horsemen closed. Caught without time to shoot Kane blocked a blow from a ball-headed club, throwing up the Foley with his right hand, then fired the piece one-handed so close to its target he could see dark skin blister in the muzzle-flare. Then he reversed the carbine and swung the butt ax-style to smash the feather skull of a warrior aiming a hatchet blow at him from the other side.

A racket like the sky ripping across like a giant sheet tearing unfurled over their heads. An invisible influence ripped apart five riders and their mounts in miniature whirl-winds of red earth and yellow grass. The Gatling guns mounted on the Aero-Dreadnought's deck had joined the fray.

Like their counterparts on Kane's Earth, these Lakota were capable of completely foolhardy bravery. But flesh imposed its limits. The horsemen pursuing Kane and Rodríguez-Satterfield whirled and dispersed so as not to make themselves an invitation for the quick-firers to turn the Assinboine airfield into an abattoir.

Captain Martin held *Liberty's Lady* daringly close to the ground. Although his main guns outranged and out powered the tanks, and his crews were used to hitting moving targets from a moving platform at long range, the tank cannon could do damage to the great warships of the air. As the smoke continuing to billow from the guts of the one craft now a thousand yards overhead attested.

An airship had begun to rise slowly, its big ducted props spun up to high, though feathered so that they pushed only enough airflow over the vertical vanes to keep her headed nose to wind. But no sky car awaited Kane and his compadre. Instead the airship crew were looking out for their compatriots on the ground. Of all things, a lasso came spinning down. Whether through cowboy skill or raw Rocky Mountain oyster luck, it settled over Kane's shoulders. He jerked in reflex alarm. He wasn't a man whose experiences had made him feel comfortable about being restrained.

Then Rodríguez-Satterfield was at his side. "Under your arms, compadre," he said, helping Kane adjust the loop. "Just for safety."

"Don't you get one?" Kane asked as the line began to lay in and snugged tight beneath his armpits.

Rodríguez-Satterfield showed him a flashing grin. "They know which fish is the biggest prize."

Then he reached out to snag another rope lasso as it dropped past his shoulder.

Reassured, Kane began to climb a rope ladder that was lowered from the airship. He felt the rope ladder sag beneath him as Rodríguez-Satterfield's weight swung on beneath his.

Then the ground fell away dizzily beneath them.

Chapter 23

The day after witnessing the massacre in the square, Brigid sat in a little nook off the ground floor of the great warehouse laboratory. She was sipping tea and talking with Norman. The scientist suffered one of his migraines; he lay on a pallet in a dark cool storeroom of the giant building with a damp towel on his face, and wished no one near him.

Norman had long since shamed Brigid by making nonsense her presumptions that, as a lifelong bodyservant, he must be an unsophisticated man of limited mental capacity and horizons. He was in fact urbane, capable and well-informed; she quickly realized he was also Miles-Burnham's bodyguard, and in all effects his master's interface to a cold and hostile reality. He came close to being omnicompetent, a Renaissance man who could converse knowledgeably and insightfully on any subject even a senior archivist knew to broach.

And if he could not grasp but a fraction of Miles Burnham's plenum of theory and endeavor, as symbolized by the monstrous clockwork swooping and circling above them with an endless surf of clacks and tinkles, then no one else on this world could, either—not even Brigid.

"The pattern of the hegemony," he said in his sad, sonorous voice, "is very much the velvet glove—and very much the iron fist beneath. It's an old story in this world—the rulers make much of their concern for the common man, the workers. But it's all a palliative, to render them insensitive to how they're being squeezed."

Brigid perched on a stool holding her mug with both hands, drawing warmth from it. Although it was still officially summer, the hegemony holding that autumn did not commence until the autumnal equinox a week away, a chill wind prowled the streets outside. A lot of it managed to infiltrate the warehouse, indifferently sealed against the elements.

Not all the chill Brigid sought respite for was of the body.

"So I was wrong," she all but whispered. She looked up at him sharply where he stood leaning against the frame of the door, from which pale blue paint was coming away in long peels and flakes.

"Why does he help them, then?"

"What makes you think he does, Dr. Baptiste?" the butler asked.

"What do you mean?"

"He believes he serves all mankind—all of this world, perhaps, since he bears no intrinsic animosity to the Reptoids on it, most of whom were born here the same as we. It is not his intention to provide Her Majesty the means of conquering the planet. Never has been."

She stared at him as if he had begun speaking a strange language. "You mean he's been lying to them?"

"I assure you he is altogether too otherworldly to lie. Our Canadian hosts have merely made certain…presumptions. And if I spoke a few words in certain ears which seemed to support those presumptions—" he sipped tea "—the guilt rests upon my own immortal soul."

"WHILE IT IS PERHAPS fatuous to speak of the Great Discontinuity as unnatural," Miles-Burnham said as Brigid trailed him along a brass-railed catwalk two stories above the concrete floor, as he adjusted gears with his shirtsleeves rolled up past his elbows, "it strikes me most urgently as possessing an adventitious quality."

"Adventitious?"

He nodded, never taking his eyes from the intricate intermeshing of metals within the brass box opened at just above the level of his face. Dust motes swam like midges in a shaft of light falling from the skylights high overhead. "Although perhaps not in the normal sense of the word, in which something has been added. Rather as if something has been subtracted."

He shut the box with a clack, turned away, wiping his hands on a rag from one of the many pockets of his lab apron. The apron appeared to have begun life as some shade of olive, but was now almost black from accreted grease.

Yesterday Norman had refused to explain more about what the great scientist thought he was doing, if not empowering Fiona to take over the world. Today Miles-Burnham was back to himself again. Or, as Brigid suspected, feeling well enough to fake it.

"What are you saying, Doctor?" Brigid asked. "Surely

the stray piece of cosmic string called the Great Destructor caused the dislocation in reality."

"Perhaps. Perhaps not." He turned to stand gripping the rail with both hands, gazing up. Miles Burnham shook his head. "There must have been another agent involved. And I believe I have perceived it—or him."

"Perceived? How?"

"I cannot tell you," he said. "Not in any way you would accept. I can only show you."

She looked right and left. The restless mechanism turned and turned about them. "I'm ready."

Again he shook his head. "Not here. Not now. Rather in your dreams."

"My dreams?"

"Open your mind to me tonight. Simply decide before you go to sleep to yield your defenses. That is all. No harm will come to you—I shall see to that."

"But what does that have to do with—with reality?"

"Nothing or everything, depending. How do you think I knew you were coming?"

"You said you saw it in a vision."

He nodded crisply. "And now I shall share my visions with you. If you are willing. And now if you will please excuse my rudeness, dear child, I must go. My head is ready to split asunder."

He turned and walked away, the perforated metal springing slightly beneath his step.

AND SO SHE OPENED herself to him in sleep. And as promised he came.

Beyond, Brigid could see the planets, and the Sun—

and more. The stars, their planets, the galaxies out to the extent of the universe.

"What is it?" she asked him when the upwelling of emotion had subsided enough to form directed thought.

"Everything," he said, and she could feel his smile. "The world of matter. But come, we have much to see. What this sphere has to show us we will discern upon our return."

They began to rise. Brigid had a definite sense of movement but no sense of surroundings. It struck her as how an electron might feel, were it able to do so, in the interval in which it vanished from a low energy level to reappear on one higher.

Opalescent clouds swirled around her like jeweled fog. She watched in wonder, borne upward by Miles-Burnham's strong arms. She felt human intellect and awareness as a tangible thing, as a form of energy, as a plasma which suffused her with warmth and electricity.

They passed through the glittering clouds to find themselves passing a great orange ball. They seemed to accelerate. She sensed that Miles-Burnham felt especially at home here.

They passed through a green realm and into one of shining gold. She felt a sense of purification.

Above waited a red realm. She felt heat upon her face and breasts and thighs as from a furnace. Alarm clutched at her throat like unseen fingers. She felt intimidation and something like disappointment, as if after the golden sphere she should never experience fear again.

Miles-Burnham's firm touch reassured her. She sensed that no harm could come to her here.

Above was a realm of brilliant royal blue. She felt exalted, enlarged. Then blackness enfolded them. As they floated together peace filled her. She realized their surroundings were not truly black, but a purple of incredible depth and saturation.

They entered into another abode of clouds, white intermingling with gray. She had a sense of being in the presence of the answer to all puzzles, the key to every code. She felt oddly ill at ease here, but once more sensed Miles-Burnham's familiarity with this place.

Above, radiance glowed like the soul of a sun. The light was so intense Brigid could only look away.

Sensing this, Miles-Burnham began to descend.

Serenity and fulfillment grew steadily within Brigid. Until they returned to the hot red realm. Then terror seized her, not the tug of apprehension she had felt before, but talons of sheer fear.

Away around the curve of the sphere, like a corona rising from the surface of the Sun, she saw a figure. It was manlike. Yet it seemed made all of metal, glowing hot with the heat of this sphere. It waved an arm at them.

Miles-Burnham bore them quickly down. They broke through into golden radiance. Brigid felt peace crowd close around her like a throng, but her heart beat rapidly. The last image she had seen burned in her mind as if branded by a red-hot finger.

Down and down they went, through green and orange

and clouds that sparkled with rainbow color, as if imbued with ice crystals acting as billions of tiny prisms.

And then down again, to the vision of the world and all that moved within or without it.

"What was that?" she asked.

"I don't know for certain," Miles-Burnham said. "I have encountered him before. A powerful malignant presence who seems to move among spaces as readily as we moved among the spheres. I think he may have some involvement with what happened to this world."

"And that symbol," she said, "you saw it, too?"

"I have. The curious glyph like three inverted exclamation marks, or a stylized image of three daggers with ball pommels. I sense it is familiar to you."

Even in her mind Brigid could say nothing. She knew he could feel her acknowledgment.

"Time presses," he said. "We must seek such answers as we can find. What would you know of what happens on this world?"

"I want to know," Brigid answered, "how my friends are."

She meant, of course, Kane—and Domi. While she still felt that Domi had judged too quickly—both her and their Canadian captors—Brigid had let go concern over who was right and who was wrong. She missed the albino feral girl terribly, as she did Kane.

And Grant. She shut him deliberately from her mind. She feared to see him as he must be now, his strength and nobility corrupted by decay…or even just a jumble of scavenger-gnawed bones.

She looked down. At once she realized there was simply too much. Her mind could not assimilate the totality of all it perceived, nor filter out meaning.

"All I see are clouds," she said, "as of a terrible storm. Nigel, can you help me?"

"I shall do what I can. You are quite correct, dear child—a mighty storms gathers. And we lie at its eye."

He stretched down a hand. The clouds seemed to part to show Gloriana, glowing like a miniature fairy castle.

"At the roots of the golden city a rose blooms, white— and sends out thorns," he said.

"Domi," Brigid declared. "I should've known she'd make herself a ringleader of the anarchist underground. If they have such things."

"She prepares to lead her comrades aboveground," Miles-Burnham said. "It is part and parcel of the storm that even now swirls about the golden city. Look away to the west. I see a tall figure who seems to wade through storm clouds, with lightning by his side. He dresses all in black. Black are his hair and beard, though touched with gray. His eyes are pale, like a wolf's."

Her heart leaped. "Kane! He's coming for me."

"He carries a great weight of doom, child. He brings great blood and sorrow. For his friends and for this city."

"That's Kane."

"From the south I see another figure striding like a dark colossus. He comes with the host of the lizard folk, but he is no Reptoid. He is their human champion, and none can stand against him."

"Will the Reptoids conquer Gloriana?" she asked.

"I cannot see. The future is largely hidden from me—all I do for you now is help you see the present. I can only see what lies below, and lines of force and convergence. There are other forces stalking…stalking you, I'm afraid. There shall be a mighty collision."

"Stalking me? Why am I so important?"

"Because of what you might tell me."

Her thoughts spun. "What can I do?"

"The best you can. You are strong. *Be* strong. As I say, I can but poorly glimpse the future. I know that you are to be sorely tried. I have every faith that you will persevere."

His words warmed her even as they chilled. I hope you're right, she thought.

She saw his classically sculpted profile elevated. His godlike brow frowned as he stared into the infinite heavens. She tried to follow his gaze. But as below, so above—it was too much for her mind to resolve detail. She was simply overwhelmed by ultimate immensity.

"There is yet another trial intended for this world," he said, "and for this city. A piece has been broken off of Heaven, and may yet come hurtling down. Perhaps I can avert it. Perhaps another shall. And perhaps it shan't be averted at all."

Dread immersed her like an icy bath. She started to ask what he meant.

But a hand closed on her arm, hard and cruel as iron, and snatched her from her sleep.

Chapter 24

The great iron steamship entered the St. Lawrence River beneath the mighty stronghold of Fort Wolfe and prowled upstream at half power, monstrous even among the cargo vessels that plied the waterway. It flew the peacock flag of the Khedive of Morocco, a nation that had maintained its independence and neutrality in the face of European, Arab and Pan-Turanian aggression by an adroit combination of bribery and a facility for ruthless and fiendishly clever guerrilla warfare.

One of its most secure sources of income derived from its sale of its national registry to outlanders willing to donate generously to the Khedive's favorite charity: upkeep of his immense harem and even more immense army of offspring. It was a costly hobby.

All vessels entering the great waterway were supposed to be boarded at Wolfe and investigated by royal hegemonic inspectors. But traffic was heavy; it often was this time of year, as ships strove to make profitable runs before the North Atlantic weather turned from foul to monstrous. The inspectors were harried. They were also not well paid. The urbane, swarthy, turbaned master of the *Great Elephant* was not so crude as to offer outright bribes, of course. He was very subtle about it. The end result being the same: the ship was passed along with scarcely a glance at its manifest and a few holds full of industrial machines and spices, both imported in quantity from certain Asian potentates.

Because many powers in the world resented or envied the hegemony's compassionate system of social welfare, cargoes were supposed to be investigated again, and if possible even more minutely, in Montreal. But Montreal, like most of the former Quebec, had been gradually repopulated by francophones, who had drifted back over the centuries after the brutal ethnic cleansing that had followed the Ontarian reconquest of eastern Canada in the late nineteenth and early twentieth centuries. Mostly they had come from the Republic of Assiniboina, and spent the time intervening wondering why. Nevertheless the French Canadians enjoyed under the hegemonic charter the same rights and privileges as their English-speaking fellow citizens, such as the duty to defer to and obey to the nobility, to pay high taxes and to be tried by juries of anglophones. Being surly and ungrateful by nature, they failed to appreciate these boons.

While the administrators of the huge port of Montreal were impeccably English-speaking Ontarians, the middle and lower ranks of the civil service were dominated by the French. So it was that no keen scrutiny of the Moroccan-registered vessel took place there, either. Possibly certain inducements were offered, these not necessarily of monetary nature.

Indeed, perhaps they involved no more than hints of the *Elephant*'s true cargo.

On to Lake Ontario the vessel cruised, then down most of its length. And so, along with a dense snowfall early even for this latitude and the postcatastrophe world, the *Great Elephant*, riding so low in the water it skirted hegemonic regulations concerning maximum displacement for river traffic, made landfall at the docks of golden Gloriana.

THE BLUE-UNIFORMED TORSO of the crewman next to Kane erupted in a spray of blood, almost black in the clouded light. Kane threw himself down on the dirigible's exposed weather deck as bullets struck the brass rail with deep, musical *pongs*.

Their tribulation began over the eastern shore of Lake Nipigon, north of the arch of Lake Superior, with a stinging swarm of gliders and ultralight battery-powered aircraft.

The bulk of the hegemonic fleet was disposed in an arc along the southern frontiers, from the frontier with Minnetonka in the southwest to the ever expanding border with the Dutch-speaking Patroonate of Albany, now ruled in exile from Philadelphia, in the east. The Cíbolan flight path had been chosen with that fact in mind. Though powerful, the republic's airships were called Aero-Dreadnoughts primarily because all warships of the sky were called that: they were more in the class of frigates and cruisers of the air. The Canadians deployed of truly gigantic air warships, some with envelopes a third of a mile in length, shipping upward of thirty rifles and sheathed in armor twice as thick as that of the doughtiest Cíbolan craft. Although the Cíbolans claimed their armor was more adamant per weight than the hegemonic plate, their shells' penetration deeper, which Kane had no way of evaluating, but was inclined to accept. The Cíbolans seemed to be this world's human high-tech enclave, at least on the North American continent.

But despite the relative qualities of plate, guns and crews, the Cíbolan fleet, impressive as it was to Kane's eyes and indeed by republican standards, was a lightweight force that could not live an hour in the sky in broadside-to-broadside contest with a squadron of Canadian behemoths.

Fortunately they had yet to face any. The air-defense system had been alerted to the intrusion into Canadian airspace by spotters on the ground in eastern Ontario. The lightweight fighting craft were hoisted aloft to meet them by tethered balloons from Fort Wycliffe on the Nipigon shore.

Constant shattering noise assailed *Liberty's Lady's* deck. The fort's guns were trying to take the fleet under fire with time-fuzed shells. Their reach was too short. Airbursts cracking off hundreds of feet beneath the gondolas' armored bellies filled the sky with black smoke blossoms, and their reports echoed between the gas bags with such force they made the envelopes shimmer like the flanks of a horse shedding a horsefly.

Kane heard the roaring snarl of the nearest Gatling change pitch. He popped up to one knee in time to send a pair of blasts booming from a lever-action shotgun into the underside of a gossamer flyer with an electric pusher-motor. Whether he hit a structural spar, the pilot or nothing at all he couldn't tell; the little craft was already wheeling out of sight and down from its strafing run at the deck.

Cautiously, Kane rose to his feet. When the flyers had appeared Commodore Watts, who had his flag on *Liberty's Lady*, ordered the Aero-Dreadnoughts, now thirteen with the departure of the damaged *Wildfire*, into a roughly cubical formation with the airships about a thousand feet apart, with the *Lady* at the center. It allowed them to support each other with their Gatlings and canister shot in the main guns, which didn't carry far before their trajectories sent them plummeting toward Earth, and would do little damage to each others' self-sealing *ballonets*, much less their armor-plated hulls. At the same time it didn't make them a big bunched target for the enemy flyers, whose rockets were short ranged like their own quick firers. He withheld the fleet's own individual craft. They would be needed over Gloriana.

If we ever get that far, Kane thought, hunkered down stuffing shells into his shotgun's tubular magazine. The Aero-Dreadnought's guns fired individually as their crews spotted targets. He saw a white sailplane struck by a full charge of canister from a four-inch rifle. It broke like a stepped-on toy. One wing was shredded, the other snapped vertical in relation to the podlike fuselage. The stricken craft dropped like a brick.

"Don't be fooled, my friend," Rodríguez-Satterfield called out to him. He had stepped up to the port side rail, to a Gatling whose beautiful brass fittings and polished steel barrels were spattered with the gore of its gunner, whose cranium had been evacuated by a hit from behind. "At this stage of the game it's mostly sound and fury signifying nothing. It doesn't get serious till later."

Rodríguez-Satterfield began working the coffee-mill crank of his weapon with joyous fury, blazing straight into the face of another electric-powered pusher plane headed straight for him. The Canadian aviator's bullets left shiny soft-lead smears on the brass railing to either side, and across the corrugated metal deck plating all around.

"Get your head down, you fused-out jolt-runner!" Kane shouted, running up firing his shotgun from the shoulder as he did. He ran at an angle, not straight at the oncoming flyer; he liked Rodríguez-Satterfield fine, but was far from fused-out enough himself to dash right into the stream of thumb-sized bullets.

He didn't know if either his shots or the colonel's hit the ultralight. Humming like a giant mutant mosquito, the aircraft flew right over Rodríguez-Satterfield's head, between the railing and the gas bag's bulging belly. It struck about midships, ten yards behind Rodríguez-Satterfield and Kane. It went skittering across the deck with a grinding and screeching of metal on metal, popping and banging as struts and wires gave way. A pair of blue-suited crewmen at a Gatling at the far rail spun around at the racket. They barely had time to begin to scream in chorus before the hurtling wreck smashed into them, broke through the rail and bore them and their heavy gun out of sight and dropping to destruction.

Kane already faced outward, tracking left and right with his longblaster, looking for targets. As he'd already found out, any kind of heated battle on this world created its own smoke screens in short order. Wisps and banks of smoke floated between the giant sausage shapes in shades of white and gray. The air was crisp and thick with the scent of burned black powder.

Despite the impaired visibility the reason Kane saw few small hostile shapes flitting through the smog seemed to be that for the moment at least they were concentrating their efforts elsewhere in the formation. Shaking his head, he lowered the shotgun.

"Bit too exciting for my taste."

Rodríguez-Satterfield was still hunched behind his gun, turning the crank slowly to keep the barrels rotating so he wouldn't have to strain to get them up to speed again if he needed to shoot in a hurry. "You could've stayed safe and snug belowdecks," he pointed out, "like a sensible man."

"Yeah, well." Kane shrugged. "When it comes to air combat I'm used to taking a more active role. Playing cargo is too much like waiting to die."

Straight away off the port beam an orange flash lit the inside of an artificial fog bank. "Down!" shouted Rodríguez-Satterfield, abandoning his weapon to dive aside, dragging Kane to the deck by the yoke of his black leather greatcoat. A heartbeat later a hot breath of shock wave rolled over them. Chunks of shattered metal spanged off the rail, thumped on the deck, made the envelope above Kane's head boom like a drum. Not seven yards away a bluejacket lay on the deck amid a spreading pool of scarlet, thrashing around a jagged shard that had impaled his belly from right to left.

"Damn," Rodríguez-Satterfield said as a pair of medical orderlies appeared out of a hatch, dashing to attend the spitted crewman with a stretcher. Medical corpsmen in the Cíbolan fleet wore dark maroon tunics and black trousers, so that they wouldn't show the blood of those they aided. "That must've been the *Front-Range Fanny*."

"What was all that about the sound and fury signifying nothing?" Kane still lay prone on the deck. He wore his shadow armor beneath his coat, but didn't see a lot of reason to tempt fate. A fifty-pound chunk of armor moving at a couple hundred yards a second would push the flexible fabric armor of his shadow suit right through him, and it wouldn't matter a pinch of dried birdshit if it penetrated the cloth or not.

"A poorly chosen Shakespeare quote," Rodríguez-Satterfield admitted. He shook his head. "Some lobsterback must've got a lucky rocket hit—down an open hatch, maybe. What with the magazines and the boilers, there's a lot to blow up in these beauties."

"Strike," Kane said.

BRIGID BIT BACK a scream as a gauntleted hand lifted the iron from its bed of glowing coals. The chamber was so dark she could see ghostly blue flames dancing above the embers. The iron's tip was a yellow eye in the gloom.

Brigid was naked and bound to a board. Perhaps torture table would be a better description. It was conveniently adjustable as to angle and was currently at forty-five degrees. She remained totally exposed to her captors' mercies, should they turn out to have any after all.

The iron bracelets that held her wrists and ankles were padded with leather. In itself Brigid perceived that as a sinister touch: the interrogators intended no incidental pain or even discomfort, but intended to carefully meter every joule. Or perhaps they wished for nothing to distract the subject's attention from the main event.

The still yellow iron tip swung toward her full right breast, drawing a purple afterimage trail in her retinas. Then it was broken entirely by a touch that made her body jerk with reaction and a gasp escape her lips. But the touch was not hot iron, but cool skin, and soft. Fingers, gentle.

A face came into view, at once inhumanly beautiful and simply inhuman, underlit by yellow metal glow.

"This might strike you as barbaric," said the Queen Fiona. "Even trite. But while we pride ourselves on being a thoroughgoing modern monarchy, we have found that in some cases the old ways really are the best."

"What do you think you're going to get out of me?" Brigid asked. Her voice was steady.

Fiona smiled. She had a strange V-shaped smile. She wore a white blouse of coarse linen and dark trousers. She was still the only female Brigid had ever seen who dressed in man's clothes in the hegemony.

"What we want, Dr. Baptiste."

"And you think torture is an effective way of getting me to tell you?"

"Gentle means has brought us weeks of genteel con-

versation with our esteemed guest, the saintly Dr. Nigel.
We're running rapidly out of time. We have no more leeway for circumspection."

"What do you mean?"

A burly figure standing in the nearly solid shadow behind Fiona said, "We ask the questions here," in a brusque
male voice.

Fiona cocked and eyebrow over her shoulder. "My toler-
ance for cliché is not limitless, Buford. Kindly restrain your
remarks to the original, if you cannot muster meaningful."

She turned back to Brigid. "We are being invaded, Dr.
Baptiste. On at least two fronts simultaneously. Both the
lizards and those prairie plutocrats from Cíbola have penetrated our airspace with war fleets of significant size. Not
significant enough to conquer and hold any appreciable
amount of territory, mind. But enough—or so they manifestly hope—to carry out a desperate raid. They want
you, Doctor. And I doubt severely it is on account of your
undeniably substantial charms."

One of the other male presences in the room—Brigid
could hear several sets of breathing, out of synch, smell at
least three distinct body washes of a flowery sort she had
come to associate with hegemony males—made a slight
noise of disapproval. Or his sovereign thought he did.

"Really," she snapped, turning to glare into the dark. "I
can appreciate feminine beauty in a purely abstract sense.
There's nothing unnatural about it. Nothing whatever."

She tossed her head and turned back to Brigid. "We
have been extraordinarily forbearing with you, despite
the defection of your female companion to the terrorists.

We know that one of your associates survived and was taken into custody by the Cíbolan bandits."

"He's coming for me!" Brigid burst out. "Kane. I knew he would."

"Kane," Fiona repeated. "That's the name of the other survivor, then."

"Yes."

She shrugged. "He'll not survive long. Although, should he be so careless as to fall into our hands alive, he will find himself surviving far longer than I think he'll find congenial."

"You're a lot less likely to break him with torture than you are me."

Fiona laughed. "You're quite the pair, I must admit. You're not lacking in brass—nor is he, either, to fly clear across the continent on a mad attack against the greatest nation on Earth to rescue you. What one might expect from interdimensional adventurers, I suppose. No occupation for weak sisters."

She turned away. "You were an intelligence analyst on your Earth, Dr. Baptiste. You disclaim expertise in matters technical. But clearly you have some understanding of them, beyond your remarkable memory—you are not simply an idiot savant. That is how I know you are holding out on us."

"You really believe I know the secret to completing the Apocalyptic Engine?"

Fiona turned back to her with a brassy laugh. "Dear lady, I don't give a donkey's arse for Santa Claus, the Philosopher's Stone nor the Apocalyptic Engine, either." This time at least one of her male entourage gasped openly. "I want a *weapon*. Some marvel of your advanced technology that will work here. If not a weapon, a tool, perhaps—some way to accelerate the manufacturing process. Or perhaps even means to surmount the great barrier that lies between the energies we can command and those disposed of by Almighty God."

She was right up face-to-face with Brigid, leaning toward her. Brigid fought the desire to cringe away from the still hot, if no longer glowing, iron rod clasped in her leather-gloved hand.

"I want something real. Something concrete. Not some nonesuch!"

She reached her bare left hand to caress the side of Brigid's skull, letting strands of red-gold hair trickle through her slim, strong fingers. "Somewhere in this skull lie the secrets to make me mistress of this world. I want them. You can give them to me."

She put her face close to Brigid's. A lock of her own hair had come free; it brushed ticklingly against Brigid's nose. "And you shall," she softly said.

"In the meantime," she said, straightening and turning crisply away, "this was all for show—this time. I believe you will find your own most agile and active imagination subjects you to far greater torments than I might inflict upon your shrinking flesh. Especially as you contemplate the question—will I decide to crack you by torturing this Kane before you? Or seek to learn what secrets he may know by torturing you?"

She tossed her torture iron aside without looking. It landed in a water kettle on the floor with a sinister hiss of steam.

Chapter 25

Dead ahead, a mile away and perhaps a hundred yards lower, an Aero-Dreadnought drifted out of control. Yellow flames boiled out to the sides between its armored gondola and its spheroid *ballonets,* exposed by the envelope's having burned or melted away. The engines of the *Foreclaw of the Race* labored to drive the great airship to clear the flaming derelict upwind, as its stacks dumped hot air into reserve containers in its own envelope for extra buoyancy. Flying above the burning craft was obviously a questionable idea, in that heat rises, but it was preferable to flying beneath it, given the tendency of debris, flaming or otherwise, to fall. And much better than failing to clear it at all.

Combat survival, Grant knew too well, often consists in making the least bad decision from an unpalatable set of options.

"I can tell you're eager to be at grips with the enemy, Mr. Grant," Ishmael said. He rubbed his taloned hands together gleefully, seemingly oblivious to the imminent danger as to the yellow embers that dusted the deck of their own airship like early snow. Grant had no idea whether it was a lizard gesture or another affectation his handler had picked up from men.

"We got to stay alive," Grant said, "to get to grips."

All around them vast armored airships swerved and boomed and struggled and died.

THE NEST-MASTER had taken Zirak's counsel seriously enough to launch a full-scale aerial assault against the Canadian forces north of St. Louis. It was all, in effect, a diversion. In the confusion attendant on a vast aerial fleet action, a small squadron, including the vessel carrying Grant, Zirak and a troop of Reptoid special-operations troops, would attempt to break through and make its way north to Gloriana. The battle was timed to take place late in the afternoon; the squadron would attempt its penetration around or after sunset. With no wireless communication other than visual signals it would be hard for observers on the ground to tell Reptoid Aero-Dreadnoughts from Canadian ones in the dark, if they even spotted them.

That, in any event, was the theory. Zirak had been unable to think of any better scheme. He basically preferred not to think about it. After all, they would succeed or they would not; a certain fatalism was implicit in the outlook of the Race's dominant culture.

GRANT FELT dragon's breath roll up over the gondola's side at him. The Aero-Dreadnought rose rapidly in the heat welling from its burning compatriot. Black smoke surrounded them, crowding in between deck and envelope. He squinted his eyes against the stinging smoke, breathed shallowly against the stink of burning rubber and black powder and the aroma of human flesh combusting.

Then they were through. Lizard men air crew in bright monochrome one-piece suits dashed around pushing burning chunks of debris overboard with utensils like bristleless push brooms, and hitting areas of residual fire with white blasts from compressed carbon-dioxide canisters. It was an oddly homelike touch.

Ishmael wiped his forehead with a handkerchief from a pocket of his jacket. That was no affectation: sweat was visible sheening his hairless scalp, so oddly similar in coloration to a human's. Just slightly yellower than any human's ever was, and somewhat faintly mottled.

Klaxons blared. The Reptoid crew began darting in different patterns. A Canadian Aero-Dreadnought approached on their level from the port bow, closing rapidly.

"Perhaps," Ishmael said, "you should get below."

Grant stepped up to the rail. He wore a long black coat over his shadow suit. Its leather tails whipped around his calves in the wind of the airship's passage.

"If the ship blows," he said, "does it make a damned bit of difference where we are?"

Clouds off far to the west cast gray-and-purple shadows across the sky. In the high twilight the muzzle-flare of an enemy bow chaser was a brilliant crimson stab with a blue heart. A shell streaked toward them, passing to Grant's left, just above the rail, with a crack like a gunshot. Its course intersected that of a crewman trotting to his battle station. The middle section of his drab-uniformed torso, held level with stumpy tail raised for balance, vanished in a geyser of blood. An armor piercer, the shell didn't detonate, but passed on beyond the far railing.

The shock of its passage stung Grant's bare cheek; the wind of it rocked him as he stood.

"Well," Ishmael said, "no."

So Grant stood by the rail, glaring like an angry black god, gripping it as if to leave dents in the immaculately polished brass, as the enemy airship closed in. The *Foreclaw*'s own bow gun began to bang out replies. Ishmael dithered next to him, obviously more fearful for the fate of his prize pony than his own.

The Canadian vessel was bigger than the *Foreclaw*, which was a sixteen-gun Aero-Dreadnought built for comparative speed. Grant could see the pale ovals of Canadian faces above the rail on the deck. Several Gatling guns began to grind as the ships rushed together. Quick firers began to roar back from the *Foreclaw*.

The twin bulges of the gas envelopes would hold the gondolas separate if the bags brushed like amorous whales. The two opposing captains chose to maneuver to avoid that, but the torpedo-shaped bags almost came in contact. The respective gondolas were still less than a hundred yards apart when they passed broadside to broadside.

Thunder crashed as the ships volleyed death into one another. The *Foreclaw* shuddered as heavy shells smashed her plate. The fact that her captain had made no attempt to swerve to avoid the contact seemed to take the enemy captain by surprise, or at least his gunnery officer: most of the shells that hit the Reptoid vessel were fused with too long a delay, and smashed their way out the far-side armor to explode in air rather than bursting inside her belly. It didn't mean the shells were harmless, though: anything in their path, whether mechanism or vulnerable human flesh, they smashed.

The Reptoid gunners had anticipated the range perfectly. Grant could feel, as well as hear, secondary explosions from within the larger gondola as the *Foreclaw*'s seven-gun broadside crashed home. Orange flashes lit gun ports from within. Flame jetted from hatches. A crewman, caught on a ladder, ran about the Canadian deck wreathed in flame, his shrieks clearly audible at this distance above the mingled engine throb and the crackle of cannonading.

An enemy Gatling began to chew the gleaming rail to Grant's right to twisted ruin: its gunner was zeroing in on the tall, unmistakably human silhouette standing in clear view. Ishmael clutched his sleeve.

"Run for it!" the Reptoid shouted.

With his right hand Grant drew one of the lizards' autoloading handblasters from a holster beneath his left armpit. He braced right hand with left, locking into a modified Weaver combat stance, with his left foot advanced so his body angled about thirty degrees toward his target. As brass chips flew from the rail with a continuous harsh ringing, right up toward him, he sighted carefully through curtains and tendrils of dense gun smoke.

He squeezed off a single shot.

Transfixed despite his fear for his prize and protégé, Ishmael stopped and stared toward the enemy ship. He actually saw red mist fly out from behind the pillbox-capped head of the enemy gunner, saw the head fly black. The man fell from view. His gun swung muzzle down, its barrels rotating, but silently.

The big broadside rifles in both Aero-Dreadnoughts were breechloaders; the Reptoid and hegemonic aerial navies were nothing if not thoroughly modern. They were quick to reload. But each crew had time for but a single volley before the vast craft slid past one another. The *Foreclaw*'s gondola shuddered as a last shot from an enemy broadside gun at the extent of its firing range punched through her armor near the stern. Another exploded on the elevated afterdeck in a searing yellow flash, eliciting odd whistling shrieks from scorched and shredded Reptoid crewmen.

A fresh thunder burst of firing erupted from aft of the *Foreclaw*: one of her escort Aero-Dreadnoughts had crossed the bows of the Canadian airship and was raking her. The Reptoid gunners were skilled. Looking back through gaps in the black smoke boiling from the *Foreclaw*'s stern, Grant saw yellow flame spurt from the enemy's gun ports as gun positions were smashed by exploding Reptoid shells.

Another Reptoid Aero-Dreadnought came up to help her sister finish the stricken Canadian. Her own injuries not mortal, the *Foreclaw of the Race* continued to steam into a rapidly darkening sky, leaving the battle behind.

She had successfully penetrated the powerful Canadian defensive line. Barring the unforeseen, her sailing from here onward should be clear.

Dawn would find Gloriana agleam before her bow.

Chapter 26

Dawn slid into the golden city almost furtively between chill, dew-slick streets and sidewalks and slate-gray clouds.

As ash-colored light seeped across the docks, ramps were lowered from two anonymous freighters docked within a few hundred yards of each other. From one streamed infantrymen in the maroon coats and white trousers of the Royal Danish Army. Denmark and its Scandinavian holdings were the last bastion of civilization against the Reptoid-backed barbarian hordes who had overrun Western Europe and Britannia in the past several years.

From the other great grimy vessel emerged files of white-coated soldiers serving the czar of all the Russias.

A few drowsy watchmen patrolling the wharfs were quickly clubbed down with rifle butts. The immediate threat to the invaders, however, came not the Canadians, but from each other. As soon as they spied one another through the wisps of mist off the lake, the two forces turned and fell on each other like swarms of red and black ants. Rifle flashes stabbed through the fog. The crump of gunfire was oddly muted by the heavy, humid air.

Both commanders knew their enterprise was desperate and probably doomed. They couldn't afford to bleed their forces away on anything but trying to force passage to their goal through the red-coated Canadian forces who would soon come swarming to stop them. But the prize was not just too great to be left to the hegemony: it was too great to be shared.

Instead of flowing off the docks and into the streets of the waterfront district, the lines of while and maroon streamed toward one another, each bent on destroying its rival.

TWO MILES to the southwest, the huge freighter with the Moroccan flag flying from its staff also lower ramps. Figures poured down these, as well, small brown-skinned men carrying muskets, spears, clubs and wavy daggers. They wore only turbans of scarlet or black—to honor the skin and eyes of their deity—and loincloths, as though inured to the chill of the morning and the desultory sleet that had begun to drift down toward the cobbled street.

Meanwhile a powerful crane transferred an immense canvas-covered object from the depths of a hold amidships down onto the dock. The stout timbers bowed noticeably beneath its weight, with pipe-organ groans of protest.

As men in white tunics, trousers and khaki puttees busied themselves beneath the canvas covers, several hundred Sino-Indian devotees of the goddess Kali began trotting in meaningful silence toward the hegemonic palace.

"HERE THEY COME," Colonel Randall Rodríguez-Satterfield said, putting a cheroot in his mouth and lighting it. He stood with one boot up on the rail, Kane at his side.

A line of dark shapes dotted its way across the clouds before them. A dozen, swelling to twenty as Kane saw more shapes resolve out of the white backdrop. Their own fleet was down to ten vessels from running battles.

Below their boots Gloriana appeared, glittering like a toy in the light of new day.

"Imposing odds. And they're likely to get worse." The colonel cocked a brow at his companion. "Think we got a chance?"

Kane shrugged. "We're alive, aren't we?"

"For the moment." Rodríguez-Satterfield laughed. "I like your style, Kane. Sometimes style's all we've got."

His right shoulder hunched in his own shrug. "And sometimes style's enough. We'll see."

The fleets swept together. The invading craft, nine Cíbolan and one Kai-Gwe, had the height advantage. The Canadians kept vessels on station above the capital, but they patrolled relatively low, primarily to keep an eye on events in the streets. It was beyond belief that anyone would be so rash as to challenge the world's mightiest power in its own sky.

But once such a challenge appeared, the defenders were prepared to respond with crushing force.

The Cíbolan commodore once more had *Liberty's Lady* at the core of his formation, although he had transferred his flag aboard *Freedom's Fire*. Kane watched the Canadian line sweep toward them like a scythe. He had no understanding of the subtleties of naval tactics in play here. The basic truth was blatant enough: they were outshipped and outgunned.

The fleets swept together. The *Liberty's Lady's* deck jumped beneath Kane's boots as the Aero-Dreadnought let go with both broadsides simultaneously. The good luck that sometimes rewarded sheer balls-before-brains brashness had brought two defending airships at once into the deadliest of killzones, worse even than a stern-to-bow rake. They were below the Cíbolan vessel at a range and height differential that exposed their thin top-deck plating.

Looking down to portside, Kane saw black holes appear in the enemy deck. Tiny figures in blue and hegemonic scarlet were tossed around like toy soldiers by invisible hands of blast-wave. Flame spurted out through the holes, and then the great gas bag was wreathed in a twisted, swelling black cloud.

A great cheer went up from the *Lady's* weather deck. Kane even imagined he could hear cheers from below. It had an edge of something more than the atavistic thrill of victory.

"Why the excitement?" Kane shouted to a green-jacketed crewman carrying a tubful of cakes of lubricant to the nearest Gatling mount.

"That's the *Overbearing* we just gutted, sir," the crewman piped happily. He looked no more than fourteen in his little bellhop cap. "She destroyed the *Lovely Rita* out of Carnuel when the Cans turned on us, down in the Mississippi Valley."

"Right before you folks turned up," Rodríguez-Satter-field said.

The sky had filled with lesser shapes, buzzing on their battery-powered engines or simply swooping. Rockets whooshed and cracked. Gatlings sang their growling songs.

A ship loomed like an airborne mountain to starboard, rising fast. Kane could see feather tails of water wisping away below it as its captain vented his tanks, in effect blowing ballast to lighten its load, trading long-term power for height, which he needed right now. The dully gleaming gray flanks of its gondola flickered with yellow glare as its seven broadside guns cracked off in rough unison.

Rodríguez-Satterfield grabbed Kane's sleeve and drew him down to a crouch as projectiles cracked past in the air. Metal and fire erupted from the deck where shells went home. Bodies and their components were scattered to lie stinking and smoking on twisted deck plating.

The *Lady*'s own broadside roared response. Kane saw holes punched in armor, lit instantly by explosions within.

"We're safer on deck than below," Rodríguez-Satterfield shouted during the brief lull to reload. The stillness was only comparative, what with men screaming and Gatlings pounding everywhere, and Kane could barely hear through the ringing in his ears. "They don't bother aiming up here."

Kane nodded. He preferred being up here. If he was no more master of his fate than if he had been prematurely entombed amid glossy-paneled steel bulkheads below, at least he could see it coming. And he could act.

"Screw fate, anyway," he said aloud. His companion laughed and slapped him on the shoulder.

The *Lady* and her enemy passed in opposite directions. Captain Martin, below in his armored bridge in the prow, ordered no maneuver to avoid the enemy dirigible crossing his stern. Nor was his ship ripped from the rear with a devastating broadside. Evidently the Canadian Aero-Dreadnought had found something else to occupy her. Kane couldn't see for black smoke pouring up through a pair of shell holes in the deck aft of where he and Rodríguez-Satterfield hunkered.

Seeming to have taken no serious damage despite the holes and the smoke, the *Lady* steamed on at full speed. She traded long-range fire with another enemy airship. To no great effect to either side, although Kane saw a pair of gun monkeys' upper torsos shattered into sprays of blood and yellow bone from the blast of a shell exploding without penetrating on her armored hull below the gunwales where they stood.

"That's the bitch about battle," Kane said, as much to himself as to anyone else. "Light casualties aren't so light when you're one of them."

"You got that right, amigo," the colonel said.

Of all the Cíbolan fleet and its sole Kai-Gwe ally remaining of three—the fourteen-gun *Red Horse*—the *Lady* wasn't here to fight, but to reach its destination at all costs: the Royal Hegemonic Palace, where intel indicated Brigid Baptiste was being held captive. Although no one ever articulated it, Kane understood from early on that none of the Cíbolans setting out on this expedition expected their expensive and precious Aero-Dreadnoughts to survive. Nor, for that matter, themselves.

Their whole and sole hope was that the airships would get some of them alive to the prize so that they could liberate her and then somehow escape. Perhaps exfiltrating overland, perhaps by water. Kane had to admire the go-for-broke ballsiness of it all, as well as the Cíbolans' infinite regard for their own resourcefulness.

They were traits he shared.

Still, although the double-tapered gas bags were relatively aerodynamic, tail or headwinds made a substantial difference in their speed over ground. A stiff wind from dead abeam, meanwhile, could shove them sideways almost as rapidly as they progressed forward. Although they boasted powerful engines, the Aero-Dreadnoughts were almost as much at the wind's mercy as sailing ships of old, and the weather gauge held supreme tactical importance.

Thus, *Liberty's Lady* and her surviving escorts—down to seven now—swung south of the city's center to catch the wind, which at this altitude on this dreary morning blew out of the southeast, to bear them over the palace grounds.

As they made a turn over the river district, Rodríguez-Satterfield suddenly pointed downward into the streets. "*¡Mira!*" he exclaimed.

Kane bent forward to peer down. "What the fuck, over?"

"LET 'EM HAVE IT, BOYS!" a tenor voice cried. Yellow flashes sprang from the muzzles of bolt-action rifles in a ripple of thunder.

Company Albert of the Second Battalion of Her Majesty's Halifax Fusiliers—the Twenty-Seventh Infantry Regiment—crouched behind improvised barricades of sandbags meant to stem flood waters. And they were being used to stem a flood of sorts: that of dusky human flesh, advancing down broad Water Street toward the center of Gloriana.

Armored in nothing more than their skins, the Sino-Indian Kali worshippers fell like scythed wheat as the copper-jacketed lead bullets tore through them. The infantry, red-coated, faces pale and sweat sheened beneath white pith helmets despite the cold, worked the actions of their rifles with feverish intensity and fired repeatedly. Small boys scuttled bent over behind them, handing out fresh magazines. The stubby three-inch howitzer squatting on rubber tires behind its metal splash plate at the center of the barricade seemed altogether unnecessary, and its khaki-jacketed crew had yet to fire it.

The smell of burned powder and ripped intestines was so thick in the heavy air it was almost palpable. From above came chill, desultory rain, and the growl of great engines, as fleets of Aero-Dreadnoughts clashed overhead. The infantrymen kept their heads to their sights. They had their own battle to wage, even if it was more slaughter than combat....

Water Street crested before them in a hill before falling away to the docks. From the hump's far side came a strange blast of sound, like the bellow of an outraged beast, but enormously magnified. A plume of gray-black smoke appeared just above the hill, rising and swelling.

Then the men at the sandbags began to feel rhythmic vibrations, slow and measured, up through the cobblestones of the street and the soles of their mirror-polished boots. Their rate of fire slackened perceptibly as they exchanged wondering glances.

With a vast metallic clattering and creaking like a giant drawer full of cutlery being shaken, a shape mounted into view: like a bull Indian elephant, but larger than the greatest African bull had ever stood. At least twenty-five feet from the pads of its broad feet to the crown of its sloped head, it glared at the soldiers with eyes like blazing red lamps.

Without needing command from their red-faced captain or the pallid subalterns the company switched fire to the bizarre apparition. But their bullets bounced off the behemoth like rain. For its flanks were metal, not hide, the planes of its face the finest armor plate. A smoking stack rose from its high back. Its tusks were high-velocity rifled cannon with two-inch bores. And its curving trunk, all of overlapping armor sections, rising now with a metal-on-metal squeal as the steamophant emitted another whistling roar and a cloud of white steam...

A section of the barricade defenders were engulfed in yellow-and-blue flame as a stream of blazing liquid hosed them from the trunk.

"Fire!" the gunnery lieutenant shouted. The howitzer roared and jumped on its tires, the recoil of its firing being mostly absorbed in the oil tube beneath its stub barrel.

But the ammunition loadout had not been reckoned to oppose an armored foe; perhaps it would have made small difference if it had. The shell struck the steamophant full in the face, just inboard its right eye, with a white flash and a blast wave that made the flesh of the fanatics nearest it to splash like pudding. But the steamophant came on, not even marked, eyes still blazing. As the gun crew yanked open the breech and began furiously to feed in a fresh shell, the length of an arm and shaped like a giant bullet, the brass of its casing gleaming wetly in the dim dawn light, the monster's own paired cannon spoke. Howitzer, crew and most of the middle part of the barricade—and its defenders—vanished in a dazzling flicker of primary and secondary explosions as the shell, half-inserted, and its own ammo stocks exploded.

Those soldiers who could turned and fled. The steamophant strode without pausing through the black pillar of smoke rising where the howitzer had stood, raising its flame-drooling trunk and trumpeting triumph.

The land battle for Gloriana—and for Brigid Baptiste—had begun in savage earnest.

Chapter 27

"Gentlemen," Queen Fiona said in a voice that rang like a clarion. "I have decided to assume personal command of the defense of my city and my palace."

So saying, Fiona let drop from her broad shoulders the heavy indigo robe she had worn concealing her body. Several of the high-ranking officers gathered in her mahogany-paneled counsel chamber winced. It would not have been altogether out of character for their monarch to be nude beneath that robe.

But what she revealed to the yellowish glare of the gas lamps was almost as shocking as the sight of her milky bare skin would have been: the pink tunic and red-striped breeches of an Eleventh Hussar, a Cherrypicker.

"A woman in command?" burst out a red-coated general, almost slobbering in fury, his jowls shaking like an aged bloodhound's. "An outrage. Impossible!"

With the smooth speed of a practiced gunfighter Fiona drew a .51-caliber Lifeson automatic revolver from a black patent-leather holster on her right hip and shot the man through the forehead. He fell back against the wall, then slid downward, leaving a darker smear on dark-stained wood.

Fiona tipped the smoking weapon back in her feminine but undeniably powerful white hand. "Does anyone else," she inquired sweetly, "wish to express doubts of my ability to conduct myself in battle?"

Silence and strained white faces answered her. "Good. Now listen closely, and listen fast. I have a certain matter to attend to before taking the field myself. But here is the plan...."

THE DANES AND RUSSIANS had broken off their fight as by mutual accord and begun a dash toward the palace, scattering police and uncoordinated cavalry counterattacks in their berserk fury.

In King Brian XII Park, named for Fiona's late, illustrious father, two small land ironclads from the Duke of Newfoundland's own cavalry were burning, one by the fountain with its naked marble nymphs, the other by the birdlime-streaked bronze equestrian likeness of King Brian himself. In exchange the Newfies and their First Border Infantry support had managed to smash the right eye of the rampaging steamophant.

Gloriana was the heart and stronghold of the mighty Canadian empire. Had an opponent sought to invade and conquer it, he would have faced hordes of disciplined, well-motivated troops and obdurate defenses.

Because, of course, an open invasion would have required enormous time and effort and been opposed every foot of the way. By the time the hundreds of miles of ground had been won, or a waterborne attacker somehow managed to force passage of the colossal forts at Fort

Wolfe—once Quebec City—and Montreal, Canadian forces would have fallen back upon their glittering capital to man concentric iron rings of redoubtable defensive works.

Gloriana was a virgin queen armored mostly by distance, and by the bodies of troops dispersed outwards along the frontiers she commanded. Against an attack by stealth, against foes with no intent of actually seizing terrain, much less holding it, she lay open and naked as a gaudy slut on a rump-sprung bed.

To a degree. Caught unprepared, Gloriana was far from defenseless. The hegemon's valiant troops, augmented by the civil police and the RHMP, could have defeated and eradicated ten times the attackers they faced today—given time. Even accounting for the thousand fearsome Zulu warriors who had issued from the iron guts of the *White Bull*, the royal kwaZulu vessel ostensibly waiting to return the persona non grata Prince John to his homeland.

The question was how much damage the fanatically determined attackers would do before they were destroyed. And whether they would succeed in their desperate aim.

Thousands of men had come covertly to Gloriana for the sole purpose of kidnapping Brigid Baptiste. They had, in effect, already spent their lives for it.

And if they couldn't have her, they would spend their lives to kill her.

KANE BARELY HAD TIME to gawk at the bizarre giant metal elephant stamping panicked redcoats into mush and torching them with liquid flame from its trunk, while Canadian land ironclads steamed and clanked through the streets to confront it, before the klaxons began to blare again. Captain Martin announced over a bullhorn from his bridge that a fleet had been sighted closing rapidly from the south.

"Our friends the Reptoids," Rodríguez-Satterfield said, "arriving late to the party."

Kane drew his paired automatic revolvers in turn, checked their load and tucked them back under his arms. "We'll make 'em feel real welcome."

His friend forbore to comment on the apparent absurdity of checking handblasters on the verge of a fight between multiton armored behemoths a thousand feet long.

A sound like the sky being ripped across signaled that the aerial combat had caught up with them. A guy line parted with a musical twang not ten yards from Kane as a shell clipped it through. Whether the parting of a single strand out of myriad could possibly have made the gondola lurch beneath Kane's boots, it sure seemed to. The backlash of the wound steel cable, suddenly released from fantastic tension, cut through the right shoulder of a stretcher bearer, sliced his body in two to the left hip and bisected the chest of a moaning casualty with a bandage showing two red spots where his eyes probably used to be.

Looking around, Kane could see three other Aero-Dreadnoughts streaming the blue, green, and black banners of the Cíbolan republic trailing them to left and right. Were they all that was left?

"There's the palace," Rodríguez-Satterfield called, his voice audible over a flash lull in the firing. He pointed with his chin to port of their line of progress. The compound spread wide, a square bite from the cityscape, with parks of trees all color—drab now in the damp, dim light—and a fantastic pile of towers and spires rising in the midst of it, so white it was almost dazzling even in the murky dawn.

Then the *Lady* was dueling with two vessels who came alongside simultaneously from fore and aft, and Kane and Rodríguez-Satterfield got busy battling enemy fliers swarming like locusts looking to settle on the last bean patch for a hundred desert miles. Kane blew his shotgun's seven-shot tubular magazine dry, tossed the wep without thinking to a crewmen who looked twelve years old at most to reload, then drew both his Taliaferro automatic revolvers and fired them both at the goggled face visible behind the yellow fire dance of a Gatling mounted on an ultralight diving on them. Kane felt a bullet pluck at his left sleeve like a ghostly finger. Then he hit the enemy aviator, or someone did, because he saw a goggle lens star, saw fluid gush out black in the dawnlight. The leather-helmeted head slumped forward and the aircraft slammed into the armored hull right below Kane's feet with a mighty whack.

Kane threw up his arms, still holding his now exhausted handblasters, to cover his face from the inevitable rush of flame. Which never came. Only creaks and scrapes and pings and silence as the wreck slid down the work-hardened steel cliff and away. He slowly lowered his arms and gave a sheepish look to Rodríguez-Satterfield, who regarded him with long narrow head cocked to one side like a curious hound pup. He didn't try to explain.

Somehow they were clear again. At least there were no

foes immediately upon their ship, although crashes and ringing clangs indicated hits were still coming in from somewhere. The gondola now sagged appreciably, at least a few degrees to aft and portside. Overhead the gray synthetic-silk envelope that contained the helium-filled *ballonets* that gave the airship buoyancy looked as if the moths had been at it in places; in others the fabric hung in rags, revealing the dark oily gleam of the *ballonets* themselves.

The deck around the two men was gouged, scored and holed. Great sections of the railing gaped like an indigent's teeth. Bodies and disconnected parts of bodies lay strewed on laminated wood decking that ran with blood and rain. One crewmen had been hurled with such force into an intact section of railing that he seemed fused to the brass, which had been driven deep into his torso. Kane had the impression the poor bastard was still moving, hoped it was random motion induced by wind, or the increasingly disharmonic vibrations from the engines and fabric of the great craft herself.

"Whoa!" Kane said. The deck abruptly took on a new cant, down by the bows at least ten degrees.

"Captain's descending," Rodríguez-Satterfield commented. He slapped the rail affectionately. "Old girl's dying around us, but I reckon she'll get us down within reach of your lady-love, Kane."

Kane finished reloading his second handblaster with a moon clip of cartridges and stuffed it into its holster. "She's not my lady-love, damm it."

Rodríguez-Satterfield's gloved hand made a suave gesture. "Whatever you say, partner."

Kane felt an odd twinge at his calling him that. It was a common expression among friends along the Front Range. But in the past only Grant had called him that before. It left him an odd hollowness within, a sense that he had failed his real partner—his only real friend. For some reason the desolation of having left him to rot on that hillside near the Mississippi so many weeks ago now came flooding full into his mind, so that he grabbed the rail and flexed his knees to absorb the psychic impact.

"You all right?" the colonel asked solicitously, moving close to support him if he went down.

Kane warded him off with an upraised hand. "I'm fine," he lied. "Just…dizzy spell. Fumes."

Between the spilled guts and burned powder and lubricant and the clouds of various dull colors of smoke pouring up from the violated decks, there were plenty fumes to go around. Rodríguez-Satterfield nodded.

"Better snap it tight in a hurry," he said. "The lizard boys are about to join the fandango."

Kane's head snapped around. A quartet of Aero-Dreadnoughts approached at speed from the south. They didn't look any different from any other, but they trailed the white-red-gold-black banners of the Reptoid Mississippi occupation zone, and half a dozen Canadian dirigibles and a midge swarm of fliers harassed them. All the same their bows flared with yellow spots of light as they fired bow-chasers at *Liberty's Lady* and her companions. Kane heard shells roar by with a freight-train rush.

A strange urgency filled him to look closer at those oncoming craft. "Spyglass!" Kane exclaimed. "Don't you carry a telescope in your pocket?"

Rodríguez-Satterfield dug inside his long voluminous coat and came up with a telescoping brass tube, which he handed without remark to Kane. Kane extended it to full length and raised the lens to his eye.

He swept the deck of the nearest Reptoid vessel. It was deadly close already, barely over half a klick and closing. As the *Lady* finished her sweep to the southeast and began her turn to ride the wind down to the palace, the Reptoid Aero-Dreadnought was catching her up.

The lizard ship's deck was a worse shambles than *Lady's*. Her gondola's armor plate was holed and heaved by shellfire. War-fliers, their batteries or ammunition exhausted, were still being grappled by complicated claw arrangements beneath the gondola, or landed physically atop the tattered envelope to be replenished by frantic crew. But it was the deck that drew Kane's eye.

Two figures stood at the rail near the bow. One stood in the unmistakable stance of a creature with a heavy counterbalancing tail—forward-tilted posture of a Reptoid, his chunky torso wrapped in what appeared to be a gray trench coat whose tails snapped like pennons in the wind. The other was just as unmistakably human, tall and straight and clad all in black. The head was distorted by a bulky black pair of binocs it held before its face.

But that face was the color of the mahogany paneling omnipresent in this world's interior design.

Kane felt as if his body were encased in ice. Yet some jet of fire blazed at his core.

"It isn't fucking *possible*," he said.

Chapter 28

"Kane," Grant said, his deep voice calm amid the demonic symphony of screams and explosions.

"What? What's that you say?" his Reptoid handler demanded. He looked up at the man in alarm. Although his ears—far more attuned to nuance of tone in the human voice than the vast majority of humans ever were—had detected no consciously registering change in the man, alarm bells rang in his skull to drown out the din around them.

Grant lowered the field glasses. "It's Kane," he said, staring at the deck of the rapidly approaching Cíbolan warship. "I should've known he'd be here."

Zirak leaned forward over the rail, squinting. His distance vision was poor. "Are you certain?"

Grant nodded. The scowl lines never absent from his face had deepened. His knuckles were pale where his great hands gripped the rail.

"Follow that ship," he said. "Wherever Brigid being held, that's where he's going."

"No, WAIT," said the skinny guard. "You can't. Orders."

His taller, larger-bellied partner shoved him with the

palm of his hand. The scrawny jailer stumbled back, yelping as he put his hand on the brazier full of still glowing coals in a blind attempt to steady himself. It failed, and he went down on his backside on the dungeon floor.

"Serves you right, you ninny," said the heavy one, who had never taken his tiny close-set blue eyes off Brigid's nude body, strapped to the torture frame. "Leave off."

"But we'll get in trouble—"

The large man turned his big saggy face toward his partner. "Bugger off about orders, will you? No one cares what we do—there's a war on."

He turned back to Brigid with a wide smile. Saliva trickled down his chin and dotted the front of his dirty white undershirt. Both men had stripped off their tunics; the brazier made it quite warm in the small subterranean chamber.

"As for you, yer ladyship, the Queen's quite out of patience with you, in't she? You been coddled quite enough, now, what?"

He reached a big hand to cup Brigid's right breast. "'Sides, it's a traitor and spy's word against ours, long's we don't leave no marks, eh, Markie?"

"B-Bill," his partner stammered.

Bill scowled ferociously. "Oh, go wank in the corner, then, you pathetic little—"

His word flow stopped. It didn't trail off; rather it trailed up, rising until it turned to a squeak, then inaudible, possible beyond human hearing. His large face turned white and knotted into mask of hideous anguish.

He let go of Brigid's breast to reach behind his lower

back with both hands. A series of high-pitched squeals like bat cries escaped his bulky body. He dropped to his knees and toppled to the side, where he began thrashing and shrieking.

Behind him stood a short, slim young woman dressed in a white blouse and form-fitting black trousers. A bright red shout of fresh blood was streaked across the front of the blouse.

It matched her ruby eyes.

"Domi?"

The feral girl smiled and gestured with the red-dripping knife in her hand. "Like the look? People here don't take girls seriously if they look too much like boys. You know the old saying—when in Rome, light Roman candles."

Before Brigid had a chance to correct the aphorism Markie scrambled to his feet. His eyes were big as a frightened cat's. "M-murder!" he exclaimed. "You done murder on a queen's sworn officer."

He lunged forward, a pipestem arm swinging wildly toward a red alarm button set on the wall.

He stopped midway. His eyes rolled up to look at what had just sprouted from the center of his forehead. It appeared to be a short, thick arrow.

He collapsed like a rag doll.

Brigid's eyes snapped to the door. Bending slightly to step through the short doorway came Chrissie Battersea, lately queen of Britannia, political refugee and student of philosophical sciences. She was clad in rough, drab men's dress. She carried a spent pistol-style crossbow in one gloved hand.

"Hullo, Dr. Baptiste," she said cheerfully. "I see we came just in the nick of time."

Bill's shrieks, now rising to a crescendo, made it hard to hear what the dark-haired woman was saying. She stooped. The horrific screeches gradually faded as he succumbed to the injuries inflicted by Domi's knife.

Chrissie was cocking the spring steel bow with what looked like practiced expertise, pushing the bow with one hand forward while holding the thick cord string with the other. She noticed Brigid staring at her. "These were quite the vogue back home, before things all fell apart. For hunting, you know."

Brigid continued to stare. Chrissie flicked her eyes to the man she had shot.

"Oh, him." The bolt caught on the cock and she nipped another quarrel into a metal spring-clamp which held it in place in the groove. She rotated the weapon left and right to make sure the projectile was secured. "I had to defend myself more than once during the fall of my kingdom, and my flight with Nigel."

"It's a stone coldheart world," Domi said, "no matter which world it is." She had retrieved a heavy iron ring of keys from Bill's belt and was deftly unlocking the leather-padded cuffs that pinioned Brigid's ankles. Then she stood and moved up to do the same for the redhaired woman's wrists.

As she did she ran her eyes appraisingly up Brigid's naked body. "Looks like you gained a kilo or so," she murmured. "They ain't been starving you, anyway. Fattening for the kill, mebbe."

"Consorting with royals, Domi?" Brigid asked. She slid down the board until her feet touched the cool floor. She began massaging her wrists. "I thought you'd become an anarchist."

"Who says," Domi said, biting into a pear she'd taken from a pocket of her trousers, "Chrissie isn't one, too?"

Brigid looked to Chrissie, who blushed prettily and shrugged. "Who has had a closer look at the iniquities and inefficiencies of government?" she asked. "But I don't think this is the time for polemics. We have to get you out of here quickly."

Domi held up the capacious scarlet tunic Bill had hung on a rack. "This is all we got on hand."

"Thank you," Brigid said, standing unsteadily and supporting herself with an arm on the torture board while Domi draped the garment around her shoulders. "What about pants?"

"Skinny's won't fit you," Domi said matter-of-factly. "And the big fella here dumped quite the load in his. Your call."

Brigid shook her head, making her locks swing around the shoulders of the purloined tunic. "I'm fine. But I'm not going anywhere without *that*."

Both jailers were unarmed. The only readily available weapons in view were the several torture rods, basically pokers, stuck in the brazier. Donning the heavy gauntlet hung on a peg near the brazier, Brigid chose the long longest, which was perhaps thirty inches long. Its tip glowed yellow.

"I'm ready," Brigid announced grimly.

Chrissie led off through what appeared to be catacombs beneath the sprawling palace complex. "I was a terrible tomboy as a little girl," she said. "I loved to explore strange and mysterious places. I never really got over it—never grew up, really, I suppose. But it's stood me in good stead."

Brigid rolled her eyes toward Domi. She clung to the smaller women's shoulders for support. Her legs felt rubbery and uncertain still. Domi grinned back.

Unless there was some advantage in it, Domi suffered fools probably less readily than anybody at Cerberus, including the irascible Lakesh with his infinite regard for his own genius. But the slight albino girl wasn't rolling her own eyes or making faces at the fugitive noblewoman's rattling on. Obviously she accepted Chrissie as a comrade.

The woman just saved me from what at the least would be painful degradation, if not being tortured to death, Brigid told herself. She just took a life to save all our lives. If she runs on a bit nervously, so what, basically? Brigid realized she needed to readjust her preconceptions about the young brunette. Again.

They weren't the only prejudices that needed realignment, she decided. Although the hot poker still clutched determinedly in her left hand endangered Domi's leg, the albino didn't flinch or complain. Almost despite herself, Brigid felt a swelling sense of comradeship for the small, fierce, ruthless—but endlessly loyal and resourceful—young woman. Despite their differences, Domi had risked all to rescue her.

"We're coming up to where we left some good lads on

guard," Chrissie was saying. "Domi suggested we go by ourselves—she thought they were more likely to attract attention than the two of us alone...."

The door that confronted them at the end of the round-roofed corridor seemed distinctly out of place for a faux-medieval dungeon: it was steel, with a metal wheel to open it and an obvious gasket sealing it. Leaving Brigid momentarily to lean upon Domi, Chrissie moved forward to open it.

The sulfurous smell that rolled out over them left no doubt what they'd found. "Main sewer junction for the whole damn palace," Domi said. "Makes a great highway if you aren't too picky."

Domi couldn't keep a tinge of relish out of her voice: she knew full well that Brigid had a wide squeamish streak. Although she also knew the erstwhile senior archivist never let it slow her down.

Brigid resolved not to give her the satisfaction of so much as pinching her own aristocratic nostrils. "Where are you taking me?" she asked.

"Home," Domi said.

Brigid looked at her with shock like a ripple of cold passing through her body. "Domi, we can never *go* home. Our interphaser won't work here. You know that."

Domi shrugged and grinned a private grin. One thing that hadn't changed was her boundless capacity to be infuriating.

"More directly," Chrissie said, resuming her place helping Brigid keep her feet, "our destination is Nigel's laboratory."

Turning sideways, they worked their way through, Domi first, Chrissie last. "Once we get there, who knows what might happen?" Chrissie said.

"I shouldn't make plans yet," a female voice said.

They straightened. About ten yards ahead of them the corridor opened into a space that looked blindingly lit after the tunnel gloom. There was a great noise of rushing water and potent stench. It was, as Domi said, the confluence of sewers from beneath the palace.

In front of it all stood Queen Fiona I in full Hussar's uniform, bareheaded, with a saber in her hand.

Chapter 29

The Aero-Dreadnought *Liberty's Lady* shuddered like a dying horse as a salvo exploded in her guts. Kane grabbed a guy line stretched taut between the deck and the envelope overhead. In his other hand he held a handblaster.

"Why don't they finish us?" he shouted.

A Reptoid airship hung like an elongated moon hard to their starboard, trading body blows with the *Lady*. Crouching behind the rail popping shots at its distant deck with his own automatic revolvers, Rodríguez-Satterfield called, "Don't you see? They're trying to force us down."

He clicked his eyes upward to their own gas bag. Its envelope was shredded, several of its *ballonets* sagged noticeably, holed beyond their ability to seal themselves. One had collapsed entirely to lie pooled in the bottom of the envelope, with bits of its tough slate-gray fabric bulging down through rents in the envelope.

"It's working," Kane said. "What now?"

A boy in Cíbolan uniform with a pillbox cap held under his chin by a strap appeared beside them and braced to attention. "Captain Martin's compliments, sirs, and he regrets to inform you that our ship cannot keep the sky much longer." Tears swam in his green eyes, and his chin quivered within its black leather strap.

Rodríguez-Satterfield glanced at Kane. "Colonel Rodríguez-Satterfield's and Major Kane's compliments to the captain, and please tell him that if he gets us down within the palace grounds he's done his job. But we have to make it there!"

"Sir!" The boy saluted and dashed off for the nearest windbreak hatch-shield. His assignment was fairly safe, the Reptoids were scrupulously keeping their fire away from the *Lady*'s weather deck. Kane didn't like the implications.

"Can he do it?" he asked.

"If it's humanly possible," Rodríguez-Satterfield said, unwrapping a fresh cigar. Kane declined his offer of one; he was so wound up tobacco would make him puke for sure. "And even if it's not, we've got a shot. Martin didn't win this command in a raffle. He's the best airship driver we have, with balls of brass." He rapped his knuckles on the railing for emphasis.

"Why we hired him. What about your friend?"

"I don't know," Kane said. "It's hard to imagine him working for those lizards." Almost as hard as imagining him alive.

Rodríguez-Satterfield looked out toward the enemy vessel. "They say the Reptoids have special techniques to take control of a man's will," he said. "It could be your friend's mind is not his own."

"That's hard to imagine, too."

"But if they brought him back from the dead, as from

your account they must, who can say? He may have been, in effect, reborn."

Kane grunted.

The Reptoid Aero-Dreadnought's envelope abruptly released a cloud of fliers like spores from its top. The *Lady*'s much diminished air escort swooped down on them firing furiously with Gatlings and rockets, to be engaged by air-defense quick firers mounted atop the gas bag. The Reptoid craft, Kane quickly saw, were all of the electric-engined pusher variety.

"So that's their game," Rodríguez-Satterfield said, tipping his cheroot skyward between his teeth. "They're looking to board us. And isn't that your friend, there, piloting the lead airplane?"

"I STILL DON'T SEE why you have to do this?" Zirak shouted. Squeezed between Grant's broad black-clad back and the motor as he was, the thin mosquito whine of the engine was actually a substantial growl to his ears.

"You want Brigid," Grant shouted back. He didn't turn away from the task of piloting the unfamiliar aircraft. Despite never having seen the controls of a Reptoid electric ultralight, much less checked out on one, Grant contemptuously dismissed the notion there was *any* fixed-wing aircraft he couldn't fly, much less one so rudimentary in design. Zirak, whose People possessed attack helicopters of their own even though no one had been able to design one that would function on this wretched ball of mud, knew enough about the difficulties of flying rotary-wing aircraft to agree. But it was intellectual agreement only, his guts were knotted into literal pain with the conviction they were about to plunge to their deaths.

Nothing about this planet and its cursed energy discontinuity banned employment of the modular swap-in/swap-out design philosophy the Race had brought with them from Beta Coma Berenices. Zirak insisted on going wherever his prize primate did, even in total defiance of his own inclination and better judgment. Techs had accordingly been able to hastily yank the Gatling from Grant's machine and slide the pilot's seat forward on rails to allow a pad-seat to be improvised between it and the motor mount. The controls had been quickly adjusted and the machine became airworthy for carrying both beings. Allegedly.

"Kane will find her for us," Grant yelled. "Why else do you think he's here?"

A burst of gunfire shredded the aircraft's high-mounted wing. Zirak shouted as it plunged....

Its landing skids glanced off the Cíbolan Aero-Dreadnought's railing. It struck on the deck, skidding across it amid a shower of sparks from steel rivet heads, slewing counterclockwise.

Before it had stopped against a hatch shield Grant was out of the pilot's seat, twin autopistols in his hands. Another hatch flipped open nearby. A Cíbolan militiaman started to emerge, fixing a bayonet on the end of his carbine. Grant blasted him with both weapons. The man threw up his hands and fell back down the hatchway.

Zirak crawled from the wreckage to find the deck alive with battling figures.

KANE AND RODRÍGUEZ-SATTERFIELD hurled themselves opposite ways as Grant's flier swept over the rail, clipped it and went scraping away across the deck.

A dozen or more other aircraft were in process of landing on the *Lady*'s weather deck with varying degrees of success as Kane picked himself up. Jarring impacts vibrated up through his boot soles as others, slammed into the armored hull.

Beneath him, *Liberty's Lady* was dying by degrees. Smoke, steam and unidentifiable vapors streamed out every hatch and shell hole and even seemed to seep through seams in the decking. The deck was tilted downward at what Kane, who had a combat aviator's precise feel for such things, judged at no less than ten degrees. The gondola was also heeled over several degrees to port. With the wood underfoot running with freezing rain, machine oil and blood, the footing was unbelievably treacherous.

Through shifting gray vapor curtains a hunched shape appeared. Its stocky forward-tilted body was encased in blouse and short trunks of a pattern of white mottled with gray and black. Kane felt a stab almost of homesickness: it was obvious urban camou, like something from his Earth, incongruous after weeks surrounded by people who seemed to live their lives and fight their battles in fancy dress.

He didn't have long to savor it, nor his first close-up look at the dinosaurid aliens. The Reptoid commando held a stubby two-hand blaster in his taloned but startlingly human-looking hands. When he saw Kane he pointed it in his direction and opened up, with a full-auto burst.

Kane dived behind an armored ammo bin built by the rail, belonging to an uncrewed Gatling. He landed on one of its erstwhile operators, sprawled gracelessly against the base of the bin minus his head.

The existence of fully automatic weapons went against everything Kane knew about this world's tech. Then he recalled a conversation in the great Rodríguez-Satterfield manor house in which Ned Barker and Henry Purcell discussed recent intel that claimed the Reptoids were meeting success in overcoming the fouling problem inherent in black-powder weapons. The development of true semi-automatic firearms was an obvious first stage for such a breakthrough. But true machine guns, full-on automatic weps, wouldn't be far behind, as Reptoids, had already developed that technology centuries before, out beyond the Great Discontinuity.

Given the leaky-sieve security prevalent on this world, even though the lizards' was apparently better than anyone else's, functioning machine pistols had to be spanking new tech. Which meant—

Elite lizard commando or not, the alien fired himself dry as quick as his blaster action would cycle, slamming copper-washed lead slugs into the steel box behind which Kane sheltered and leaving smears of silver and orange, but not even denting the metal. As soon as the jackhammer clamor ceased, Kane popped up like a prairie dog on the Rodríguez-Satterfield spread, throwing his right arm out to full extension just as he had been trained to deploy his Sin Eater. And even though it was no Sin Eater, and had but iron combat sights instead of a laser-pointer assist, the Taliaferro automatic revolver was a fine blaster, not a milligram less deadly than the Mag's constant companion.

Kane's emergence had caught the Reptoid trooper just as Kane expected: fumbling as he tried to reload with a still unfamiliar box magazine under battle stress, gobbling to himself in a snarling guttural language.

Kane didn't even need the flash sight picture he caught to slam two quick .50-cal slugs into the flat plate of the creature's lowered forehead. The Reptoid dropped like a poleaxed steer.

More Reptoids charged from the smog, blazing enthusiastically from the hip with their novelty chatterguns. Even the Cíbolans, who suffered no self-esteem problems that Kane had been able to spot and were no slouches as warriors themselves, admitted freely that lizard for man, the common Reptoid soldiers were the planet's most proficient. Only their extreme rarity had kept them from overrunning the planet already. But the new technology had shot fire discipline all to hell. And as Kane's firearms instructors had told him back in the Cobaltville firing ranges, you can't miss fast enough to catch up.

With bullets whanging off the ammo bin and moaning like demons as they tumbled away, Kane picked his shots and dropped three Reptoids in succession with three quick bullets. One thing about these Neolithic handblasters: when one of their outsized slugs hit you square, you went down.

In exchange a bullet pierced Kane's black leather great-coat and glanced off the ribs on his right just above the level of his navel. The hit probably would not have pene-trated even without his shadow armor, especially given the low velocities of this Earth's slugs. But the shadow suit fabric flexed. He took a hammerblow and the impact site immediately began to smart like a wasp sting. He cursed, figuring he'd cracked a rib.

Elite alien death commandos or not, the Reptoids re-coiled from his murderously effective counterfire. More yellow flashes probed through the smoke; the Reptoids were trying recon by fire.

Kane lit off his last two cartridges at the flames, thought he heard at least one hoarse cry in response. It was hard to tell for all the screaming and shooting going on around him. Evidently the fliers Grant had led across were just the first wave.

As Rodríguez-Satterfield had reminded Kane in Assini-boina, the reason Cíbolans carried two handblasters was not to indulge in two-gun bullet-spraying antics like a character from a twentieth century John Woo vid. Simply put, the quickest reload of all is a second blaster. But Kane wasn't the only one with enough combat sense to wait until a foe had fired himself dry. Knowing most human handblasters carried six shots at most—and given the huge bores, many cylinders held only five—the Reptoids had counted Kane's shots right back. They rushed him before he even had chance to draw his second piece, firing and shouting.

He knew at once he was facing more than six attack-

ers. He threw down his empty piece and flung himself at
the brass aiming bar at the rear of the unmanned Gatling.
He caught it with both hands as his leap carried him over
the bullet-torn brass rail and inertia swung him out above
empty white space.

Finely counterbalanced, the Gatling swung easily on its
bearings. He stopped his clockwise progress with a left
boot planted against the steel plate of the gondola's hull.
Then, bracing both feet, he clung like a monkey to the bar
with one hand and worked the crank with the other.

The charging Reptoids fell like bowling pins as the
heavy bullets pounded into them.

He kept cranking for all he was worth until no living
enemies remained in sight. Though Kane's training kept
him at a degree of fitness like a professional athlete's, his
right shoulder and elbow had quickly started hurting from
the unfamiliar exercise. He held his fire just as a lone figure materialized out of the smoke and fog. Tall, unmistakably human, with a black greatcoat like Kane's hanging
from broad shoulders. A coat reminiscent of nothing so
much as a Magistrate's greatcoat.

It was Grant. The Gatling was aimed at his powerful
chest, but Kane had stopped turning the handle. The barrels continued to freewheel with a metallic hum.

There was no time for even an abbreviated greeting.

"Brace yourself," Grant shouted, and pointed to the
rapidly approaching ground, indistinct amid the smoke of
battle below them.

Chapter 30

"I thought I detected a whiff of foulness about you, cousin," Queen Fiona said to a white-faced Chrissie Battersea. "It turned out to be treason—and something more, shall we say tangible, as well. You forget, it would seem, who pays the servants who handled the clothes you discarded after your jaunts through the sewers, my dear."

Weariness landed on Brigid like a crushing weight. The weariness of despair, of hopes raised and hopes crushed. It all comes to…this?

She realized the light silhouetting Fiona's wiry but highly feminine form was mostly natural, sunlight leached to white pallor by the overcast. She had the sense of an atrium behind the youthful monarch, a sort of Gothic vaulted space. Apparently it rose upward to a skylight at ground level and beyond; she guessed at stairs from above, for maintenance access. And who knew what Gothic purpose had been in the minds of the Palace's builders, who included in their design such pulp-novel touches as catacombs and subterranean torture chambers?

Directly behind Fiona streams of sewage converged from three great openings to pour into a great circular hole with a rushing roar. Below evidently lay the sewer proper, conducting the gathered waste water away from the Palace.

Brigid glimpsed at least two figures lying on the flagstones in the utter stillness of death. "So much for Frank and Eric," Domi said under her breath.

Four soldiers appeared to stand flank their monarch in pairs: not gilded-cock palace guardsmen, but Hussars in red coats and pink pants like Fiona's. Unlike her they wore light steel breastplates. They held carbines leveled at the trio of women with bayonets fixed, but covered with brass scabbards.

"Take them alive," Fiona commanded, "and unmarked. The public—and protracted—traitor's deaths suffered by my treacherous cousin and the notorious White Rose of Anarchy will be highly edifying to my people, as well as most entertaining."

"On my world they called that 'edutainment,'" Brigid said.

"Such mistreatment of language!" Fiona said with a smile. "And I'll warrant you thought my torture chamber barbaric. You'll notice I did not actually apply pain. I merely wanted to help you focus your recollections more crisply, as it were."

"I notice you maintain a torture chamber, Your Majesty," Brigid said, voice rising as if borne upward on the anger welling inside her. She stalked forward. She felt the knuckles of the hand holding the now cooled poker threaten to burst through the skin with the tightness of her grip. "With braziers and coals and hot irons and all. And you didn't scruple to subject me—a fellow woman—to brutal degradation in the presence of men, and the threat of obscene abuse and agony!"

She was almost shouting now—and midway between Fiona and her own friends, who stood staring open-mouthed at her outburst. The Cherrypickers stepped forward, menacing with their carbines.

Fiona restrained them with a languidly raised white hand. "My privilege, gentlemen. You have your tasks—see to them."

They trotted past Brigid, a pair to either side. She ignored them. Her attention was focused upon the queen.

"I feel angry, *Majesty*," Brigid spit. "I feel violated. And what I really feel moved to do right now, Queen Fiona, is shove this poker straight up your ass!"

That shocked the unflappable young queen. Doubtless no one had ever even conceived of speaking such words to her. Far less had she even conceived anyone might say them. Her face went white, her muscles slackened in surprise.

Screaming like a banshee, Brigid raised her poker and charged. Face snapping into a fighter's fixed grin, Fiona rushed to meet her, swinging her saber overhand. Steel met steel in a scream of sparks.

As BRIGID ENGAGED Queen Fiona, the four Hussars closed up and entered the narrow passageway behind her. Shoulder to shoulder they advanced, capped bayonets held at waist level.

Chrissie raised her crossbow and loosed a bolt at one Hussar's face. He ducked his head to the side. The bolt missed.

She slumped in disappointment. He smiled. He was a young man with extravagant side whiskers. "Give up now, Your Worship. Make it easy on yourself."

From her boot she drew a dagger with a straight tapered blade. "I won't! I'm through with running, and I'll never surrender."

The Cherrypicker glanced at the companion to his left, who had black hair and mustache. "Have it your way."

Domi menaced the soldiers with her knife with the serrated back. "Interesting toad sticker you got there, miss," a third said. "Hand it over now, nice and easy."

Her ruby eyes narrowed. She looked at the soldiers, now quite near. She looked at the taller, dark-haired woman to her side.

She backed up two quick steps. Before her companion could react she took a short run and flung herself at Chrissie's back. Larger though she was, Chrissie was propelled right between the two soldiers on the women's left. As taken by surprise as she was, neither Hussar managed to jab her with a sheathed bayonet. Flailing for balance, she flung her arms about the waist of the one to her right. Off balance, he staggered back.

Chrissie's legs had fouled those of the man to her left, nearest the wall. He fell against it. He let go his rifle with his right hand to brace himself.

Domi sprang. With her right hand she grabbed the rifle by the wooden forestock. With the knife in her left she slashed the hand with which the soldier still clung to his carbine. With a curse he let go. Possibly she had severed tendons, disabling his hand.

She struck at him with the butt. Then she swung the butt horizontally against the side of the head of the trooper Chrissie had inadvertently half tackled. He fell down.

The first Hussar had fended Domi's attempt to club him with his own carbine, which in any event had been relatively weak. With a wild laugh of triumph he grabbed her and hugged her close against his breastplate.

She brought up her left hand and, almost slowly, cut his throat.

His blood splashed her face and snowy blouse. He released her to clap his hands to his spurting neck. He sank to his knees.

Chrissie had assumed a creditable mount position astride the supine second Hussar and was pounding him in the face with the pommel of her dagger. The other two soldiers, appalled, stood back.

Then, as one, they racked the actions of their carbines, each chambering a round.

Chapter 31

Almost as soon as she crossed her black iron poker with the queen's saber, Brigid realized the younger woman, though shorter and more lightly built than she was, possessed substantial wiry strength.

But her rage, still erupting, paid no attention to the thoughts that skittered through a detached segment of her mind, nor to the accompanying pang of self-doubt. Something primal had awakened within her. It would not go back to sleep until it had destroyed or been destroyed.

"You have strength unlooked-for in one so studious," Fiona said. Her voice was clearly strained.

But she pushed, and Brigid staggered back three steps on her bare feet. Fiona performed a moulinet with her curved blade and brought it to the guard position. "But do you really think you can best me?"

Brigid didn't answer. Her breath already came raggedly, whether from passion or incipient exhaustion. She held the poker out before her warily and began circling, instinctively moving away from Fiona's sword arm.

"I'd love to play with you, Dr. Baptiste," Fiona said, "but there simply isn't time. I've battles to win, a rebellion to crush. Your little albino friend has done me a service, leading her ragtag band up out of the sewers where I can catch them and exterminate them like the rats they are."

"Don't underestimate her," Brigid said, "either."

Fiona thrust for Brigid's face. Brigid seized her poker in both hands and brought it up almost vertical before her. The thrust was a feint; Fiona rolled her wrist and cut diagonally across her own body at Brigid's bare left thigh. But Brigid was skipping back as she blocked. The tip drew a line of scarlet transversely above the knee.

Brigid glanced down to see a line of tiny red mounds growing, stark against her pale skin. "Not such a lark when you see your own blood, is it?" Fiona asked.

"I've seen it before," Brigid said grimly. "You ever seen yours?"

Fiona came on, slashing forehanded and backhanded, high and low. Brigid kept clutching the poker two-handed and kept it near the centerline of her body.

She lacked skill, whereas her royal opponent was clearly accomplished. But she was strong, had fast reflexes and was well motivated. Also she had long since learned to keep her wits about her in a fight. She felt neither apprehensive nor angry, but elevated, her mind working with clarity uncommon even for her.

But just because she wasn't engulfed by the expanding bubble of her rage didn't mean it was gone. She could not have said she was truly in control of it, but rather rode the fury like a surfer on a tsunami.

Fiona's flashing saber opened a half-dozen cuts and took off the left epaulette of the tunic Brigid had appropriated as her sole garment. At the same time the queen pressed her backward until her shoulders came up hard against cool damp stone.

Fiona paused. She was breathing hard now. Brigid felt her energy, sapped by the incredible stress of combat as much as exertion, seeping away through her superficial but persistent wounds.

"And now," Fiona said with a mocking smile, "time to finish this. And then to deal with your faithless friend, Dr. Miles-Burnham."

The rage blew. Brigid let it. Only instead of giving into it, she made it *propel* her.

Straight at Fiona. Screaming again, oblivious even to shots echoing from somewhere behind her, she charged, hacking with all her substantial strength and weight with her poker. The sheer force of Brigid's fury drove Fiona back. For all her skill and youthful strength, it was all the queen could do to keep her blade interposed between her bones and that cold black iron—and to keep her guard from being beaten down by Brigid's manic strength.

Closer to the yawning pit of sewage she backed. At the last instant, instead of trying to recover her saber for a strike or even another parry, she dug her boot heels in, threw herself forward and clipped Brigid on the jaw with her saber's bell handguard.

Brigid reeled. Red lightning laced blackness that suddenly swam behind her eyes. Her arms drooped; the poker felt as if it had turned to pure neutronium from the heart of a collapsed star. Its head fell to the slimy pavement.

"And now," the queen said, gloating with that odious

V-shaped smile, "I think you can answer my questions quite well with both arms off."

She raised the saber.

Brigid seized the poker halfway along its length with her right hand. Still holding the grip in her left, she threw herself forward, more falling than charging. But she got a bare foot planted, and driving with the last strength of her legs, propelled the head of the poker through stiff scarlet fabric and deep into Fiona's flat belly.

Fiona gasped and bent double. Her saber clattered on stone. When she raised her head to look at Brigid, there was neither fear nor pain in her eyes but astonished outrage.

This wasn't supposed to happen to the queen, who was meant to rule Earth.

Fiona's mouth opened, a red wound in her paper-white face. "You—" she said accusingly. A line of blood trailed from her mouth like drool.

"I," Brigid said, "send you to seek your own level."

She kicked the queen in the face. Fiona the First fell backward into the pit with the poker still buried in her stomach. A beat later, Brigid heard a splash over the roar of the mingling sewage streams.

Footsteps clocked behind. Unarmed and utterly spent, Brigid made herself stand erect and square her shoulders before turning to meet her fate.

THE PROTRACTED IMPACT hurled Kane tumbling toward the *Lady*'s bow. The great airship still had forward momentum; its armored gondola now scraped the ground, shrieking like a dying Titan. Kane fetched up against an air tube sticking up hard by the prow, clung to it.

The bow struck a high wall of gleaming white stone. Its mass smashed right through. But riding up and over the remnants of the wall braked it. Kane was flipped forward over the rail.

Something caught his right wrist. His arm wrenched in the socket. His face slammed against the wet armor plate below the gunwales.

Beneath him the gondola raised a wave of sparks as it skidded over pavement. Had Kane fallen—if he fell now—he would instantly be ground to maroon paste beneath its steel-shod mass. He looked up.

Grant bent over the rail, hanging on to his wrist with an unbreakable grip.

With a grunt of exertion he hauled Kane up over the rail and onto the deck. "Thanks," Kane said. "I think."

"Later. If we get out of this—"

The gondola began to slew sideways. As it did it heeled over to starboard. Grant and Kane raced up the steepening deck for the port side rail. They managed to heave themselves over as the gondola went all the way onto her starboard side with a slam of impact and an even louder grinding screech.

The careening mass slowed. Stopped. Snow fell. So did a great silence.

For a moment Kane and Grant lay side by side on what had been the hull of the great Aero-Dreadnought. A gun port yawned open nearby. A few tongues of yellow flame licked out of it.

Hearing returned. There was creaking and pinging as the vast mass of metal settled into buckled concrete, a hissing of steam venting from ruptured boilers, the crackle of flames. And gunfire, shouts and screams.

Kane looked around. The gondola had come to rest in the midst of a vast expanse, alternating pavement with park: grass, mostly colorless under slushy snow, trees with leaves starting to color and go dry, but mostly damp and dark from the sleet. "We're actually on the palace grounds. Or if it's not the palace, they got some really huge yards in this ville."

Grant and Kane stood up. Off to their right rose an unlikely fairyland castle, with mock-medieval spires and turrets and crenellated walls. It was partly masked by yet another curtain of smoke, whether from large fires or just the usual smoke-screens automatically generated by this world's black-powder firefights, Kane had no idea.

Certainly there was a lot of running, hollering and shooting going on. Kane glimpsed cavalrymen in potlike breastplates chasing men in ragged civilian clothes near what they took for the palace itself. Off to the right camou-clad Reptoid commandos skirmished with humans in outlandish uniforms of white and gold.

"Can't tell the players without a program," Kane said, leaning forward with hands on thighs to suck wind. "Speaking of which—what side are you on, partner?"

"What side do you think? I saved your ass."

Kane squinted at him. "Why were you fighting with the lizard boys, then?"

"Wouldn't give me a ticket here without it."

"What about all that brainwashing stuff I heard?"

Grant laughed mirthlessly. "They tried. Lord, did they try. Pretty piss-poor stuff, though."

"What the hell did you tell them?"

"That I'd do anything to get Brigid."

"They didn't ask if you meant to let them have her afterward?"

"Reptoids are pretty much like humans, Kane," Grant said, "though they pretend real hard to themselves they're totally different. They mostly believe what they want to, same as us."

"Yeah."

"Now we better move," Grant said, "before that shit falls on our heads."

Kane looked back and up. The synthetic-silk envelope containing the Aero-Dreadnought's *ballonets* was fire resistant but not fire-proof. Not only was it sagging seriously, settling toward the wreck of its gondola as the last of the helium leaked out of the often violated miniballoons, but the envelope itself had started to burn with a smoky blue flame. It was beginning to drip in places like dragon drool.

"Yeah."

They started to trot toward the palace. As they passed the bow of the capsized gondola a voice called, "Kane."

INSTEAD OF two dead allies and four angry Hussars, Brigid saw Domi, dancing over four fallen soldiers, pumping her fist in the air. The fist in question held a squat snubnosed revolver. "Chilled *you*."

"But if you had a side arm all along," asked Chrissie, standing up off one of the bodies and looking distinctly ill, "why didn't you use it before?"

"Didn't want them to start shooting," Domi said, tucking away the blaster. "More of them than us."

Brigid found herself running to her. They embraced quickly, fervently.

"Thank you," Brigid said huskily.

"Yeah, just remember it next time I start to piss you off," Domi said.

Chrissie had composed herself. "Come with me, please, Dr. Baptiste. I'll take you to Dr. Nigel."

"What about you, Domi?" Brigid asked.

"Need to find the boys," she said, "before they get in too much trouble."

Before it occurred to the still dazed Brigid to ask what she meant by *boys*, plural, the tiny albino woman had scampered halfway up the stairs to what passed for daylight.

THE CRY WAS FEEBLE but familiar, and snapped Kane's head around.

Colonel Randall Rodríguez-Satterfield lay on the ground by the *Lady*'s rail. Or the upper half of him did. The lower part was hidden in a crumple of metal ruin where one of the big stanchions that held the main cables that attached gondola to envelope had folded on him. By the quantity of blood in the mud beneath the visible part of him, he wouldn't last long even if he could be extricated.

"I'm done for," he said matter-of-factly. He thrust his left arm into the puddle to drown with a hiss the flames that had sprung up where a drop of quasinapalm had fallen on his sleeve from the flaming envelope, now settling inexorably toward him. "I got a question for you, Kane."

Kane didn't look up at the burning gas bag. "Ask."

"You never cared about us getting your lady friend, did you? You intended to take her and your friend here back to your home world all along if you possibly could, no?"

"That's right, amigo," Kane said.

Rodríguez-Satterfield grinned. "I forgive you, amigo. Under the circumstances, I'd've done as much. Like to think so, anyway."

He grimaced but quickly recovered, although his normal dark complexion had gone ashen. "Whole...point of this expedition was to keep what she knows from being used by the damned Canadians—or the lizards. If that happens it was worth everything—the money, the ships, the lives. Mine, too."

"What about your family? Didn't they mortgage your ancestral estate to help finance the expedition?"

"They'll be fine. They knew the score. Tía Cecilia always does. Drop her naked on an ice floe, inside the year she'd own the Arctic, fee simple, charge the Eskimo usage fees for ice and snow. Before we ever left, she sewed up exclusive contracts for the rights to the story of our mad and brave endeavor, whatever the outcome. And our family spies will ensure that enough of the tale gets home to make it a global best-seller. I've a cousin down the Rio Grande in New Mexico, a man not young, yet whose verve and vigor of prose has won him some small repute. He'll know what to do with our story."

A blazing rain fell steadily about them now, with a reek like burning plastic. "This must be the estimable Grant," the dying man said. "Congratulations on your… survival."

He rolled his eyes upwards to the flaming envelope. "Now you two better shift out of here before that all comes down on us. But if I might beg a favor or two?"

"He's right, Kane," Grant said. "We better go or we're gonna get buried and cremated all at once here."

"Ask," Kane said.

"First, get a cigar our of my inner coat pocket, put it in my mouth and give me a light. Second, if I might, ah, borrow a pistol."

Kane knelt and complied with the first wish, unwrapping a cheroot and placing it gently between the colonel's bloodless lips. He picked up a shard of metal with a blob of burning synthetic on the end to light the cigar.

"You're down to one handblaster," Grant said to Kane. He proffered his left-hand autopistol. "Use mine."

"Much…obliged, Grant," Rodríguez-Satterfield said, accepting the blaster from Kane. "A new radical design, I see…a true autoloading pistol. I hope our spies will get word of the design back home.

"And now—*vayan con Dios*—and haul ass outta here!"

They complied. As they raced away the gas bag, now fully involved in flame, draped itself over the wreckage with a final giant whoosh. Over the dragon sigh they heard a single gunshot.

"Good man," Kane said. He didn't look back.

"They're always first to go down."

"So what's the verdict?"

Grant stopped and held out a hand. "Guess I won't retire for a while, anyway."

Kane shook in forearm to forearm grasp, disregarding the heat from the inferno now roaring where the gondola lay. "First we better see about getting home."

"At least getting Brigid," Grant said, "and the hell outta here. Especially before the magazines blow."

They trotted toward the palace. No one paid them particular attention. A pair of unattached men weren't worth paying attention to, it seemed. Kane saw redcoats fighting with whitecoats off by what looked like some blown-in iron gates a good half klick away. "Who are they?"

"Who knows?" Grant said. "What Ishmael said, half the world was headed to this party."

"Ishmael?"

"What the lizard who handled me wanted me to call him. I think he was a human wanna-be at core."

"What happened to him?"

Grant shrugged.

"Now," Kane said, "all we got to do is figure out where in that fairyland nightmare of a castle Baptiste is. Then how the hell to get back home."

"I think we're stuck here for good, Kane. Little tough to power a Mat-trans on steam."

Kane shrugged. "We're still alive, we got a chance."

"Classic one-percenter," Grant said.

Kane tipped a forefinger off an eyebrow. "You got it."

"*Grant!*" A small shape darted from a smoke wall and struck the big man amidships before even his catlike reflexes could respond.

Chapter 32

Grant looked down at a head of tousled white hair. "Domi?"

"Oh, Grant, I'm so happy to see you. I thought you were dead." the small pale woman said.

"So did I, for a while," Grant said, peeling her off.

"Where's Baptiste?" Kane asked.

"She's gone ahead to the lab," Domi said. "She left me here to look for Kane."

"You knew I was coming?"

She shrugged. "I always figured if you were alive, you'd be coming for Brigid. Never thought you'd make it quite so spectacular."

"How'd you know he'd be right here, right now?" Grant queried.

"Because Nige told us," she said.

WHEN BRIGID and Chrissie emerged from the ladder leading up through a hole in a back room of the warehouse laboratory, Norman awaited them with a great zinc tub of steaming water and towels.

"If the young ladies would care to refresh themselves," he said, unpeturbed neither by Brigid's near nakedness nor the reek streaming off them like heat from a coal-burning stove.

Brigid accepted the offer gratefully, and Norman discreetly withdrew. Chrissie, to Brigid's surprise, deferred to her.

Brigid dropped her befouled tunic down the hole before closing it up, then scrubbed herself off as best she could using soap and brushes left for the purpose. She dressed in some comfortably shabby but clean men's clothes that Norman had also set out and emerged into the warehouse as Chrissie took her turn in the tub.

Miles-Burnham stood in the midst of the floor gazing up at the slowly turning clockworks of his great mechanism. He wore a stained shop apron. His heavy wavy auburn hair was tied back. He held a stopwatch in one hand and a notebook in the other. He would frown from one to the other, look up at the turning gears and the great swooping dials they drove, cycled through again.

He noticed her, smiled an abstracted smile and nodded. "Dearest Brigid. I'm ever so pleased you were able to make it." He grinned. "Although I admit I was fairly certain you would."

"You've had another of your visions?"

He nodded. "Oh, yes. I have seen many things from the lightning path. The convergence of dark champions, your rescue and return, unlooked-for reunions. Also the possible threat of an evil star falling from the heavens. There are many things still cloudy to me, too many...."

His words trailed off and he frowned at his notebook. Brigid approached a few steps. She hated to break in upon his thoughts, but the fact was, the situation was urgent.

"What's going on?" she asked. "Why did you have Chrissie bring me here? I don't mind that it's danger-ous—it's nothing compared to what she and Domi pulled me out of—but we should all be packing to flee. The lo-cation of this lab is no great secret. Sooner or later, espe-cially when they don't find me at the palace, someone will come here looking for your chimerical Apocalyptic En-gine everyone's so afraid of."

He looked at her with his head tipped to the side like a curious pup, hazel eyes large. Then he burst into uproar-ious laughter. "Ah, dear child, there's nothing chimerical about my Apocalyptic Engine at all. Look up, dear girl—it's all about you!"

"WHAT THE FUCK," Kane said, "is that?"

The unlikely object was blocking their arrival at Miles-Burnham's laboratory. It was a two-story monstrosity in the shape of an Indian elephant. Its tusks were cannon and its trunk a flamethrower. A stack jutted from its back, belching black smoke into a gap in the swirling snow cre-ated by the heat it emitted.

"Looks to me," Grant said, "like a giant metal elephant with a smokestack sticking out of its back."

"That's what I was afraid you'd say."

All around it lean brown men in turbans and loincloths hunkered down. Some of them fired bolt-action longblast-ers from doorways, and behind carts and crates at redcoat infantry crouched behind similarly improvised barricades of steamcoaches and carriages. At least a hundred Kali worshippers lay strewed dead or dying down the block, attesting both to their mad courage and the folly of attacking repeating blasters in good defensive position. The three extradimensional travelers could see the whole scene because they had paused their mounts atop a low rise behind the Canadian defenders.

Kane, Grant and Domi rode cavalry horses appropriated at the palace. There had been a lot of them available. Attacked from several directions at once, including above and below, the hegemonic defenders were taking heavy casualties. From all Kane knew of the mighty Canadian military, the redcoats would eventually overwhelm the raiders and crush the rising commoners back into the pavement of the Gloriana City. But they were finding it a long, hard slog.

The building Domi pointed out as the lab lay on their right. Even from about a quarter klick off Kane could see it was something of a fortress, stoutly built of yellow brick, with slit windows at the lower levels and narrow pointy-arched ones higher up. A steel plate covered its front door; there must be some relatively easy way for those behind to shift it out of the way, but at this range Kane couldn't see any.

"You sure we can get in?" Kane asked Domi.

"Brigid can be a stiff-necked, self-righteous pain in the ass," Domi said, "but when did you ever know her to let us down?"

"Girl's got you, Kane," Grant said. "Brigid's as hardcore as you are in her own way. Though you'd probably rather die than admit it."

"Yeah. Well how do we get in, then?"

The puzzle of why the steamophant didn't just wade down the street and stamp on the defenders it couldn't torch was answered when a crew of artillery men in dirt-colored tunics wheeled some kind of light howitzer around a corner and blasted off a shot at the leviathan. The shell flashed off harmlessly on the monster's forehead glacis, and the crew barely wheeled the piece back in time—aided by the retro-rocket effect of its recoil—before an answering shell blasted brick dust from a corner of the building where they had been an eye blink before.

"Chinese standoff," Domi said. Both men looked at her. She smiled cryptically.

"There's always the sewers," the albino girl said.

"I been through enough shit the last few weeks to last me a lifetime," Grant said.

Domi shrugged. "Sooner or later the bad guys are going to figure to try the underground route, too. Especially the way my anarchists have been popping out of them today."

"By 'bad guys,' you mean…?" Grant said.

"Everybody but us."

"Right."

"Okay, if the smart, indirect path is closed," Kane said, "there's always stupid but ballsy."

"And there you have it," Domi said brightly.

"DAMN," KANE SAID.

Burning valuable minutes, they had circled around, hoping to bust through the numerous but lightly armed Kali-ites from the rear and hit the doorway before being cut down by the Canadians, who would surely be a lot more concerned with a steam-and-flame-belching metal behemoth two stories tall than three random civilians on horseback. But the Sino-Indians were far more numerous than the three had anticipated, fairly clogging the streets for several blocks behind the standoff before the warehouse. And also they were beset from both sides themselves. From one direction troops in unfamiliar maroon-and-white uniforms were pressing them with bayoneted rifles. From another direction Zulu warriors approached.

"Zulus?" Grant said.

"Their prince tried a commando snatch on Brigid a few nights ago," Domi explained. "They were gonna deport him, so he was cooped up on board the ship that brought him, supposedly getting ready to steam back to Africa. Apparently he decided to try again."

"Jesus," Kane said. "Is anybody on Earth *not* after Baptiste and this Apocalyptic Engine?"

"From off Earth, too," Grant reminded him.

"And you're putting us right at the center of this nuke-blast, Domi?" Kane demanded.

"We're already a moving ground zero ourselves, and we're not getting in this way," she said. "So now what?"

"Obvious," Kane said.

Grant looked at Kane. "You are *not* thinking what I think you're thinking—"

"That's affirmative, big guy." He tipped a finger off a brow. "Just a standard everyday one-percenter. SOP."

"Christ."

"Our only possible road home is through the door of that warehouse," Domi said. "So lead on."

"I don't see how there's any way home for us," Grant said. "But anything's better than being stuck here. Let's ride!"

THE CANADIAN FORCES, composed of First Hegemonic Ontarian Rifles and dismounted troopers from the Duke of New Brunswick's Light Horse, had their attention focused on the monstrous steamophant and the thousand screeching fanatics of its infantry support.

Thus they were taken utterly by surprise when three horses bearing riders in mufti burst through their ranks from behind and charged straight up the block toward the steam beast and those thousand fanatic dagger men.

The steamophant crew, who must have been half-dead from heat exhaustion and entirely deaf from the cracking of their own cannon and the boom of enemy shells off their battered but intact armor, were alert and possessed of rapid reflexes. Suspecting the riders' intent, they sent a jet of flame spewing at the doorway to the contested warehouse/laboratory, barring it with a wall of red-and-blue flames and black smoke.

But the riders rode straight toward the steamophant itself. Instinctively reacting on the principle that the enemy of my enemy is my friend, the Canadians opened up with all they had left, firing wide to either side of the riders in hopes of repelling the half-clad Sino-Indians.

The steamophant fired both its tusk cannon. They knocked chunks of pavement from behind the Cerberus trio. The horses, galloping all-out with foam streaming from their mouths, were already too close for the guns to depress enough to bear. Domi vaulted her mount over an overturned handcart and then they were at the columnlike legs of the mechanical monster.

Barely reining in, they swung off their horses. Now free, the half-panicked creatures stampeded through the barricades, scattering Kali devotees. Grant ran to the steamophant's side and stooped, cupping his powerful hands with fingers interlaced. Kane put a boot in and was boosted up to stand on his partner's wide shoulders. Then Domi swarmed up them both like a white monkey and scaled the sloping back of the monster using welded handholds.

A hatch popped open right behind the skull. A turbaned head emerged. Domi fired a shot from her bulldog revolver into a startled face. It went away.

Down on the street Grant and Kane were blasting away at the befuddled Kali-ites, each man with a blaster in either hand. Neither bothered aiming: for one rare instance brute firepower counted more than accuracy, and anyway, it was a target-rich environment.

Capable of facing overwhelming expected danger with suicidal courage, the Sino-Indians were stone demoralized by this bizarre and utterly unexpected attack. They fled in panic from the pair of men who towered over them in black greatcoats and spewed death from either hand.

Domi grabbed one of the Reptoid frag grenades Grant had provided her from a trouser pocket, yanked out the pin and dropped it down the hatch. A startled cry from within testified that it had bounced off somebody's upturned face. She followed it with a second, then stood up, armed a third and rolled it down the black smokestack. Then she turned and leaped into space, and the three Cerberus raced for the warehouse at full speed.

A weird *crump* sounded from the metal monster behind them. It wasn't loud so much as it was big, like God slamming the door to the solar system, out beyond the orbit of Planet X. The smokestack shot straight up into the air like a skyrocket, and the armor-crystal eyes, one broken, one still unmarked by bullet or shell, blew out on jets of yellow-white flame.

White steam vented out the monster's back. Liquid fire poured from its empty eye sockets like tears. Somehow the steamophant held together as secondary explosions rumbled and cracked within, though smoke and steam and fire streamed through a hundred seams of armor plate or joints.

The flames had mostly died away from in front of the warehouse door when the three hit it at a dead run. The Canadians were all standing and cheering and throwing their pith helmets in the air at the destruction of their terrifying foe. By the time it occurred to them that their duty might be as much to prevent the three plucky interlopers from reaching the laboratory of Dr. Nigel Miles-Burnham as keeping the Sino-Indians away from it, the metal plate had slid aside just far enough to admit them, then slid shut again with a final ringing clang.

Chapter 33

"Welcome," said a tall, cadaverous man with sweeping grey mustache and side-whiskers and a patch over one eye. "Lady. Gentlemen."

"Thanks, Norman." Domi stood on tiptoe to kiss him on the cheek.

"My pleasure, Mistress Domi," the butler said.

Initially the interior seemed dark even after daylight filtered through clouds and a pall of brown smoke that overlay the entire city. Then the three passed through into the main structure, which seemed to blaze with light.

"What *is* this?" Kane asked, stopping to stare in amazement at the giant clockworks turning above his head.

"Looks like the insides of a giant clock," Grant said.

"Or a model of the solar system," Kane said.

"Very perceptive, my friends," said a short, spare man with a stained apron and red-brown hair tied back at his nape. "It *is* that, and more—a model, after a fashion, of the multiverse itself."

"The multiverse?" Kane said.

"*A* multiverse, actually," the man said in his precise English accent. He managed not to make it sound stuffy. "The one most readily accessible to us—as in, to the people of your continuum, as well as ours. There are actually an infinite number of them, as of universes within them—a transfinity, as it were."

"You lost me already, mister," Grant said.

The man laughed. "I'm Miles-Burnham. Professor Nigel, to be stuffy about it. Please don't be."

Someone stepped up behind him. "Kane," said Brigid in a muted voice. "Grant."

"You don't seem surprised to see him alive," Kane said.

The woman nodded at the scientist. "Nigel told me he was."

Grant raised a brow at Kane, who shrugged.

"What is all this, Baptiste?" Kane asked.

"I'm glad to see you, too, Kane."

"Yeah, well, we can do joyous reunions once we don't have the whole world about to land on our necks. What the hell's going on?"

"Don't you see, Kane? It's the Apocalyptic Engine. It's what everybody's looking for."

"Where?"

She gestured up at the giant moving parts of brass and chromed steel. "Here. There. Everywhere."

"The clockwork?"

"Yes, Mr. Kane," Miles-Burnham said, wiping his hands on a rag.

"I don't see anything real apocalyptic," Grant said. "Just machinery."

"In ancient Greek, 'apocalypse' meant 'prophecy', or 'unveiling.'"

"This is how you saw we were coming?" Kane asked.

"Ah, no. That is a different unlikelihood altogether. What it's meant to 'unveil' is the working of the universe—the *universes*."

He turned away and strode a few steps. "It is a talisman, of sorts. A representation of reality at its most fundamental. To the extent it is accurate in certain key correspondences it is capable, in a minute yet significant way, of affecting the very working of the multiverse."

"What do you do with it?"

"He thinks he can send us home," Brigid said.

"How?" Grant asked. "Magic?"

Miles-Burnham smiled and nodded. "Magic, if you like. A few simple alterations of possible state. Brigid has shown me the way to achieve far more than I hitherto dreamt possible."

"I?" Brigid said.

"Speaking of your experiences," the scientist said. "The quincunx effect, your so-called jumps. Even your feelings—the sickness, the visions."

"Hallucinations," Grant said.

"I beg to differ, my friend. *Perceptions.* All helped me to calibrate my engine."

A dim pounding from behind made Kane stiffen. He spun, snaking out his right-hand automatic revolver.

Norman stood by looking calm. Thuds sounded, followed by shots, then a cry that ended in gurgling.

"The door is secured against anything except a sizable explosive charge," the butler said. "Currently battle continues to rage without. A contingent of what I suspect to be Russian Imperial Marines has just ambushed several of

Her Majesty's soldiers on our step. They should occupy one another for a few minutes yet. However, if I might urge a picking up of the pace of these proceedings… Sooner or later one faction or another will triumph—or at least obtain sufficient local superiority to demolish our door."

Miles-Burnham nodded, not a whit more disturbed than his man. "Quite so, Norman. Thank you." He looked to his guests, who stood in a bemused clump, and gestured toward an open-sided stairway mounting upward into the mechanism from the midst of the stained and crack-seamed shop floor. "If you will accompany me, we shall see about returning you whence you came."

Kane noticed a striking dark-haired woman hanging behind the others. "Who's she?"

"I'm Christina Battersea," she said diffidently. "Honored to meet you, Mr. Kane, Mr. Grant."

"Ex-queen of England," Domi said. "They call it Britannia in this world. Except it isn't there anymore. She's okay, in spite of being queen."

"Just when I think it can't get any weirder…" Kane shut his eyes, very briefly, shook his head then mounted the stairs in the wake of Miles-Burnham.

"Among the invaluable insights your most remarkable Dr. Baptiste imparted was the insight of Dr. Heisenberg, from your twentieth century, that the act of observation itself helps to determine reality, at least at a vanishingly small scale. However, I had already begun to learn, in my halting way, that such an observation, though true and profoundly important, does not go nearly far enough. In truth, observation can determine reality on a grand scale indeed, from the proper vantage. The key—" He stopped at a catwalk almost ten yards above the floor. "—lies in the selective observation of possible states of being."

"And your engine enables such observations?" Brigid asked in what seemed to Kane a reverent tone.

"It serves to provide points of reference. Upon learning of your imminent arrival from Miss Domi, I took the liberty of setting the coordinates for the current set of states that constitute the consensus reality I currently share. I have also set the mechanism—" he gestured overhead at a great dial, a flat brass ring a good eight yards across, inscribed with journal marks, numbers and symbols that looked vaguely familiar to Kane "—to approximate the states that constitute your reality. I hope I can be forgiven possible fatuity for failing to be surprised that they are not altogether dissimilar."

"What do you mean?" Grant demanded. "This world isn't anything like ours."

"Ah, but I beg to differ, friend Grant."

The words, thought Kane, were similar to Lakesh's, but whereas the Cerberus director seemed to veer none too predictably between patronization and smarmy obsequiousness, the displaced Brit sounded sincere. It didn't mean Kane was going to take the sawed-off little guy at face value, but Miles-Burnham had just won some points.

"For example, your cultural and technological progress were catastrophically interrupted by events of a global scale. Both worlds have been strongly influenced by non-human beings. And the events that altered our respective worlds, although one was ostensibly natural and the other man-made, both appear to bear the imprint of a transdimensional actor, an individual identified by Brigid as C. W. Thrush."

"Thrush," Grant said. Kane felt his lips peel back from his teeth in a reflex snarl.

"The similarities between our worlds set up resonances that appear to have made it relatively easy to transition between them. It's a major reason you're here in the first place. These resonances will enable us—I hope—to return you to your world without need for the high-energy reactions which are debarred to us."

"What about the falling star you saw in your…vision?" Brigid asked.

"Wormwood." He shrugged. "I will try what I can to divert it. Perhaps Grant's reptilian acquaintance might be of service in convincing his superiors not to carry out the attack. If my suppositions are correct, he will have survived the crash of the machine which brought Mr. Kane here. He'll not likely be very pleased to learn a rogue asteroid is aimed at his own head."

"You got a lot of suppositions," Grant said.

"He's good at it," Brigid said.

Miles-Burnham clapped his hands together. "Well. Let's get you home, then."

"Why are you doing this for us?" Kane asked.

"Because it is the right thing to do," Miles-Burnham said. "Because Brigid Baptiste has become my friend, and wishes me to do so. And finally—" he grinned "—because I can."

"Fair enough," Kane said. "When do we start."

"Is now too soon?"

It wasn't. The scientist shook hands gravely with the two men, accepted a hug from Domi, then a longer embrace from Brigid, whom he kissed chastely on the cheek.

With Chrissie Battersea at his side, he had them take up positions on the catwalk. It seemed to Kane at least that they were in the exact center of the mechanism. All around them, above and below, the marvelous mechanism ratcheted and spun.

"And now," Miles-Burnham said, stepping back to a handsome brass panel with various dials and buttons, "we will activate the engine—"

A rattle of full-auto fire from overhead cut him off. "You'll do nothing of the sort, Dr. Nigel," a familiar voice called out through the burst's ringing echoes. Kane frowned, wondering where he'd heard it before....

"*Mackenzie,*" Grant and Brigid said as one. Kane wondered fleetingly how his old partner had learned the name of the man who had got him shot down like a dog down on the Mississippi. Then he recalled that Mackenzie's fame extended as far as the Front Range, thousands of miles to the south and west. The Reptoids must know it, too.

"Quite right," the secret-police operative said, lowering himself from a skylight on a rope toward the catwalk. He aimed a stubby Reptoid machine pistol down at the group with one hand. "By the by, I'm quite confident I can contrive to drop both the professor and the charming Dr. Baptiste with one spray from this delightfully fiendish contrivance of our reptilian friends. Which ought suffice, I daresay, to secure your cooperation—"

"Wrong," Grant said. He was already in fluid motion, drawing an autopistol from beneath his left armpit.

Mackenzie was a seasoned gunfighter with razor reflexes. Unfortunately he was also in a mode to talk rather than shoot. The time it took him to switch mental gears and send his trigger finger the signal to clench measured the span remaining in his life.

Grant's big handblaster boomed out two shots as Domi fired her own bulldog from inside the hip pocket of her loose black trousers.

Kane had just lined up Mackenzie's handsome blond-mustached face over the sights of his own handblaster when the Canadian secret operator began to spin on the end of his rope. Then without a sound he plummeted to the concrete floor, where he landed with a wet-sandbag thud.

"Payback's a bugger," Grant said, gazing impassively over the rail at the body of his foe.

The catwalk swayed beneath the outlanders' feet as a huge gunpowder charge blasted the steel plate off the front door of the warehouse. Acrid smoke rolled in like a tidal wave.

"Hurry," Norman's voice called from below, "I shan't hold them long." It was punctuated by booms from a lever-action shotgun.

"Right," the scientist called, turning back from the rail with ashen cheeks. "Farewell, my friends—"

Kane got a glimpse of red-coated figures swarming in

through the cloud of smoke and dust billowing from the warehouse entrance. He felt a strange shifting, a sense of dislocation. It seemed the walls melted around them, and the half-lit space gave way to the star-shot blackness of the Void, still surrounding the elaborate and wondrous giant clockworks of the Apocalyptic Engine, as it surrounded them....

And then Kane and the others were back in the Cerberus redoubt, with Dr. Mohandas Lakesh Singh staring at them, blue eyes huge behind his glasses and his head tipped to one side like a curious baby bird's.

"My friends," he said, "whatever are you doing back so quickly?"

Epilogue

Brigid found Kane in the red eye of sunset, sitting out upon the plateau that overlooked the Darks.

"I thought I'd find you here," she said.

"Yeah," Kane acknowledged without turning his head. "It's where I always come when I'm trying to sort things out."

For a time Brigid stood beside him, allowing the rising sunset breeze to blow on her face and ruffle her mane like flames. Purplish-gray dark swelled about them. Behind their backs the night rose black out of the mountains.

"I wonder what became of Dr. Nigel," Brigid said.

"He probably made out all right. Everybody wanted to capture him. Not kill him."

He looked up at her. "You really cared for him, didn't you?"

She nodded without looking at him.

"I hope Ishmael was able to get the asteroid deflected from striking Earth. Or perhaps Nigel could use the Apocalyptic Engine to prevent it hitting."

Kane shook his head. "We're never gonna know."

"I'm not so sure," Brigid said. "Lakesh sent us there for

some reason he's not letting on. I suspect he feels he has unfinished business there."

"He's going to have to finish it himself. Without me, anyway."

"That's what we always say," Brigid said. "But then we always wind up doing what we swore we'd never do again."

"Yeah. The way Grant always winds up coming back from Shizuka's island."

It was almost full dark, now, but for a lemony band to the west. Mercury shone like a spotlighted diamond in indigo above it.

"You came for me," Brigid said.

Kane reached up and covered the hand on his shoulder with his. "Yeah," he said. "Always. In this lifetime and any other."

In silence they let the night come over them.

VANISHING POINT

A U.S. aircraft carrier carrying a top secret weapon is hijacked in the Pacific....

The USS *Stennis* has been hijacked and on board is the
X-51—the most advanced unmanned aircraft ever
built. As the carrier becomes a war zone and the crew
succumbs to a poison attack, a covert three-man unit
called Able Team is the last line of defense against
a global shock wave.

STONY MAN ®

#82

*Available
April 2006 at your
favorite retail outlet.*

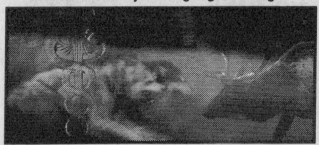

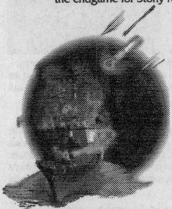

DEATH LANDS®

JAMES AXLER

DEATH LANDS

Labyrinth

*In a ruined world, the past and the future
clash with frightening force...*

NO TIME TO LOSE

It took only minutes for human history to derail
in a mushroom cloud—now more than a century later, whatever destiny lies ahead for humanity is
bound by the rules that have governed survival since the dawn of time: part luck, part skill and part
hard experience. For Ryan Cawdor and his band, survival in Deathlands means keeping hold of what
you have—or losing it along with your life.

BORN TO DIE

In the ancient canyons of New Mexico, the citizens of Little Pueblo prepare to sacrifice Ryan and his
companions to ancient demons locked inside a twentieth-century dam project. But in a world where
nuke-spawned predators feed upon weak and strong alike, Ryan knows avenging eternal spirits
aren't part of the game. Especially when these freaks spit yellow acid—and their creators are the
whitecoat masterminds of genetic recombination, destroyed by their mutant offspring born of sin and
science gone horribly wrong....

In the Deathlands, some await a better tomorrow, but others hope it never comes....

GOLD
EAGLE®

GDL73